DATE DUE

D1042098

Praise for *The Boy Who Could See Demons*

"A psychologically complex thriller, told with compassion in a marvelously suspenseful narrative that keeps you engaged from the first page to the last. This book has it all: a dark and dangerous setting, characters full of depth, rich emotions, and a clever plot. You'll fall in love with Alex—and his demons." —CHEVY STEVENS, author of *Still Missing*

"Top-notch psychological suspense. From her descriptions of a struggling young family to a recovering Northern Ireland, Jess-Cooke effortlessly draws you into one woman's fight to save a troubled boy. Beware what you think you know. It might be only the demons talking. . . ." —LISA GARDNER, author of *Touch & Go*

"Brilliant! Rich with fully formed characters, this heart-gripping novel will keep you riveted from first page to last." —JEFFERY DEAVER, author of *XO*

"Utterly captivating, this is a book I adored and savored from the first to the very last magical page." —TESS GERRITSEN, author of *Ice Cold*

"An absolute chiller, deep, moving, and utterly gripping . . . I was riveted from the unsettling beginning to the mind-bender of an ending. This is a stellar read that will stay with me for a good long while." —LISA UNGER, author of *Heartbroken*

"It's a stunning story; a well-researched, authoritative delve into psychosis, guilt, and damage. Not only does it look at the case of an individual, but it also examines how national events can shape the personality of a whole people. The book is beautifully written, with compassion and insight. . . . Thrilling, wholly plausible, and utterly satisfying." —JULIA CROUCH, author of *Every Vow You Break*

"Gripping from the opening paragraph to its final revelations, this is a brilliant exploration of the point where imagination, psychology, art, politics, and the supernatural meet and merge in a young boy's mind. Touching and painfully funny." —CHRISTOPHER FOWLER, author of *The Memory of Blood*

"A rare and intriguing book, both emotionally and intellectually challenging. The cerebral challenge is the puzzle at the heart of the novel: Whose truth is real?" —HELEN GRANT, author of *The Vanishing of Katharina Linden*

# BY CAROLYN JESS-COOKE

## FICTION
THE BOY WHO COULD SEE DEMONS
THE GUARDIAN ANGEL'S JOURNAL

## POETRY
INROADS

THE
BOY
WHO
COULD
SEE
DEMONS

DELACORTE PRESS

NEW YORK

THE
BOY
WHO
COULD
SEE
DEMONS

A NOVEL

CAROLYN JESS-COOKE

Published in the United States by Delacorte Press,
an imprint of The Random House Publishing Group,
a division of Random House, Inc., New York.

DELACORTE PRESS and the HOUSE colophon
are registered trademarks of Random House, Inc.

Originally published in the United Kingdom in paperback
by Piatkus, an imprint of Little, Brown Book Group,
London, in 2012.

Grateful acknowledgment is made to Wake Forest University
Press for permission to reprint "Belfast Confetti" from *Belfast
Confetti* by Ciaran Carson, copyright © 1989 by Ciaran Carson.
Reprinted by permission of Wake Forest University Press.

Library of Congress Cataloging-in-Publication Data

Jess-Cooke, Carolyn
The boy who could see demons: a novel/Carolyn Jess-Cooke.
p.   cm.
ISBN 978-0-345-53653-2
eBook ISBN 978-0-345-53654-9
1. Women psychiatrists—Fiction.   2. Children—Death—
Fiction.   3. Grief—Fiction.   4. Delusions—Fiction.
5. Northern Ireland—Fiction. 6. Psychological fiction.
I. Title.
PR6110.E78B69 2013
823'.92—dc23        2012038953

Printed in the United States of America on acid-free paper

www.bantamdell.com

246897531

First U.S. Edition

Book design by Elizabeth A. D. Eno

FOR PHOENIX

THE GREATEST TRICK THE DEVIL EVER PULLED
WAS TO CONVINCE US ALL THAT
HE DOES NOT EXIST.

—CHARLES BAUDELAIRE

THE
BOY
WHO
COULD
SEE
DEMONS

## ALEX

People look at me funny when I tell them I have a demon.

"Don't you mean, you have *demons?*" they ask. "Like a drug problem or an urge to stab your dad?" I tell them no. My demon is called Ruen, he's about five foot three, and his favorite things are Mozart, table tennis, and rice pudding.

I met Ruen and his friends five years, five months, and six days ago. It was the morning that Mum said Dad had gone, and I was at school. A bunch of very strange creatures appeared in the corner of the room beside the canvas we'd made of the *Titanic*. Some of them looked like people, though I knew they weren't teachers or anyone's parents because some of them looked like wolves, but with human arms and legs. One of the females had arms, legs, and ears that were all different, as if they had belonged to different people and were pieced together like Frankenstein. One of her arms was hairy and muscly, the other was thin like a girl's. They frightened me, and I started to cry because I was only five.

Miss White came over to my desk and asked what was wrong. I told her about the monsters in the corner. She took off her glasses very slowly and pushed them into her hair, then asked if I was feeling all right.

I looked back at the monsters. I couldn't stop looking at the one who had no face but just a huge red horn, like a rhino's horn, only red, in his forehead. He had a man's body but it was covered in fur and his black trousers were held up with braces that were made out of barbed wire and dripping with blood. He was holding a long pole with a round metal ball on top with spikes sticking out of it like a hedgehog. He put a finger where his lips would be, if he had any, and then a voice appeared in my head. It sounded very soft and yet gruff, just like my Dad's:

*"I'm your friend, Alex."*

And then all the fear left me because what I wanted more than anything in the whole world was a friend.

I found out later that Ruen has different ways of appearing and this was the one I call the Horn Head, which is very scary, especially when you see it for the first time. Luckily he doesn't appear like that very often.

Miss White asked what I was staring at, because I was still looking at the monsters and wondering if they were ghosts, because some of them were like shadows. The thought of it made me start to open my mouth and I felt a noise start to come out, but before it grew too big I heard my Dad's voice, again in my head:

*"Be calm, Alex. We're not monsters. We're your friends. Don't you want us to be your friends?"*

I looked at Miss White and said I was fine, and she smiled and said okay and walked back to her desk, but she kept glancing back at me with her face all worried.

About a second later, without crossing the room, the monster who had spoken to me appeared beside me and told me his name was Ruen. He said I'd better sit down otherwise Miss White would send me to talk to someone called A Psychiatrist. And that, Ruen assured me, would not involve anything fun, like acting or telling jokes or drawing pictures of skeletons.

Ruen knew my favorite hobbies so I knew there was something strange going on here. Miss White kept looking at me like she was very worried as she continued her lesson on how to stick a needle through a frozen balloon and why this was an important scientific experiment. I sat down and said nothing about the monsters.

Ruen has explained many things to me about who he is and what he does, but never about why I can see him when no one else can. I think we're friends. Only, what Ruen has asked me to do makes me think he's not my friend at all. He wants me to do something very bad.

He wants me to kill someone.

## 2
## WAKEFUL
## DREAM

## ALEX

Dear Diary,

A ten-year-old boy walks into a fishmonger's and asks for a leg of
salmon. The wise fishmonger raises his eyebrows and says, "salmon
don't have any legs!" The boy goes home and tells his Dad what the
fishmonger said, and his Dad starts to laugh.

"Okay," the boy's Dad says. "Off to the hardware store, pick me up
some tartan paint."

So the boy goes off to the hardware store. When he returns, he is
feeling very humiliated.

"Okay, okay, I'm sorry," the Dad says, though he's laughing so hard
he almost pees himself. "Here's a fiver. Go get us all fish fingers and use
the change for some chips for you."

The boy throws the fiver back in his Dad's face.

"Here, what's all that about?" the Dad yells.

"You can't fool me," the boy shouts back. "Fish don't have any
fingers!"

• • •

This is a new diary that Mum bought me for my last birthday when I was ten. I want to start every entry with a new joke so I can keep in character. That means I can remember what it feels like to be the person I'm playing, which is a boy called Horatio. My acting teacher Jojo said she's rewritten a famous play called *Hamlet* as a "contemporary retelling of twenty-first-century Belfast, with rap, street gangs, and kamikaze nuns" and apparently William Shakespeare is okay with that. Mum says my getting into the theater company is a really big deal but not to tell anyone on our street as I might get beaten up.

We're performing the play at the Grand Opera House in Belfast city, which is cool 'cos it's like a ten-minute walk from my house so I can make rehearsals every Thursday and Friday after school. Jojo said I can even make up my own jokes. I think this joke is funnier than my last one about the old woman and the orangutan. I told it to Mum but she didn't laugh. She is sad again. I have started to ask her why she gets sad, and each time the reason is different. Yesterday it was because the postman was late, and she was waiting for a Really Important Letter from social services. Today, it's because we've run out of eggs.

I can't think of a more stupid reason to be sad. I wonder whether she's lying to me, or if she actually thinks that it's fine to burst into tears every five seconds. I think I'll ask her more questions about what the sadness is like. *Is it because of my dad,* I wanted to ask this morning, but then I had what the bald counselor called a Wakeful Dream and remembered my dad the time he made Mum cry. Usually she was really really happy when he came to visit, which wasn't very often, and she'd make her lips red and her hair would look like ice cream piled up on her head and she'd sometimes wear her dark green dress. But there was this time that he came and all she did was cry. I remember I was sitting so close to him that I could see the tattoo on his left forearm of a man who Dad said starved himself to death on purpose. He was saying to Mum, *Don't give me that guilt trip,* leaning across the kitchen sink to tap his cigarette into the sink. Always three taps. *Tap tap tap.*

*Aren't you always going on about how you want a better house than this? This is your chance, love.*

And just as I reached out to touch his jeans, the left knee almost worn through from where he'd always bend down to tie my shoelaces, the Wakeful Dream faded and it was just me, Mum, and the sound of her crying.

Mum hasn't talked about Dad in about a million years, so I think she might be sad because of Granny, because Granny always looked after us and was tough with nosy social workers and when Mum got sad Granny would slam her hand on the kitchen counter and say things like "if you don't stand up to life it'll knock you down," and then Mum seemed to snap out of it. But Granny doesn't say that anymore, and Mum just gets worse all the time.

So, I do what I always do, which is ignore Mum as she walks around our house with her face all dripping wet, and I hunt through the fridge and kitchen cupboards and under the stairs for something to eat, until finally I find what I'm looking for: an onion and some frozen bread. Unfortunately I don't find any eggs, which is a pity because it might have made Mum stop crying.

I stand on a stool and chop up the onion underwater in the sink—like Granny taught me, so the juices don't make my eyes flood—and then fry it up with some oil. Then I put it all between two slices of toasted bread. Trust me, it is the best thing in the world.

The second best thing in the world is my bedroom. I was going to say drawing skeletons, or balancing on the back legs of my chair, but I think they're third best, because my bedroom is so high at the top of our house that I don't hear Mum crying when I come up here, and because it's where I go to think and to draw, and also to write jokes for my part as Horatio. It's freezing up here. You could probably store dead bodies. The windowpane is cracked and there's no carpet and all the radiator does is make a big yellow puddle on the bare floor. Most of the time I put on an extra sweater and sometimes a coat, a hat, woolly socks, and gloves when I get up there, though I've cut the fingertips off my gloves so I can hold my pencils. It's so cold that Dad never even bothered to rip all the old wallpaper off the walls, which he said has been up since Saint Patrick kicked all the snakes out of Ireland. It's silver with lots of white leaves all over it, though I think they look like an angel's feathers. The last person who lived here left all their stuff, like a bed with only three legs, a wardrobe, and a tall white chest of drawers that was filled with lots of clothes. The person who left them was probably just lazy but it's worked out okay as Mum never has any money to get me any new clothes.

But that's just the best thing about my room. You know what the best *best* thing about my room is?

When Ruen comes, I can talk to him for ages. And no one else can hear.

So when I found out that Ruen is a *demon* I wasn't scared because I didn't know a demon was a *thing*. I thought it was just the name of the shop near my school that sold motorbikes.

"What's a demon, then?" I asked Ruen.

He was Ghost Boy then. Ruen has four appearances: Horn Head, Monster, Ghost Boy, and Old Man. Ghost Boy is when he looks like me, only in a funny kind of way: He has my exact same brown hair and is as tall as me and even has the same knobbly fingers and fat nose and sticky-out ears, but he has eyes that are completely black and sometimes his whole body is see-through like a balloon. His clothes are different from mine, too. He wears trousers that are puffy and gather in at the knees and a white shirt with no collar, and his feet are bare and dirty.

When I asked what a demon was Ruen jumped up and started shadowboxing in front of the mirror on the back of my bedroom door.

"Demons are like superheroes," he said between jabs. "Humans are like maggots."

I was still sitting on the floor. I'd lost our game of chess. Ruen had let me take all his pawns and bishops and then checkmated me with just his king and queen.

"Why are humans like maggots?" I asked.

He stopped boxing and turned to me. I could see the mirror through him so I kept my gaze on that rather than look him in the face, because his black eyes make my stomach feel funny.

"It's not your fault your mum gave birth to you," he said, and started doing jumping jacks. Because he's like a ghost his jumps looked like scribbles in the air.

"But why are humans like maggots?" I asked. Unlike humans, maggots look like crawling fingernails and they live at the bottom of our wheelie garbage can.

"Because they're stupid," he said, still jumping.

"*How* are humans stupid, then?" I said, standing up.

He stopped jumping and looked at me. His face was angry.

"Look," he said, and held out his hand toward me. "Now put yours on top of mine."

I did. You couldn't see the floor through mine.

"You have a body," he said. "But you'll probably waste it, everything you can do with it. Just like free will. It's like giving a Lamborghini to an infant."

"So you're jealous, then?" I asked, because a Lamborghini is a really cool car that everyone wants.

"A baby driving a sports car would be a bad idea, wouldn't it? Somebody needs to step in, stop the kid from doing more damage than it needs to."

"So demons look after babies, then?" I said.

He looked disgusted. "Don't be ridiculous."

"What do they do then?"

And then he gave me his Alex Is Stupid look. It's when he smiles with only half his mouth and his eyes are small and hard and he shakes his head as if I'm a disappointment. It's the look that makes my stomach knot and my heart beat faster because deep down I know I *am* stupid.

"We try and help you see past the lie."

I blinked. "What lie?"

"You all think you're so important, so special. It's a fallacy, Alex. You're *nothing*."

Now I'm ten I'm much older so I kind of know more about demons but Ruen's not like that. I think everyone's got it wrong about demons, just like they did about rottweilers. Everyone says rottweilers eat children but Granny had one called Milo and he always just licked my face and let me ride him like a pony.

Mum never sees Ruen, and I haven't told her about him or about any of the demons who come into our house. Some of them are a bit strange, but I just ignore them. It's like having loads of grumpy relatives tramping through the place, thinking they can order me about. Ruen's okay, though. He ignores Mum and likes poking around our house. He loves Granddad's old piano that sits in the hallway. He'll stand beside it for ages, leaning down to have a closer look at the wood as if there's a miniature village living in the grain. Then he lowers down to press his ear against the bottom half, as if there's someone inside trying to talk to him. He tells me this was a *stupendous make of piano,* once upon a time, but he's very irritated by the way Mum keeps it pressed up against a radiator and doesn't get it tuned. *Sounds like an old dog,* he says, rapping it with his knuckles like a door. I just shrug and say, *big deal.* Then he gets so cross that he vanishes.

Ruen sometimes turns into the Old Man when he gets cross. If I look like him when I get older, I'll honestly kill myself. When he's the Old Man he's so skinny and withered he looks like a cactus with eyes and ears. His face is long as a spade with lots of wrinkles grooved so deep he looks sort of scrunched up, like tinfoil that's been reused. He's got a long hooked nose and his mouth reminds me of a piranha's. His head is shiny as a silver doorknob and is covered in wispy tufts of fine white hair. His face is gray like a pencil but the bags under his eyes are bright pink, as if someone's ripped the skin off. He's really ugly.

But this isn't as bad as what he looks like when he's Monster. Monster is like a dead body that's been underwater for weeks and is dragged up by the police onto a small boat and everyone pukes because the skin is the color of an eggplant and the head is three times the size of a normal person's head. And that's not all; when he's Monster, Ruen's face isn't a face. His mouth looks like someone blew a hole there with a shotgun and his eyes are tiny like a lizard's.

Here's another thing: he says he's nine thousand human years old. *Yeah, right,* I said when he first told me, but he just tilted his chin and spent the next hour telling me how he could speak more than six thousand languages, even the ones that no one spoke anymore. He went on and on about how humans don't even know their own language, not really, and don't even have proper words for big things like *guilt* and *evil*, that it was *idiotic* that a country with so many different kinds of rain should only have one word for it, blah blah blah, until I yawned for about five minutes solid and he took the hint and left. But the next day, it rained, and I thought *maybe Ruen isn't such an eejit after all. Maybe he actually has a point*. Some rain is like little fish, some is like big globby chunks of spit, and some is like ball bearings. So I started to borrow books from the library to learn some words in lots of cool languages, like Turkish and Icelandic and Maori.

"*Merhaba*, Ruen," I said to him one day, and he just sighed and said, "it's a silent *h*, you imbecile." So I said, "*Góða kvöldið*" and he snapped, "it's still only midmorning," and when I said, "*He roa te wā kua kitea,*" he said I was as obtuse as a gnu.

"What language is that?" I asked.

"English," he sighed, and disappeared.

So I started reading the dictionary to understand the weird words he uses all the time, like *brouhaha*. I tried using that word with Mum about the riots last July. She thought I was laughing at her.

Ruen also told me all this stuff about people I had to look up on the Internet. He said one of his best mates for ages was called Nero, but that Nero preferred to be called Seezer by everyone and still peed the bed when he was like twenty years old. Then Ruen told me he'd stayed in a prison cell with a guy called Sock-rat-ease when Sock-rat-ease was under a death sentence. Ruen told Sock-rat-ease that he should escape. Ruen said that he even had some of Sock-rat-ease's friends offer to help him escape, but Sock-rat-ease wouldn't, so he just died.

"That's crazy," I said.

"Indeed," said Ruen.

It sounded like Ruen had loads of friends, which made me sad because I didn't have any except him.

"Who was your *best* friend?" I asked him, hoping he'd say me.

He said Wolfgang.

I asked, *why Wolfgang?*, and what I meant was why was Wolfgang his best friend and not me, but all Ruen said was he liked Wolfgang's music and then he went quiet.

• • •

I know what you're thinking: I'm crazy and Ruen is all in my head, not just his voice. That I watched too many horror movies. That Ruen's an imaginary friend I've dreamed up because I'm lonely. Well, you'd be incredibly wrong if you thought any of that. Though sometimes I am lonely.

Mum bought me a dog for my eighth birthday that I named Woof. Woof reminds me of a grumpy old man 'cos he's always barking and baring his teeth and his fur is white and tough like an old man's hair. Mum calls him the barking footstool. Woof used to sleep beside my bed and run down the stairs to bark at people when they came into the house in case they were going to kill me, but when Ruen started appearing more often Woof got scared. He just growls at thin air now, even when Ruen isn't there.

Which reminds me. Ruen told me something today that I thought was interesting enough to bother writing down. He said he's not just a demon. His real title is a *Harrower*.

When he said it he was the Old Man. He smiled like a cat and all his wrinkles stretched. He said it the way Auntie Bev tells people that she's a doctor. I think it means a lot to Auntie Bev that she's a doctor, because nobody in our family ever went to University before, or drove a Mercedes and bought their own house like Auntie Bev.

I reckon Ruen is proud of being a Harrower because it means he is someone very important in Hell. When I asked Ruen what a Harrower is, he told me to think of what the word meant. I tried to look it up in my dictionary but it described a gardening tool, which makes no sense. When I asked again, Ruen said did I know what a soldier was. I said, duh, of course I do, and he said, *well, if a regular demon's a soldier, I would be comparable to a Commander General or Field Marshal*. So I said, *do demons fight in wars, then*. And he said, *no, though they are always fighting against the Enemy*. And I said that sounded paranoid, and he scowled and said *demons are perpetually vigilant, not paranoid*. He *still* won't tell me exactly what a Harrower is, so I've decided to make up my own definition: a Harrower is a stinky old sod who wants to show off his war medals and hates that only I can see him.

Wait. I think I can hear mum downstairs. Yep, she's crying again.

Maybe I should pretend that I don't notice. I've got rehearsals for *Hamlet* in seventy-two and a half minutes. Maybe she's just doing it for attention. But my room has started filling with demons, about twenty of them sitting on my bed and huddled in corners, whispering and giggling. They're all talking excitedly like it's Christmas or something, and one of them just said my mum's name. I have a funny feeling in my tummy.

Something is happening downstairs.

"What's going on?" I ask Ruen. "Why are they talking about my Mum?"

He looks at me and raises one of his caterpillar eyebrows. "My dear boy, Death has arrived at your front door."

# 3
# THE
# FEELING

## ANYA

The call came this morning at seven thirty.

Ursula Hepworth, the senior consultant at MacNeice House Child and Adolescent Mental Health Inpatient Unit in Belfast, rang me on my mobile and mentioned a ten-year-old boy at risk of possibly harming himself and others. Name of Alex Connolly, she said. Alex's mother had attempted suicide yesterday and has since been hospitalized, while the boy had been taken to the pediatric unit at the city hospital. Alex had spent an hour alone with her in their home in West Belfast, trying to call for help. Eventually a woman coming to collect Alex for a drama group arrived and took the pair to hospital. Quite understandably, the boy was in quite a state. Urusla informed me that a social worker named Michael Jones had already had contact with the boy and that Jones was concerned about the boy's mental health. Alex's mother has attempted suicide at least four times in the last five years. Eight out of ten children who witness a parent self-harm will go on to repeat the action on themselves.

"Typically, *I* would be the lead clinician on this boy's case," Ursula explained, her Greek accent sliced up by Northern Irish tones. "But as our new adolescent psychiatry consultant I thought I'd pass the baton over to you. What do you say?"

I sat up in bed, greeted by a swath of boxes all over the floor of my new flat. It's a four-room place on the outskirts of the city, so close to the ocean that I wake to the sound of seagulls and the faint smell of salt. It is tiled floor-to-ceiling in a tomato-red tile that burns like the inside of a furnace every sunrise, on account of the fact that the apartment faces east and I haven't had the chance to buy curtains. I haven't had time to furnish it, either, such have been the demands of this new job since moving back from Edinburgh two weeks ago.

I glanced at my watch. "When would you need me to come in?"

"In an hour?"

The sixth of May has been circled on my work schedule as a day off for the past three years, and was agreed at the point I signed my employment contract. It always will be for the rest of my working life. On this day, those whom I count as my closest friends will arrive bearing consolation offerings of cheesecake, tender embraces, photo albums of me and my daughter in happier times, when she was alive and relatively well. Some of these friends will not have seen me for months, but even when their hair color has changed and other relationships have ended, these friends will show up on my doorstep to help me purge this day out of my calendar for another year. And it will always be so.

"I'm sorry," I told Ursula, and I began to explain about my contract, about the fact that I've arranged to take this day off and perhaps she could interview the boy for today and I could catch up on his notes tomorrow?

There was a long pause.

"This is really quite important," she said sternly.

There are many who feel initimidated by Ursula. At forty-three, I like to think I am past such things as inferiority, and in any case the staggering reality of Poppy's fourth anniversary already had me on the verge of tears. I took a deep breath and informed Ursula in my most professional voice that I would gladly meet with the rest of the Child and Adolescent Mental Health Services team first thing tomorrow morning.

And then something happened that I still can't explain, something that has happened only a few times before and is so unlike any other feeling that I've named it, quite simply, The Feeling. It defies words, but if I'm to attempt to verbalize it, it goes like this: Deep in my solar plexus, there's at first a warmth, and then a fire, though not a sensation of heat or pain, that creeps up my neck and jaw, right into my scalp until my hair stands on end, and at the same time I feel it in my knees, my ankles, even my pelvis, until I am so conscious of every part of my body that I feel like I'm about to lift off. It's like my soul is trying to tell me something, an urgent, tingling message that so fills my capillaries and cells, it threatens to burst if I don't listen.

"Are you all right?" Ursula asked, and I told her to give me a moment. I set the receiver on my dresser and wiped my face. In ten years of training I have never come across a single piece of literature to inform me why this thing happens to me sometimes, nor why it tends to happen on the most significant of occasions. I only know that I have to listen. Last time I didn't, my daughter decided to end her life and I was not able to stop her.

"Okay," I told Ursula. "I'll be there this morning."

"Appreciate it, Anya. I know you'll be wonderful on this case."

She told me she would contact the boy's social worker, Michael Jones, and have him meet me in the lobby of MacNeice House in two hours. I ended the call and glanced in the mirror. One of the effects of Poppy's death is that I now wake frequently during the night, resulting in sallow patches beneath my eyes for which no makeup seems to compensate. I studied the jagged white scar in my face, the flat of my cheek there sucked inward by the ribbed pattern of dead tissue. Usually I spend a considerable amount of time each morning arranging my long black hair in a way that shields this ugliness. Today, however, I made do with sweeping my hair into a chignon spiked by a pen and threw on the only items of clothing that I'd unpacked—a black trouser suit with a crumpled white shirt. Finally, of course, I draped my silver talisman around my neck. Then I left a note for the friends who would come and find, to their astonishment and fear, that I had actually crossed the threshold of my home on the anniversary of Poppy's death.

• • •

I took the coastal road instead of the motorway in an attempt to distract myself from thoughts of Poppy. Maybe it's a consequence of approaching middle age, but my memories of her these days are not visual. They come to me, instead, as sounds. Her laughter, light and infectious. The melodies she used to make up on my old Steinway in our Morningside flat in Edinburgh, using one finger. The phrases she'd use to describe her condition. *It's like . . . it's like a hole, Mum. No, like I am one. A hole. Like I'm swallowing darkness.*

MacNeice House is an old Victorian mansion located in an acre of wilderness high in the hills that look down on Belfast's bridges named after British monarchs. Recently renovated, the unit offers inpatient and day patient treatment for children and young people between the ages of four and fifteen suffering from any mental illness noted in textbooks—anxiety disorders, autism spectrum disorders, behavioral disorders, depressive disorders, obsessive compulsive disorder, psychotic disorders, and more. There are ten bedrooms, a common room with computers, an art room, an interview or therapy room, a toy room, a dining room, a swimming pool, a small apartment for parents who need to stay over occasionally, and a restraining room—strictly referred to in-house as *the quiet room.* Inpatients require education, and so an on-site school is available and staffed by specialist teachers. After completing my training at Edinburgh University I worked at a similar unit there for two years, but the reputation of MacNeice House attracted me back home to Northern Ireland—a move I am still unsure about.

I spotted a new vehicle parked beside Ursula's gleaming black Lexus in the parking lot—a battered bottle-green Volvo with a 1990 registration plate—and I wondered if Alex's social worker, Michael Jones, had already arrived. I was racing across the gravel lot using my briefcase as a shield against the pouring rain, when a tall man in a navy-blue suit stepped out from behind the stone pillars, opening a golf umbrella in my direction.

"Welcome," he called. I stepped underneath the umbrella and he shielded me until we were inside, where Ursula stood waiting. She is tall with an imperial air, her red suit, thick black Diana Ross mane

streaked with gray and handsome Greek bone structure more sugges-
tive of a high-powered businesswoman than a clinical psychologist.
She was also one of the panel members at my interview for this post,
and it was because of her that I was sure I hadn't gotten the job.

*You originally trained to become a GP. Why the shift into child psy-
chiatry?*

At the interview I had slipped my right hand beneath my thigh,
looking over the faces of the panel—three male psychiatrists and Ursula, internationally renowned as much for her work in child psychology as for her boorishness.

*My original interest lay in psychiatry,* I had replied. *My mother had a
long battle with mental illness, and I wanted to find answers to the riddles
posed by such illnesses.* If anyone knew the devastation caused by mental
illness—its social taboos, disgraces, its ancient, fearful association with
shame at just how far the human mind can plummet into itself—it
was me.

Ursula had watched me carefully from behind the panel desk. *I
thought the cardinal sin of any psychiatrist was to suppose that all
the answers can be found,* she had offered lightly—a joke with a knife
thrust. The panel chair—John Kind, head of the Psychiatry Depart-
ment at Queen's University—had glanced uncomfortably from Ursula
to me and attempted to forge a question out of Ursula's thinly veiled
joke.

*Do you believe you've found all the answers, Anya? Or is that your in-
tention in taking up this position?*

My heart said *yes.* But at the time, I smiled and gave the answer they
were looking for.

*My intention is to make a difference.*


Ursula gave me an overly wide smile, then extended a hand and shook
it firmly for the first time since my interview. It is not entirely uncom-
mon for psychiatrists to clash with psychologists, given the disparity in
our approaches, though I assumed from her phone call that whatever
issue she had with me at the interview had been resolved. She turned
from me to the man in the navy-blue suit, who was shaking out the

umbrella and slotting it into the coat stand. "Anya, this is Michael, Alex's social worker. He works for the local authority."

Michael Jones turned and flashed a crooked smile. "Yes," he said. "Someone has to."

Ursula regarded him through heavy eyelids before turning to me. "Michael will talk you through the details of the case. I'll meet with you later to discuss its management." She nodded curtly at Michael before walking away down the corridor.

Michael held out his hand. "Thanks for coming in on your day off," he said. I wanted to tell him it was more than a day off—it was the anniversary of my daughter's death—but found a lump forming in my throat. I busied myself with signing my name into the register.

"You know, we've already met," he told me as he took the pen from my hand to sign in.

"We have?"

He signed his name with an illegible flourish. "At the child psychiatry conference in Dublin in 2001."

The conference was six years ago. I had no memory of him at all. I saw he was rangy and wide-shouldered, with steely green eyes that held a stare several seconds longer than was comfortable. I guessed him to be in his late thirties, and there was a weariness about him that I'd encountered many times with social workers, a cynicism detectable in his body language, the thinness of his smile. His voice bore the rough edge of too many cigarettes, and from the cut of his suit and the shine of his shoes I suspected that he had no children. His blond hair was worn messy and long over his collar, but a scent of hair gel told me this was deliberate.

"What was a social worker doing at a child psychiatry conference?" I turned toward the corridor that leads to my office.

"Psychiatry was my original discipline, after a spell studying for the priesthood."

"The priesthood?"

"Family tradition. I liked your paper, by the way. 'Addressing the Need for Psychosis Intervention in Northern Ireland,' wasn't that it? It struck me that you're passionate about changing things around here."

"Change is probably a bit ambitious," I said. "But I'd like to see the way we handle younger cases of psychosis."

"How so?"

I cleared my throat, feeling an old defensiveness rise up. "I think we're missing too many signs of psychosis and even early-onset schizophrenia, allowing these kids to flail and even harm themselves when treatment could very easily help them live normal lives." My voice started to wobble. I heard Poppy's efforts on our piano in my head, her voice softly humming the melody she was trying to match on the keys. When I looked back at him I noticed he was staring at the scar on my face. *I should have worn my hair long,* I thought.

We reached the door to my office. I tried to remember my entry code, given to me the week before by Ursula's secretary, Josh. After a few seconds I punched the gold number on the lock. I turned to see Michael looking up and down the corridor.

"You never been to MacNeice House before?"

"Yes. Too many times, I'm afraid."

"You don't like it?"

"I don't believe in psychiatric institutions. Not for kids."

I opened the door. "This isn't a psychiatric institution, it's an inpatient unit . . ."

"tomato, to-mah-to, eh?"

Inside, Michael remained standing until I gestured toward two soft-backed armchairs at a white coffee table and offered him a drink, which he declined. I poured myself an herbal tea and sat down in the smaller armchair opposite. Michael leaned back in his chair, paying rapt attention to a poster on the wall by my bookcase.

*"Suspicion often creates what it suspects,"* he said, reading the poster. There was a question in his tone.

"C. S. Lewis," I said. "From *The Screwtape Letters.* Have you read—?"

". . . yes, I know," he said, his face twisting at the sight of my herbal tea. "I'm wondering why you framed a quote like that?"

"I guess it was one of those things that made sense at the time."

He smiled. "I have the T-shirt for that one."

There was a pause as he pulled out a file from his briefcase. The name on the label read ALEX CONNOLLY.

"Alex is ten years old," Michael told me, his voice softening. "He lives in one of the poorest parts of Belfast with his mother, Cindy, who is a single parent in her midtwenties. Cindy has had a hard life herself, though that's probably a conversation for another time."

I nodded. "Where's Alex's father?"

"We don't know. There's no name on Alex's birth certificate. Cindy's never been married and refuses to talk about him. He didn't seem to play any role in Alex's life. What we do know is that Alex is deeply worried about his mother's health. He acts fatherly toward her, exhibiting all the hallmarks of a child deep in the grip of the trauma of parental suicide."

He spun a document around on the table to face me—a compilation of notes from Alex's consultations with several different pediatric psychiatrists.

"Interviews with his mother and schoolteachers have flagged multiple psychotic episodes, including violence toward a schoolteacher."

I looked up, startled. "Violence?"

Michael sighed, reluctant to divulge. "He lashed out during an outburst in the classroom. He claimed he was provoked by another child and the teacher didn't wish to make a big deal out of it, but we still document these events."

A quick scan of the notes told me that Alex had all the classic first-rank symptoms of mild high-functioning ASD—autism spectrum disorder—such as being intensely concrete in his thinking, prone to misunderstandings, violent outbursts, language that is slightly more sophisticated than his age, no friends, and eccentricity. I noticed a detail about his claiming to see demons. Then I saw that no medication or treatment had ever been prescribed, and for a moment I was lost for words. I had been warned repeatedly by colleagues in Scotland that *things are different in Northern Ireland,* "things" being the practice of psychiatric intervention. That warning rang in my ears as I scanned the file.

After a few moments I became aware that Michael was watching me. "So what brought you back to Northern Ireland?" he asked when I caught his gaze.

I sat back in my seat and clasped my hands. "Short answer, the job."

"And the long answer?"

I hesitated. "An offhand remark from a PhD candidate doing a placement at the unit I worked at in Edinburgh. She mentioned that even those kids in Northern Ireland who have never experienced the Troubles, who have never been fished from a swimming pool and wrapped in tinfoil during a terrorist threat, who have never measured distance by the sound of a bomb, and who have never even seen a gun are experiencing psychological effects because of what the older generation has suffered."

"*Secondary impact*, isn't that what it's called?"

I nodded. For a moment my memory heaved up the muffled thud of a bomb. From my bedroom window in Bangor—a coastal suburb on the outskirts of Belfast—I could hear the explosions; sickening, hollow. A memory I had never shaken.

"There's a higher prevalence of psychological morbidity in the adult population here than anywhere else in the UK."

"Well, that explains a lot about my job, then." He rubbed his eyes, taking it in. "Did *you* ever get fished out of a swimming pool during a bomb hoax?"

"Twice."

"So you reckon every poor soul who's been involved in the Troubles has a higher chance of a mental breakdown?"

"No one has any ability to estimate the impact of an experience on a person's mental health. There's too many other factors . . ."

He frowned. "Alex has never been involved in the Troubles."

"No?"

"We've interviewed him and Cindy about things like that. I mean, yes, they live in a rough neighborhood, but Cindy has made it clear that it was the abuse she suffered at home as a child that impacted on her so greatly."

*Another form of secondary impact*, I thought. "How long have you been involved with Alex's case?"

Michael sighed. "I've had intermittent contact with him since he was seven. His family situation is very vulnerable, and his living conditions aren't exactly ideal, either. The powers-that-be threatened to place him in foster care last time Cindy attempted suicide."

It struck me that this might not have been as bad an idea as Michael clearly believed, though I figured I would give him the benefit of the doubt for the time being. I noticed his voice had hardened at the mention of foster care, his pale face beginning to flush red around his jaw.

I tapped the thick wad of notes on the table in front of me, thinking.

"What's needed?" I asked quietly.

"A Statement of Special Needs, for a start." He paused. "When I heard we had a new child psychiatrist in town . . . well, you can only imagine my relief." He smiled, and suddenly I felt afraid of letting him down.

"Be specific, Michael. Please."

He leaned forward, elbows dug into his knees, sliding a sliver ring up and down his index finger, deep in thought.

"The thing is, Dr. Molokova, I'm an advocate of Signs of Safety."

I stared at him. He stopped sliding the ring.

"You know, the Australian model for child protection . . . ?"

". . . I know what Signs of Safety is," I said flatly. It was in my interests to. Signs of Safety is a type of child protection plan based on working closely with families to build a system of safety and, ultimately, family-centered treatment. Most of its advocates staunchly reject the types of intervention that form the basis of my job.

Michael seemed agitated. "Look, I need you to promise me you won't separate this family. Trust me, these two need each other, not some bureaucratic, by-the-book, form-ticking procedure that lands this boy in care . . ."

"My only agenda is to find out what treatment the boy needs." I said it clear and slow, hoping it would reassure him. If we were to work together on this case, we needed to sing from the same hymn sheet.

He eyed me with a degree of nervousness in his face, a hint of pleading. This boy meant a lot to him. Not just professionally, either—I saw that Michael had become personally involved in this case. I perceived he had a touch of the hero complex about him—that weathered, tired air was a result of his frustrations. After a long pause he broke into a smile, before pouring himself a mugful of my nettle tea and gulping it with a prolonged shudder of disgust.

I stood up to leave, noting our appointment with Alex was in twenty minutes' time. Michael shuffled his notes and slid them neatly into his briefcase.

"You look tired," he remarked, smiling to show the comment was born from empathy, not criticism. "Shall I drive?"

# 4
## "WHO GAVE YOU THAT SCAR?"

## ANYA

And so we headed off in Michael's Volvo—which, oddly, bore a strong smell of fertilizer inside—to the pediatric unit of the Belfast city hospital.

It was crucial that my approach was gentle and provided Alex with a high degree of space and assurance. Before leaving MacNeice House I had instructed Michael to contact Alex about where he would like to meet with me, and to confirm that the time was suitable, so that my arrival did not cause anxiety. Alex had not been concerned about either; he simply wanted to know how his mother was doing and when he could see her at hospital. He had subsequently been promised a visit with her once she had been treated medically.

Michael entered the room first after a knuckled *rat-a-tat-tat* on the door. Children's interview rooms in psychiatric units are always the same: a corner full of sensory toys and, invariably, a doll's house. In this case the room held just a doll's house, a child's whiteboard on a stand, a sagging blue sofa, and a table with two chairs. Over Michael's shoulder I spotted a boy on a chair behind the table, balancing on its hind legs.

"Hello, Alex," Michael said lightly. At the sight of Michael the boy slammed the chair back down on all four and shouted, "Sorry!" Michael waved his hand in the air to indicate no harm done. Then he held both hands toward me as if presenting the prize on a quiz show.

"I'd like to introduce you to Dr. Molokova," he told Alex, who nodded in my direction, smiling politely.

"Call me Anya," I told Alex. "It's nice to meet you."

"An-ya," he repeated, then grinned. I looked him over briefly. I noticed he had a touch of the street urchin about him: chocolate-brown hair in need of a haircut and a good wash; pale, Northern Irish skin; wide denim-blue eyes; a cheeky mushroom nose splattered with fat freckles. More striking was his dress sense: an oversized man's shirt with brown stripes, buttoned up wrong; brown tweed trousers with thick cuffs at the hems, a man's plaid tie, and black school shoes that had been carefully polished. I spotted a waistcoat and a blazer slung over the sofa. I wouldn't have been surprised if I'd spotted a cane and pipe. Alex had clearly been independent for a long time, and was trying to be much older than his years. To support his mother, I guessed. I was anxious to determine whether this was a manifestation of another personality, or if he was just plain eccentric. The room was filled with the smell of onions.

Michael pulled a chair close to the door and sat down, careful not to intrude on my meeting with Alex. I walked toward the table.

"Very cozy in here, isn't it?"

Alex watched me, visibly nervous. "Is my mum okay?" he asked. I glanced back at Michael, who nodded.

"I believe she's safe and sound, Alex," I said, choosing my words carefully. It is always my utmost resolve to be honest with my patients, but when it comes to young children, tact is highly important. Alex had seen me hesitate and glance at Michael, and the smile he offered back was fractured with worry. This was not surprising, given what he had been through. It is rare for me to work with children who have had pleasant childhoods, yet despite the catalog of traumatic life stories I've racked up so far it's still upsetting to find myself part of yet another narrative that is marred by so much harm at such a young age. Too many times I know the ending, and I can never erase the faces of those children from my eyes. I find myself mulling over their life experiences in my sleep.

But Alex did not appear what we in the psychiatry field call "flat." His eyes were lively, questioning, and haunted.

A psychiatry consultation is a little like an interview with a celebrity: It moves in inward-bound spirals, circling the crucial issue throughout a series of related topics. The only difference is that a psychiatry consultation needs to achieve that by allowing the interviewee to steer the conversation. I looked for cues. On the whiteboard beside the doll's house a picture of a house had been sketched in blue marker with noticeable care. I pointed at it.

"What a beautiful drawing. Is this your house?"

Alex shook his head adamantly.

"Is it a house you've seen before?"

He got up from his seat and walked carefully toward the whiteboard.

"It's the house I'd buy my mum if I had enough money," he explained, rubbing a stray line around the carefully arched front door. "It's got a yellow roof, and there's flowers in the front garden and lots of bedrooms."

I was keen to pursue this topic. "How many bedrooms?" I asked.

"I'm not sure." He picked up his blue marker and continued adding to the house with surprising artistic skill—a cockerel-shaped weather vane on the roof, two small bay trees beside the front door, a dog running up the garden path. I watched, saying nothing, mentally taking notes.

He drew a small circle in the front garden of the house and filled it with dots—a strawberry patch, he said, because his granny used to grow strawberries to make jam. His final addition to the drawing was a huge set of wings at the top of the picture in the sky above the house.

"What's that?" I asked.

"An angel," he replied. "To protect us from bad things. Though I've never seen an angel." As soon as he said it he appeared to shut down, withdrawing eye contact and raising a hand to his mouth, as if he was afraid he'd given something away.

I asked Alex if it would be okay for me to open a window. I find an open window often acts as a reassurance to patients that they are not trapped, that there's a physical exit, should they require it, even though it would take a set of ladders and a Spider-Man dexterity to climb out these windows. He nodded and took a deep breath. Already, he was relaxing. Step one.

I sat cross-legged on the multicolored floor tiles and pulled out a notebook and pen from my satchel. Alex fidgeted a bit, glancing at Michael sitting on the other side of the room. Eventually, Alex sat down opposite me.

"Do you mind if I take notes during our conversation, Alex?"

He made himself comfortable, crossing his legs and holding on to his ankles. He nodded. "I write stuff down, too."

"You write?" I asked. "Stories? Poems? A diary?"

At my third suggestion, his eyes lit up.

"Me too. I find writing things down helps me clarify things," I said, holding up my notebook, but he was staring at the corner, deep in thought.

"How did you get that?" he said when he spotted my facial scar.

"It's nothing," I answered, touching the jagged groove on my cheek, reminding myself to keep my emotions in check. "Have you ever fallen off your bike?"

"I cut my knee once." A long pause while he reflected on this. Then: "Why are you wearing a bottle top for a necklace?"

He was looking at the silver talisman around my neck. I held it up. "It's not a bottle top. It's called an SOS Talisman. It's to tell people what treatment I need in case I experience something called an anaphylactic shock."

He repeated the words *anaphylactic shock*. "What is that?"

"I'm allergic to nuts."

His blue eyes widened. "Even peanuts?"

"Yep."

He considered this. "And peanut butter?"

"That too."

He cocked his head. "Why?"

"My body doesn't like them."

He held me more firmly in his gaze now, inspecting me like I might explode at any moment or grow a second head.

"So what would happen if you ate like a Snickers or something?"

*I would probably stop breathing,* I thought, but instead I said: "I would fall straight to sleep."

His eyes widened. "Do you snore?"

I laughed out loud. "Michael tells me you've got some great jokes. I *love* jokes. Can you tell me your favorite?"

He studied me and, after a moment of contemplation, shook his head slowly. "I can't," he said, very seriously. "I've too many favorites."

I gave him a minute to think, then: "Shall I tell you one of my favorites?"

"No, I've got one," he said, and cleared his throat. "Statistically, six out of seven dwarves aren't Happy."

It took me a second or two to get it, but when I did, I laughed so hard that Alex's face lit up like a Chinese lantern.

"I didn't write that one," he said quickly.

"You write your own jokes as well?"

"It's for a play I'm in. I'm playing someone called Horatio."

"You're in *Hamlet*?"

He informed me that the play was a modern version of Shakespeare's original, that he would be performing it at the Grand Opera House in a week and a half, and would I like to come along?

"I'd *love* to," I said, and I meant it. "I bet your mum is really proud. Have you shared any of your jokes with her?"

He nodded and looked immensely sad. "She hasn't laughed in a long, long time."

"Sometimes people don't laugh on the outside," I offered, "but they still laugh on the inside."

He contemplated this, but I noticed his right hand had crept up to his shirt collar and was tugging at it as if it had suddenly become too tight. I allowed the silence to move past the point of discomfort.

"You mean, people laugh *internally*?" Alex said at last. "Like, internal laughing instead of internal bleeding?"

The association startled me, a little. I let him continue.

"I think I know what you mean," he said slowly. "I used to laugh internally when my dad was still alive."

I trod lightly on this topic. "Can you tell me what you mean?"

Alex glanced at me warily. His hand had not dropped from his collar.

"Sort of. Or more like, I'd do stuff that I liked to do but when he was around I'd do it quietly. Like writing and drawing. That made me happy in *here*"—he pressed a fist against his chest—"even though my granny said my dad should go to Hell for what he did."

He slapped a hand over his mouth as if he had revealed something of himself that he didn't wish to.

"It's okay," I reassured him. "You can say that. I'm not here to punish you."

He nodded and fidgeted.

"I run," I said to break the tension. "Running makes me happy."

I laughed, but Alex's face dropped.

"I don't want to," he said tensely.

I cocked my head. "What?"

He glanced at the corner, as if someone was there. Then he sighed. "Okay," he said resolutely. I waited for him to continue. Finally, he smiled warily and said: "Ruin wants me to say hi."

*"Ruin?"*

"Ruin's my friend," Alex said. There was a hint of confusion in his voice, as if he expected me to know already. "My *best* friend."

*"Ruin,"* I said. "Well, thank you. Hello back to Ruin. Can you tell me who Ruin is, though?"

Alex chewed his lip, his eyes dropping to his knees.

"Ruin's an unusual name," I said. Then, after a long pause: "Is Ruin an animal?"

He shook his head, his eyes focused beyond me. "Some of them are, but Ruin's not. He's . . . we're just friends."

*"Some* of them?" I asked. He nodded but said no more. *Imaginary friends,* I decided. "Can you tell me a little bit about him?"

Alex looked up, thinking. "He likes my granddad's piano. And he *loves* Mozart."

"Mozart?"

Alex nodded. "But Ruin can't play the piano." A pause. "He says you do, though."

"Yes," I said, feeling my smile wither. "I've played the piano since I was a little girl. Mozart's not my favorite composer, though. My very favorite is Ra—"

"Ravel," Alex said, matter-of-factly finishing my sentence for me. "Ruin says Ravel was like a Swiss watchmaker."

"A *Swiss watchmaker*?" His accuracy shocked me. Ravel had been my favorite composer for decades. I set down my pen and folded my arms. This kid was full of surprises.

Alex leaned sideways, as if he was listening to something. Then he straightened. "He means Ravel wrote his music like he was making a really expensive watch." He lifted his hands and twisted imaginary dials. "Like all the cogs fit."

It wasn't out of the question that this child might know about Ravel, though still fairly astonishing. I was intrigued. "And how does Ruin know all this?"

Alex didn't blink. "Ruin is over nine centuries old. He knows lots of stuff, though most of it is really *boring*."

"Does he tell jokes, too?"

Alex raised his eyebrows and started to laugh, his head arched right back. When he recovered he said, "No way, Ruin thinks my jokes are *stupid*. He's more serious than the Terminator."

I must have looked puzzled, because Alex read my face and told me, "You know, the film? With Ah-nuhld?" He put on a surprisingly decent Arnold Schwarzenegger voice: *"It's in your nature to destroy yourselves,"* he growled.

I gave a sufficiently generous chuckle. "Does Ruin look like Arnie, too?"

"No, he . . ." His eyes searched the room. "He says you are *delectable*."

Alex's voice had a tone of surprise to it, and he pronounced *delectable* in a lowered tone and slightly English accent.

"Do you know what that word means, Alex? Delectable?"

He searched his mind. "No," he says. "I skipped most of D." His fingers crept to his collar again. "Can we talk about something else now, please?"

I nodded, but when I looked up I realized it wasn't me he was asking. He was still addressing the empty space in the corner.

"We can talk about anything you like," I said, but he was starting to shake his head furiously. "Stop it!" he shouted. I felt Michael rise to his feet behind me, and I raised my hand to prevent him from intervening.

"Take it easy, Alex," I said calmly. His face was pale, his eyes wild. "Is Ruin bothering you?"

He was rocking back and forth now, rubbing his hands together as if he was trying to start a fire from the friction. I set a hand lightly on his arm. After a moment, his body stilled and his eyes cleared.

"Sometimes he does," he said, when he had calmed. "He says he's a superhero but really he's just a pain."

"A superhero?"

Alex nodded. "It's how he describes what he really is."

"And what is that?"

He hesitated. "A demon," he said innocently. "My demon."

I thought back to the notes Michael showed me in my office. A mention of demons, though I am certain the note was dated three years ago, when Alex was seven.

"Is Ruin a character, like the one you're playing in *Hamlet*?"

He shook his head, then paused. I allowed him time to consider, but he remained adamant. "Ruin is real. He's a demon."

"You're an excellent artist." I nodded at the picture of the house on the whiteboard. "Could you draw a picture of Ruin for me?"

"What, the way he looks right now?" Alex asked, and I nodded again.

He took a few breaths, pondering. Then he stood up and, reluctantly, removed the picture of the house with the eraser. When the whiteboard was clear, he began to draw a face. As he sketched, I made a few notations on the environment, my thoughts during the interview, and a note to investigate superheroes named *Ruin*.

"There," he said, a few moments later.

I looked at the image on the board and frowned. It was a self-portrait of Alex, replete with sunglasses.

"That's Ruin?" I asked Alex.

He nodded.

"But he looks very like you," I said.

"No, he's much different. He's the bad Alex, and I'm the good Alex."

This gave me grave cause for concern. I opened my mouth to ask *What makes the bad Alex bad?* But then I closed it, aware that I had reached the core of Alex's issues, the root of this "Ruin." I needed to tread extremely carefully in order to understand how Alex conceived of himself as "good" and "bad."

"Has Ruin ever hurt you, Alex?"

He shook his head. "Ruin is my friend."

"Oh, I see." I struggled silently to come up with ways to find out why Alex had chosen a demon to project his emotions. Was Ruin the imagined figure responsible for his mother's episodes of self-harm? Did Ruin have plans for Alex to harm himself? Alex's conceptualization of "bad" might well involve self-punishment.

Just then, Alex walked right up to me and pointed at the scar swirling over my jawline.

"Who gave you that scar?" he asked.

I opened my mouth but no sound came out.

He blinked. "Ruin said a little girl did that to you because she was angry."

I glanced over at Michael, but he was looking out the glass door at several doctors walking up the corridor, too distracted to notice what had just happened. I look back at Alex, my heart racing.

*How the hell does he know all this?* I wondered.

"Ruin said you hurt that girl," Alex said, his tone questioning, puzzled.

I struggled to retain my focus. "Does Ruin say how I hurt her?"

Alex glanced to his right. "Ruin," he snapped. "That's not nice." Then he turned back to me.

"Ignore him," he told me.

"What did Ruin say?"

Alex sighed. "Something stupid. He says she was trapped in a dark, dark hole. And that there was a ladder there but you pulled it up so she got stuck."

"Is that how you feel, Alex?" I asked, though my voice had shrunk to a distant whisper. It was as if there were two of me: one asking the questions I'd been trained to ask, the other a grieving mother, my arms aching to hold my little girl again.

But, too late. Alex withdrew again, closed for business. I watched him as he walked over to the whiteboard, beginning to draw his dream house a second time.

"I'll come and see you again tomorrow," I said, rising to my feet. My hands were trembling.

But he was engrossed in his drawing, touching up the soaring wings above the house.


"How did it go?" Michael asked as we headed down the corridor toward the front entrance.

I kept three steps ahead of him so he couldn't see the strain in my face. I could feel my phone buzzing in my bag with text messages from my friends, who were all probably out of their minds with worry. I was training my mind on a series of numbers that scrolled in my mind backward from ten, but I had already reached zero and still my heart was racing, the tears pricking my eyes. I felt the wounds of Poppy awaken in their deep places. Within seconds, I knew, I'd break down.

"I'll compile my notes this afternoon and meet you and the others in the morning," I told Michael quickly.

We had reached the hospital foyer. Michael stopped me as I reached the entrance.

"Dr. Molokova," he said, his voice terse. I spun around and glared at him, rattled by his tone. He raked a hand through his long blond hair, visibly perplexed.

"Look, please just tell me you're not going to split up that family. I have one of the best therapists in the country working with his mother—"

"That's good," I interrupted. "But . . ."

"But what?"

"I believe Alex may be a danger to himself. I'd like to book him into MacNeice House for sustained assessment."

Michael's face fell. "Alex's aunt Beverly is on her way up here from

Cork. Surely he can be assessed in his own house with his own flesh and blood . . ."

I felt suddenly exhausted, full of regret at breaking my resolve to stay at home. "In my opinion, Alex could seriously harm himself if we don't keep an eye on him. Frankly, I'm appalled he's not been given proper treatment until now." A memory of Poppy flashed before my eyes. She was holding a knife at a table in a restaurant, the people around us beginning to turn and watch. The soft light from a chandelier danced on the knife blade. I turned to walk away, but Michael grabbed my arm. "I want what's best for this boy."

I stared at his hand on my bicep, my blood boiling. Finally, I pulled my arm free. "Then let me do my job," I said quietly, walking past him toward the exit.

Many of the parents I encounter in the course of my job confide tearfully in me that they worry their child is possessed. It is a very real and extremely terrifying possibility to confront: You may never have given the concept of God or Satan the time of day, but suddenly the bizarre, frightening, and occasionally violent actions of your son or daughter force you to ask yourself questions you never dared believe would cross your mind. Such questions haunted me every day for most of Poppy's life—and if I'm honest, I don't think I've ever found the real answers. After many years of watching her behavior deteriorate, I had grown tired of specialists telling me that my beautiful, intelligent, and sensitive child was merely "hyper-imaginative," a diagnosis that progressed as she got older through the apathetic and uninformed spectrum of childhood mental health disorders: attention deficit disorder, dissociative identity disorder, bipolarity, Asperger's syndrome. All wrong, and with these wrong diagnoses, the wrong meds, the wrong kind of treatment. So after medical school I trained in child psychiatry, doubled up by a PhD based on a hunch about Poppy's condition: childhood schizophrenia.

Like Michael, I had wanted us to stay together as a family. But what I wanted had cost Poppy her life.

As I pulled through the busy streets of Belfast in a taxi, I heard her voice. *I love you, Mummy. I love you.* And then I saw her, clear in my mind. Her chocolate-brown eyes curved with laughter, her thick black hair swept across one shoulder. She was turning to me, the white sheen of a curtain brushing against her face. *The hole is gone,* she said, smiling.

She was only twelve years old.

# 5
## "TELL HER WHO I AM"

ALEX

Dear Diary,

Today I met a lady doctor at the hospital who asked a lot of questions about Ruen. I felt very hot around my neck when she asked about him. I've never told anyone much about him because that was our deal. But then he asked me to introduce him and it confused me because usually he hisses at me like a cat to keep quiet and pretend that he doesn't exist, at which I say something like, "but Ruen, you're such a charming fellow, surely you want me to tell the whole world about you?" and he narrows his horrible eyes at me and says *sarcasm only gestures at one's impotence*. Then I blow a raspberry and he disappears in a huff.

When Ruen first came to stay, he said he was simply here to be my friend because I looked lonely. Then one day we had an argument and I told him to go away, and he said he couldn't. He said he'd been sent to study me because he and all his friends had never come across a human being who could see demons like I did. He said I was very special. The most anyone had ever seen of demons was a glimpse, he said, and these people usually thought they were seeing things. I remember he was very, very excited that I could see him and said it was very important that he study me, like a lab rat or something. I said I didn't want to be studied, that sounded like there was something wrong with me and all my life people have been saying that there is something wrong with me. I hate it, because I am totally fine and want to be left alone. But Ruen promised me something if I let him study me. I'm not going to say what. It's our secret.

The lady doctor had a big Harry Potter kind of scar, but on her jaw, not her forehead. She was pretty and smiley and had small dark brown eyes and long black hair that looked like chocolate sauce being poured out of a bottle. One of her teeth had a chip in it and sometimes I could see her bra through her shirt. Doctor Molokova, she said her name was, but to call her Anya. Peanuts make Anya fall asleep. I ate some after she left to see if they'd make me fall asleep but they didn't.

When Anya asked me about Ruen I think I must have blushed and got twitchy. Ruen told me to tell her who he was. I was very confused. The lady doctor asked me what was wrong. Ruen said it again: *tell her who I am.* So I did. She was very interested to hear about Ruen and Ruen must have met her before because he told me some things about her, like she played the piano quite well and that her Daddy had been Chinese and her Mum had a lot of problems. Just like mine.

When she left Ruen had a funny look in his eyes, the kind of look Woof gets when he sees Ruen. Worried. Afraid, almost. I asked him what was wrong and he said *nothing* and then started asking lots of questions about Anya and about *love.* I was *so* sick of questions by this point, though I was a bit freaked out by the fact that I had to stay in hospital when it was mum that had something wrong with her, not me, and that no one had come to get me yet. So I answered his questions, even though they were very strange.

He said: "What does love feel like?"

I said: "You'd have to ask a girl." And then I thought of Mum and how much I love her and so I said: "Like you'd do anything for the person you love." And then I stared at him for a long time and worked it out by myself.

"You love Anya," I said.

"I most certainly *do not,*" he said.

"You do," I said, laughing. "You *like* her."

I was having great fun getting even after he teased me about fancying Katie McInerny just because I let her share my locker.

He disappeared so fast he made a slight *pop,* and I laughed myself to sleep.

When I woke up, it was really dark outside. All the rooftops of the houses across the street looked like a zigzaggedy dinosaur spine against the sky. I could tell Ruen was in the room because I was colder than frozen sausages even though it was May, and sometimes he does that. All the hairs on my arms were standing straight upright. I said, "what is it now, you creep?"

He took a step out of the shadow beside the window and said, "I want you to tell Anya all about me."

I sat up in bed. "I was right, wasn't I? You really *do* like that lady, Ruen."

And for some reason I thought of my dad just then. I saw his face in my head, all blurry, his eyes blue just like mine, Mum said. Then I saw the face of the policeman, his face turning toward me in slow motion, angry and scared at the same time.

Ruen scowled at me. I snapped out of my daydream and rolled my eyes at him.

"Fine, Ruen. I'll tell her about you, okay? Does that make you happy?"

He gave a tiny nod like he begrudged even moving his head and then he vanished and I thought, *what a nut.*

I slept all night at the hospital and in the morning Anya came and said I could see mum. She was more smiley today, though her eyes looked sad and she was wearing black square glasses. I didn't tell her what Ruen had said because I was so excited to see Mum.

"How are you today, Alex?" she said as we walked through the hospital.

"I thought of a new joke," I said, and I told her it. "How do you make a hot dog stand?"

She shrugged.

"You steal its chair."

She laughed, though she sounded like she didn't find it funny.

"I bet you're excited to see your Mum," she said, and I nodded. "She might not look like her usual self, though. Is that okay?"

This to me could only be a good thing, so I gave a big grin and Anya told me to follow her. We walked down loads of hospital corridors until I thought my legs would fall off and then finally we came to a small room where Mum was in a white bed.

When I went in she didn't look up at first. She was just lying there with white bandages around her wrists and a tube in her arm. Her face looked like someone had taken a rubber to it and erased Mum out of it. Then she turned her head and smiled at me, and it was as if someone had put all the color back into her face. Her hair turned yellow again with black roots and her eyes changed from gray to sky blue, and even the tattoos on her arms and neck seemed brighter. Someone had taken out the hoop in her nose but that was a good thing because I thought it made her look like a bull. I wanted to ask if they'd taken the one out of her tongue, too, but I didn't.

"Hello, love," she said. Her voice was creaky. I felt nervous to go in, in case Ruen appeared.

"Come here, Alex," she said. I stepped forward and she put her arms around me and squeezed me. Her arms felt cold and skinny.

"Are you feeling better yet?" I said.

"I've had better days," she said after a long, long pause, and she smiled but her eyes were wet and small. "How have you been?"

I shrugged. "They don't have TVs here."

"What a shame, eh? You can watch TV when you get home."

"Yeah, but I've missed loads." And I started naming all the programs I'd missed and counting them off on my fingers.

Mum just stared at me. "How's the barking footstool?"

"Woof's okay," I said. "Though who's feeding him, Mum? Won't he be hungry?"

Mum's face looked worried. Then Anya stepped forward and touched mum's hand with her fingers.

"I'm Anya Molokova," she said, and her voice was suddenly really soothing and kind. "I'm a doctor at MacNeice House. I'm here to take care of Alex."

I wanted to say this was a lie because Anya wasn't cooking me pizza or onions on toast or anything like that. Mum nodded. I pulled a chair close to her bed and she reached out and ruffled my hair.

"Cindy, I'm aware that you'll be kept in here for another few weeks?"

"Yeah?" Mum said in a way that made me wonder if Anya was doing something wrong.

"I'd like Alex to stay at my unit for a little while. Just so I can assess him."

Mum's face tightened. "Assess for what?"

Anya glanced at me. "I wonder if we should discuss this in private . . ."

"No," Mum said loudly. "It's about him, so he should be here."

Anya sat down on the other side of the bed, then took off her black square glasses and used her shirt to clean them.

"In light of recent circumstances, I think Alex may have a kind of illness that requires ongoing assessment and monitoring. It might be in his interests to have a stay at MacNeice House." I wondered what sort of illness she meant and if MacNeice House had TVs.

"Isn't that a place for nutjobs?" Mum said.

Anya's smile turned real. "Not at all. It's where we do some of our most important work for families in the region."

"Last time some woman in a suit tried to take Alex away from me."

Mum and I stared at Anya. I noticed she was wearing a suit. She swallowed. "If we were to do this, I'd need your permission . . ."

"Well, you don't have it," Mum snapped, and her voice wobbled until I squeezed her hand and she looked at me and smiled. "I'll get myself out of here soon, I promise," she said.

"Your sister Bev is here," Anya said softly. "She came up from Cork to take care of Alex. Part of the arrangement, if Alex stays at MacNeice House, was that Bev would take care of him weekends . . ."

Mum widened her eyes. "Bev is here?"

Anya nodded.

Mum lifted a hand to her face and started to cry. "I don't want her seeing me like this," she said, and she started pressing her hair down with her fingers because it was sticking out all over the place like she'd been electrocuted.

"She'll only visit when you're ready. Everyone's very aware that you need time. I'll drop Alex home this afternoon, but if you're not happy with him coming to MacNeice House I need to get permission to visit with him every day for the next week for us to talk."

There was something about the way Anya said *talk* that sounded like she meant something much more serious. Mum seemed to think so, too. She stared at Anya very hard.

"You mean, about me?" Mum said.

Anya glanced at me. "And other things, too."

Then she stood up and said she'd see if she could get one of the nurses to let me watch TV. She went out of the room and I didn't look at Mum because just then Ruen appeared and I jumped about three feet in the air.

"What's wrong now, Alex?" Mum said.

But I ignored her. I was nervous because I could see that Ruen was Monster. Only, he wasn't looking at me. He was looking at something in the doorway. I tried to see what he was looking at but there was no one there. But Ruen was so angry that he was growling. Three seconds later he disappeared.

When Anya came back she told me they would let me watch TV, then she saw Mum was upset and I was curled up on the floor.

"What's happened?" she asked Mum, who just shook her head and whispered something.

"Is there TV now?" I said, and I saw that Ruen was gone so I stood up.

Anya smiled and started to say something, but then she just said, "follow me." So I went out and sat in a smelly room with the tiniest TV I've ever seen that had yellow lines running through all the channels. About five minutes later Anya came in smiling and told me I could come and see Mum again, but only for a little while because Mum was very tired.

I sat beside Mum and a lady came with a tray of food, which Mum didn't want.

"Do you want it, Alex?" Mum said, and I nodded and tucked into the beans and potatoes.

"Did you know Alex is in a play?" I heard Mum say to Anya.

"Yes. *Hamlet*. You must be very proud."

I felt Mum stare at me. "I could hardly read when I was his age. He's top of his class in English. He didn't get any of that from me, I can tell you. He's brilliant." Then there was a long pause as I used the last piece of toast to mop up the juice from the beans.

"Sometimes I think I'm holding him back," I heard Mum say, and her voice was very small.

"How do you think you're holding him back?" Anya said.

Mum's color looked like it was fading again. "Do you think there's ever a chance for a kid that starts out in life like me and Alex did? Or do you think it would have been better if I'd just never been born?"

Anya looked from me to Mum. Then she leaned forward and took Mum's hand. "I think some of us have really big challenges in life. But I think everything can be overcome."

Mum stared at Anya a long time. Then she leaned over and gave my cheek a gentle tap, and even though she smiled at me there was this look in her eyes that made a knot in my belly until I couldn't eat my toast. I saw Ruen in the doorway but pretended not to.


Auntie Bev is Mum's sister though she looks nothing like Mum, not even slightly. In fact you couldn't really tell they're sisters. She's older than Mum by eleven years and ten months and about two days but she looks actually younger and finds everything funny and she doesn't have any tattoos, except for a black squiggle on her left ankle, which she says happened when she was *out of her tree in Corfu*. She says weird things like "I nearly took a buckle in my eye." Her hair is short and white like Woof's fur and her job means she spends all day shining a flashlight down people's ears and mouths. She wears a small gold cross on a chain around her neck though she's not Catholic anymore and I'm never to say the name *Lawrence* in front of her because that's the name of the husband who took all her money. When she moved into my house the first thing she did was put a shower pole in the doorway of our living room. I stood for a few minutes, wondering if her brain had slipped out of her ears in the night.

"For this," she said, when she figured out why I looked so puzzled.

She held on to the pole and started pulling her head up over the bar with her arms. She did it three times before I noticed her feet weren't touching the floor.

"Oh," I said, though I still had no idea why she'd done that. Then she laughed and jumped down and next thing I knew she'd hooked both her feet over the bar and was hanging like a bat.

This morning she came up to my room and knocked on the door, and when I noticed she wasn't out of breath I said to her:

"Why don't you sound like an old dog?"

She looked at me funny and asked what I meant, and I told her Mum always made a noise like this (I went *hah hah hah* with my tongue hanging out) when she climbed all three floors of our house. The lines in Auntie Bev's forehead disappeared then and she giggled, then flexed her arm muscles, which I thought was a funny thing for a girl to do, though they were big and made me think of onions in a sock.

"That's what wall climbing three times a week will do for you," she said, slapping her arm.

"Wall climbing?" I said. "Can you take me wall climbing with you?"

"Of course," she said, her face all shocked. "We should find one close by. It's been so long since I lived here, I can't even remember where a wall would be."

"There's a wall outside our front door," I told her.

She rolled her eyes. "That's not the kind of wall I meant, Alex." Then she looked me up and down for a long time, her eyes like gumdrops. "What in the name of Mary and Joseph are you *wearing*, Alex?"

I looked down at my clothes. I'd forgotten to roll up my trousers.

"A suit?"

Auntie Bev laughed really loudly and she sounded like an owl. "We need to go shopping, don't we?"

Before I could answer she dragged me downstairs for some food but she wouldn't let me chop the onions in case I cut myself.

"But Granny taught me how," I told her, and suddenly her smile slipped off her face and she looked out the window. It was starting to rain.

"Was your Mum happier when Granny was around?" she asked very quietly.

"I think so. Though Granny didn't like my Dad so that made Mum sad." At the thought of Granny, I felt my whole body stiffen though I wasn't sure if it was just the cold. "I really miss Granny."

Auntie Bev reached down and squeezed my arm. "I miss her, too, Alex."

And when I looked back Auntie Bev's face was all misty and our breaths hung in the cold air like smoke.

## ANYA

I sleep late and avoid my morning run. My leg, back, and neck muscles feel like I've been on a rack all night and when I look outside it's raining. I make a conscious effort to compile my notes from yesterday and catch up on emails instead. I don't return any of the phone calls from my worried friends, not even Fi, my best friend, who has called nineteen times since Poppy's anniversary and left four messages ordering me to call her back. Instead, I hide behind the faceless deletability of email, cutting and pasting the same *Hey, I'm fine, sorry I missed you* message to each of the friends who knew Poppy. I will apologize and explain later. First, there is the problem of Alex. I shower quickly, then head to my office. Unpacking will have to wait.

When I moved to Edinburgh to go to medical school, people always asked, *What was it like growing up in Northern Ireland?* with an occasional sense of awe, as if I was the first person to have done it. It was only when I'd left that it struck me how dangerous the mild but otherwise down-at-heel and volatile land of my birth appeared to others— like a treasured friend whose social graces often do her a disservice in the eyes of strangers.

From a professional viewpoint, Northern Ireland's social scars run deep, and not just through the psyches of those who experienced the violence firsthand. Although the politicians are celebrating what they call "peace," those of us working behind the scenes are finding anything but. The history of violence here is usually measured in terms of its death count, but there is another silent, and more alarming, toll: One in five Northern Irish children will experience major mental health problems before their eighteenth birthday, with case studies flagging self-harm as a response to confrontation and shame for family involvement in violence. I empathize with Michael Jones for wishing to keep Cindy and Alex as a family unit, but I have not returned to my homeland to perpetuate a failing system. I am here to begin rebuilding lives.

I pull up into the parking lot of MacNeice House at 8:59 AM. For some reason I half expect to see Michael's battered Volvo parked in my space, his tense, brooding stare forcing me to sign off Alex's report as A-okay, as if he's passed an exam to qualify for a decent family life. If only it were that simple. I should have realized it sooner—Michael sees me as the enemy. He wants to keep me close so he can have a better chance at keeping Alex out of—Michael's terms—the "nuthouse." And I suppose it is in this respect that Michael and I share a common goal—despite myself, I have bonded with this child, sensed something very familiar about his predicament, something that lies close to the bone. And I feel I can help him—though it may not be in the way that Michael desires.

Inside my office I flick the switch on the kettle and browse the few shelves of books I've finally managed to stack in my bookcases. My collection comprises psychiatric journals and textbooks, naturally, but also literature, drama, and religious texts—the truth about the human psyche doesn't always reside in the factual and academic tomes. As I flick through a handful of yellowing books by C. S. Lewis and John Milton, I reflect on Alex's claim that he can see demons. As far back as the first century the symptoms of mania and schizophrenia have been linked closely to superhuman manifestations and hallucinations. God, angels, superheroes, martyrs . . . they've all played across the stage of schizophrenia throughout the recorded delusions of the last two thousand years. Patients' claiming to see demons is not entirely out of the ordinary, but Alex's case strikes me as unusual. He claimed that a demon was his best friend. And he seemed to know about Poppy. At the very least, a ten-year-old with such powers of perception is extremely rare.

The kettle trembles with heat. Poppy's voice rattles in my head. *It feels like a hole, Mum. A hole instead of a soul.*

The red switch clicks.

I think of Cindy at the hospital, her tired, thin face filled with the weariness of a woman three times her age, how she had admitted that she did not feel good enough. I jot down some notes to the effect that Alex is struggling to understand his dark colors, and most likely those of his mother. I make another note to pursue aspects of shame and guilt in his character; why he feels both of these and how I might help him come to understand that they are natural elements of his being. How to deal with them when they cause him rage and potential self-harm, as well as the risk he may pose to others. Helping him understand why his mother turns to pills and razor blades every time a black cloud passes by will be much more difficult.

I stare at my page of scribbles. On the open textbook beside me I circle a passage from Milton's *Paradise Lost*, not because of any insight it offers me into Alex's situation, but because it clouds me in an over-whelming sense of déjà vu:

> *The mind is its own place, and in itself*
> *Can make a heav'n of hell, a hell of heav'n.*

I tap my pen on the desk for a few moments, trying to remember where I came across this quote before, and why it should feel so famil-iar, and then it all comes back: I picked it up from a fellow student dur-ing the first year of my training at Queen's University, when the questions surrounding Poppy's behavior were pounding my brain, when I felt launched beyond the natural maternal impetus to make every-thing all right into a quest worthy of Super-Woman: to make Poppy's hell a heaven. It never happened.

That doesn't mean it *can't* happen, I remind myself. The hell that psychotics live with can be relocated, if not redecorated, so to speak.

"Hell" is when no treatment is given—or the wrong sort of treatment—and when the mind is left to free fall into itself without proper intervention. My thoughts turn back to Alex. Michael wants me to write a report that will enable him to give Cindy and her son the kind of family support they should have been receiving for years—counseling, better housing, care assistance. But something nags at me. Poppy's voice in my head morphs to Alex's when he's talking about Ruin: *He's the bad Alex.*

There has already been some speculation in Michael's notes that Alex is bipolar, but I am not convinced. With a deep breath I write SCHIZOPHRENIA??? at the top of my notes. In many cases before, it has virtually been ruled out from the get-go because early-onset schizophrenia affects only one in ten thousand children under the age of twelve. Some psychotic disorders may be a result of physical and/or sexual abuse in childhood. I need to find out more about the boy's father and those other relatives who have played a part in his life. Has the mother had lovers, and how much have they been around Alex? Very often, mothers in Cindy's position end up using their lovers as babysitters: Has this been the case here? Abuse will be my primary area of inquiry, although I need to explore the history of Cindy's depression and its impact on Alex; a much harder thing to investigate.

First, I find the website for Alex's school. I send an email to his teacher, Karen Holland, asking if we can meet. Then I Google the name of the theater company that Alex belongs to—Really Talented Kids Theatre Company—and discover a surprisingly sophisticated website with a photograph of several dozen children grouped on a stage, Alex's smiling face among them. A cluster of logos for local businesses are featured under the banner of OUR SPONSORS. Below that is the photograph of an attractive woman with sharp cheekbones, a melon-slice white smile, and a wild nest of back-combed red hair. I recognize her immediately as Jojo Kennings, an actress in a TV series I much admire. Like me, Jojo is originally from Belfast. She's returned after twenty years in London to encourage regional participation in the arts, enlisting the help of celebrity friends such as Kenneth Branagh to mentor the kids in the theater company. I am impressed by her passion, and feel a sense of hope that Alex is involved in the project. Her email address is on the website. I type a message, delete it, then rewrite one that sounds less formal.

From: A_Molokova@macneicehouse.nhs.uk
Date: 05/08/07 09:21 AM

Dear Jojo (if I may),

I'm writing to ask if I might talk briefly with you about one of the children in your production of Hamlet next month, Alex Connolly. I'm a consultant with the CAMHS team at MacNeice House and am assessing Alex in the light of some recent changes at home. I'd be keen to find out more about his involvement in the play, and about the performance in general. Might there be a suitable time to meet?

Kind regards,
Dr. Anya Molokova

I hit SEND and return to my notes. I glance at the word SCHIZOPHRENIA, and I sigh. I've made myself very unpopular in some circles because of the number of children on whom I've slapped the label of early-onset schizophrenia like a dentist's smiley-face sticker. *How come all these kids are suddenly coming out of the woodwork?* is the heckle I normally get at conferences. Is it because kids as young as three really are exhibiting the hallmarks of schizophrenia—severe confusion between fantasy and reality, extreme moodiness, violence, mental disturbances, paranoia, and unusual perceptual experiences—or is it just that doctors like me are overly eager to define a set of disorders that might just be, say, characteristics of a dreamy kid or merely a childhood phase?

The thing is, when you spend eighteen years of your life dealing with a schizophrenic mother and twelve years struggling to help a schizophrenic daughter, neither of whom was ever properly diagnosed or treated, you tend to have a deep investment in the correct diagnosis of what is an absolutely horrific, crippling, and misunderstood mental illness that shatters families with the force of a bomb.

My computer bleeps a tone—B natural—that indicates a new email has come through. The sender is Jojo Kennings.

> To: A_Molokova@macneicehouse.nhs.uk
> From: jakennings@rtktheatre.co.uk
> Date: 05/08/07 09:22 AM
>
> Sure no problem—having a rehearsal at GOH 2night 4-5 PM—could speak to you just before, that OK?
>
> JOJO xoxox

I glance at my calendar. I can make it. I send an email confirming the meeting and asking if *GOH* means "Grand Opera House." A reply zings back.

> To: A_Molokova@macneicehouse.nhs.uk
> From: jakennings@rtktheatre.co.uk
> Date: 05/08/07 09:24 AM
>
> Yes, Opera House. See you then!
>
> JOJO xoxox

I only half read her reply because the chime of the email hitting my inbox has sounded another tone, its echo threading back, back into the past. The curse of perfect pitch. In a heartbeat my senses have returned to the moment a B natural key of the piano in my Morningside flat was struck by my daughter four years ago.

In my mind's eye I see Poppy's dark head behind the gleaming lid of the baby grand piano, singing out the melody in her head. I had taught her piano as, first and foremost, a family tradition. *You aren't a Molokova if you don't play,* my mother used to say. But Poppy's dabblings with music—and they were, sadly, no more than dabblings—achieved something more important. They worked wonders in calming her, in channeling energy that would otherwise spark into aggression.

They succeeded in keeping her focused for more than a handful of seconds. And she loved music.

"Try a note higher, baby," I call to her, and she glances up at me.

"Okay, Mum."

I can see her face—heart-shaped like my mother's, dark eyes from our Chinese ancestry on my father's side, and a high forehead that she meticulously covers with thick blunt bangs. Even at twelve, she has the air of an older spirit about her, a soul burdened by its uncannily mature perceptions.

Several months before, she had begun an intensive program of treatment for EOS—early-onset schizophrenia—including a stay at a residential psychiatric unit. She hated me for it. But to my relief, she started to show signs of improving after she returned. For the first time in many years, I know what it feels like to have a "normal" child—a child who tells me she loves me.

Nonetheless, I can't break the habit—I glance across the open space of the living room before I leave to run her bath, checking the room carefully for any sharps, wires, breakables, or flammables. Poppy pauses, then strikes the B above middle C once more. I can hear her singing. Satisfied that she is calm and content, I head through the kitchen to the bathroom, shutting the door tightly behind me as I turn on the taps.

The rushing bathwater drowns out the chime of the piano and for a moment I wonder if I should turn back and make sure she's all right. *She is happy*, I think. *Let her play.* I think of the vacation we had booked that summer to Paris, of the possibility of getting her piano lessons with another teacher. I tried teaching her myself, but we always ended up laughing.

As I rummage through the bathroom cupboard for bubble bath I feel a sensation of warmth flood across my skin, seeping into my heart, my lungs, telling me that something is wrong. *Something is wrong.* I scan the contents of the wall cabinet—no pills or sharps. *Nothing is wrong*, I think, and I chide myself for letting my emotions dictate to my logic. It was a core part of my training, and essential to the success of Poppy's treatment—that I heed science and not my feelings.

But the sensation grows stronger. Instinct shouts at me that I need to go back into the living room and check on Poppy. Shaken, I lean down and wrench at the tap, shutting off the water. I look at myself in the mirror, frowning at the scar on my face. It is still an ugly raw pink, not quite old enough to hide under makeup. A breeze brushes my hair across my face, trapping it against my lips. I lean over and shut the window.

*The window.*

Earlier that day the sun had made a rare visit to Edinburgh in all its glory, filling Princes Street Gardens with shirtless workers and sunglass-wearing women, forcing me to open our living room window for a gust of cool air. Of course, the window has a safety catch. And Poppy has turned a corner, her doctor has assured me. Her treatment is working.

*The window.*

I glance toward the door. "Poppy?"

There is no sound of her music. I see the wing of the piano, shining with the pink and blue lights from the city. In the distance Edinburgh Castle sits at the top of black volcanic rock, as if it has evolved from tectonic clashes to become a status of Scottish victory. When Poppy's medication made her too weak to walk up the steep hill there, I would point at the castle from our living room. To her, it was more than beautiful. It was a symbol of hope.

I step out of the bathroom into the narrow hallway that leads to the living room. Our long L-shaped sofa is empty, the corner lamp beaming. I see movement at the window, a flash of white curtain.

"Poppy?"

She is on the windowsill, a silhouette obscured by the night sky, her bare legs curled up to her chest. I feel a shiver of alarm.

"Poppy, there's no need to sit so close," I say quickly. "Come on, honey, move back. You could fall." I stop. "And why is the safety catch off?"

I move forward, but as I do, she swings both legs over the ledge and looks at me. Her face is a blank.

My heart clangs in my chest. I hold up both hands. I am no longer talking to a twelve-year-old girl. I am talking to a child who suffers from schizophrenia. All that matters now is keeping her calm.

"Poppy," I say. "Can you play your music for me again?"

"Someone built a bridge last night," she says, smiling. "From our window to Edinburgh Castle. It's cool."

I stretch out my hands to her.

"It's bedtime," I hear myself say, though my voice sounds far, far away from the panic in my head. "Poppy, love, come away from that window."

She leans forward, brushing her leg against the cool air, and I cry out.

"Mum, it's fine," she says. "There's a bridge. It's made of solid iron. I won't fall."

"Poppy, there is no bridge," I say firmly. "Come back inside."

But her face has changed. "You don't believe me."

My mind is racing with ways to distract her. "Come inside and I'll make you supper. What would you like, sweetheart? Pizza? Does that sound good?"

I am walking slowly toward her, careful not to charge lest I startle her into tipping herself right over that ledge. There is no balcony, no fire escape—nothing to break her fall onto pavement ten stories below.

"Pizza, yes," she says, and I feel dizzy with relief.

"Tell you what," I say, gently, inching past the piano. "I'll make you a cheese-crust pepperoni with olives if you come inside right now."

I am close enough to feel the cool night air rushing in. If I move very quickly, there's a chance I could grab her.

"I love you, Mummy," she says, smiling.

And then I lunge at her. She leans forward and drops, she drops into the black depths, and I am scrambling halfway out of the window, screaming as I lean forward after her. For a split second she is almost close enough to my fingertips for me to grab her hand. But despite my reaching she is beyond me, and by some deep instinct of survival I remain half inside, half outside the window, crying and reaching as my daughter shrinks into the distance.

# THE GHOST

ALEX

Dear Diary,

Okay so I have a new joke I tried out tonight and everyone laughed though according to Jojo it's incorrect politically. There's an Irishman, an Englishman, and a Scottish bloke washing the side of a skyscraper. Every day at lunchtime they sit on their balcony overlooking the city and eat their sandwiches. One day the Englishman opens his lunchbox and gets really angry. "Ham *again*!" he says. "If my wife packs me one more ham sandwich I'm going to throw myself off this balcony." The Scottish bloke opens his lunchbox and finds a cheese sandwich. "Cheese sarnies *again*!" he says. "If my wife packs me one more cheese sarnie *I'm* going to throw myself off this balcony." The Irishman opens his box and finds a tuna sandwich, and *he* threatens to throw himself off, too.

The next day, the Englishman opens his lunchbox and finds a ham sandwich. "That's it," he says, and he throws himself off the balcony.

The Scottish bloke opens his lunchbox and finds a cheese sandwich, and he throws himself off the balcony. The Irishman finds a tuna sandwich and shouts "you stupid woman!" before throwing himself off, too.

At the funeral, the English, Scottish, and Irish wives are consoling each other. "I thought he *loved* ham," says the English wife. "And I thought my husband loved cheese," says the Scottish wife. "I don't understand it," sobs the Irish wife. "He always packed his own lunch."

Jojo said she didn't like the joke but then she said actually the sinister undertones probably matched similar ones in *Hamlet*. She said it's important for us to tell our own jokes because comedy is actually a way of working out stuff that bothers us. I told her I didn't like ham, cheese, or even tuna so I don't think I'm really working through anything.

Though tonight something weird happened and it wasn't just because Anya was there or because Katie McInerny kissed me.

Tonight was a full run-through of *Hamlet* and I was very surprised and pleased but also nervous because when I arrived I saw Jojo talking to Anya. Anya looked very happy when she saw me walk in and her eyes went big and her smile was huge and red because she was wearing lipstick. She looked pretty. I could see her silver necklace—the one that tells people she'll fall asleep if she eats peanuts—flashing in the spotlight, as the technician James is an idiot and is always pointing the lights the wrong way.

"Hello, Alex," Anya said to me, and Jojo said "aren't you lucky to have a groupie, Alex? A sign of things to come."

"Anya is a psychiatrist, not a groupie," I said, and Jojo didn't seem to know what to say, which I thought was interesting because Jojo *always* knows what to say. Jojo is tall and thin and she always wears a bright pink leotard and leggings with black legwarmers and an army jacket big enough for three people to fit inside. She sounds like she's reading the ten o'clock news on television even though she's from north Belfast and is really superstitious about things like saying the word *Macbeth* on stage and putting our shoes on the dressing room table and forgetting lines during rehearsals. If any of us forget our lines we are to *improvise,* she says, not just stand there in the spotlight with our mouths open like dumb twits. I gave a thumbs-up to Jojo and Anya and they smiled back.

I dumped my rucksack in the cloakroom and saw that Katie McInerny was in the male dressing room again which she says is important because she is playing a boy, which is weird. Katie is two years and one month older than me but about seven and a half inches taller. A little bit taller would be okay but seven and a half inches is like she's half giant or something. What's really wick is that she never brings her script and always asks to share mine, and I can't even open a can of Coke without her wanting some and I bet you like a million quid she's forgotten her locker key tonight and wants to share mine.

"Hiya, Horatio," she said as I walked into the dressing room.

"Hiya, Hamlet," I said, and I noticed she was wearing a white bandage around her wrist. "Did you get that from fencing?"

She looked down at it as if she had forgotten she was wearing it.

"No," she said. "I didn't get it from fencing." Her eyes had that look in them that I used to see Mum give my Dad, as if there was something she wanted to say but wanted me to guess it instead of just coming out with it. I hate games like that.

Just then, Ruen appeared. He was his Old Man self, short and baldy and his face all scrunched up like balled-up paper. I could even smell his disgusting tweed jacket. It smells like a wet dog that's been dead for about ten years.

"Are you okay?" Katie said.

"Do you want to share my locker?" I said. I needed to get rid of her and find out why Ruen was there. Her face glowed like a Christmas tree.

"Yes, that would be great . . ." And she leaned over to kiss me but I moved my face so instead of hitting my cheek she kissed my ear. No one's ever kissed my ear.

I took the key out of my pocket and pressed it into her sore hand and she yelped but I didn't say sorry because Ruen was walking away. I ran after him. He walked onto the stage and looked up.

"What is it?" I asked.

"Look, you silly boy. Use your God-given eyes," he sneered. And so I looked up and I saw Terry the technician unscrewing the old loose screws from the big brass spotlight and holding the new screws in his mouth.

"Bad idea for a boy with an attention deficit disorder to be fiddling with the set, don't you think?" Ruen said, clasping his hands behind his back.

"So?" I whispered, careful not to let anyone see my mouth moving. I saw Anya down below but I didn't say anything, though I noticed Ruen staring at her. "So what?" I asked him again.

"So. He would be easily distracted. Doesn't Katie's mother always make a big fuss at the end, coming on stage and hugging her in front of everyone on purpose?"

I thought about it. There's something about Katie's mum that I don't like. She always claps the loudest when she comes to see Katie but her smile is fake and sometimes she smells of alcohol. And even though she's small and works as a school patrol lady, Katie looks scared of her.

"I'm not doing it," I told Ruen.

"Please yourself," he said, walking away. "Only I bet Katie'll miss out on her big night."

My legs thought they were jelly for a total of nine seconds. I watched after Ruen and opened my mouth to shout after him because suddenly what he meant dawned on me like someone just poured a bucket of ice down the back of my collar. He meant that if I didn't do something to Katie's mum, Katie's mum would hurt Katie on purpose so she couldn't perform.

Just then I saw Jojo waving at me with her arm as if she was cleaning windows too high to reach. I blinked.

"Oh, you're back with us, are you?" she said, though I hadn't been anywhere.

I nodded my head.

She grinned. "Got a new joke for the rap scene, Alex?"

I said *uh-huh* and tried to remember it. I told the joke, though suddenly I felt that the word *Irishman* sounded weird inside this place and Jojo wasn't laughing like she normally did. I remembered the time last week when she came by my house to pick me up for rehearsals and instead she had to phone an ambulance for Mum. I thought of the way her hands shook when she tried to find Mum's pulse.

● ● ●

Jojo shouted at us all to regroup and run through Act Three. I ran after Ruen.

He was in the wings now, his face in the shadows.

"You could always help Katie out, couldn't you?" he said calmly. "All it would take is for you to shout up at Terry at just the right moment."

I could feel my heart beating really quickly. *Ba-dum ba-dum ba-dum.*

"Alex?" I heard Jojo call.

I stepped closer to Ruen. "But wouldn't that hurt Katie's Mum?"

Ruen's eyes were like tiny little knives in his horrible face. He smiled. "But doesn't *she* hurt Katie?"

"Alex!" I spun around and ran back across the stage to take my position. Jojo walked toward me, her eyes watching me with a strange look, and I started to panic in case she'd spotted Ruen. She bent down in front of me. "Are you okay, Alex?"

I nodded like I was definitely okay.

"You sure?"

My nod said I was *absolutely* okay. Jojo smiled and jumped up, clapping her arms above her head.

"Okay! New plan, everyone. The Opera House manager has told me we've a little more time tonight, so we're going to take it from the top *again* and smooth out the creases."

Some people groaned and some shouted "hooray!" If we were starting from the beginning then I was on first. I tried to remember the new joke I wanted to tell but I couldn't. It felt as though my brain had turned into the stuff I sometimes pull out of the pipe in the vacuum cleaner.

And then Ruen came back, but he was no longer the Old Man. He was Ghost Boy, and as he crossed the stage he turned around to me and gave me a smile and his eyes were black. The lights went down and everything went black until my eyes adjusted. Gareth and Liam stumbled across the stage with guns toward Ruen and I almost yelled, thinking they were going to run into him.

"Who's there?" Liam shouted. The smoke machine started dribbling out a blanket of silvery fog. A projector above me started to whir, but a second later James turned on some music to cover the noise. The projector threw a movie of a man—who's one of Jojo's famous friends—on the wall just behind Liam. The projection was shadowy and the man's face was hard to see and he really did look like a ghost. He was walking though he never gets any closer. Liam didn't see him.

It was my turn to go on. I stepped forward through the black curtains of the wings. "What's all this talk of ghosts?" I said in a big voice, and Gareth and Liam almost jumped out of their skins.

"We thought you were it," Liam said. He spun around, pointing his plastic gun at blank space. "Two nights in a row now we've seen this . . . *thing*."

"Thing?" I said, and as Liam told me about the ghost the fog grew thicker. Ruen was on the other side of the stage, right beside the projection of the ghost. He was just standing there, smirking. And then his voice appeared in my head.

*Alex,* he said.

I blinked, trying to ignore him. The ghost turned and started to walk again, but it looked like he really was coming toward us.

"Aye, this ghost, demon, whatever you call it," Liam said fearfully, screwing up his lines. "You'll think I'm crazy, but I think it looks like the dead king."

I took a step beside Liam, remembering what Jojo said about keeping my shoulders turned to the audience at all times. I knew my line, as it's important because it's straight from Shakespeare's play and Jojo said it was *vital to the men with money that we keep some of Shakespeare in the play* and so I made sure I learned those parts really carefully.

"It harrows me with fear," I said, but my voice sounded really far away.

Liam looked at the projection of the man walking toward us, and as he walked Ruen marched beside him, too, and I felt dizzy at seeing double. Liam started to yell and the music got louder and sounded like a heartbeat—*ba-dum ba-dum ba-dum*—and I was supposed to lift up my fake gun and point it. But instead I looked down at it in my hand and when I looked up at Ruen standing about ten feet away I saw he had one, too.

"Don't," I said as he lifted his gun, but he just grinned. The gun shone in the spotlight. The music got louder. Someone shouted.

Ruen lifted his gun higher and aimed it at Liam, and I felt the crack of the gun deep in my gut. Liam's head snapped back. Blood shot out of his forehead. He dropped to the floor.

"Liam!" I yelled, and I ran to him and fell to my knees beside his body. The blood was coming out and making a shiny puddle around his arms but it wasn't really red like in films. It was black.

Then the music stopped and the lights went up.

I looked around. Ruen wasn't there, and the projection was less ghostly and more like a home video against the wall on the stage. Liam leaned forward and I saw there was no blood on his body. He looked at me funny.

"You're shaking," he said as he sat up, and I tried to answer but I was panting so heavily that I couldn't form any words.

Jojo ran on stage and she looked really shocked. "Alex," she shouted. "That was *brilliant*! So real, so convincing! Did you just make that up on the spot?"

"I . . . I . . . ," was all I could say, and then I saw the gun in my hand and I dropped it. Jojo was using her hand to talk to the lights team. "Let's go again. Same please, Alex," she said, but I shook my head.

"I don't want to." I felt dirty and horrible and like I wanted to take a really hot bath.

Jojo looked up. "Are you okay?"

I shook my head. "I need to go," I told her, and she nodded like she understood. "Okay, everyone, back to Plan A. Act Three. Assemble!"

I whispered "thanks" to Jojo and then "sorry" and she told me "it's all right, Alex, just take it easy," but already I was running off stage and pulling open my locker and when I got home I sat in a hot bath until my fingers turned pink and squidgy.

## ANYA

Yesterday I had met Jojo Kennings and watched a run-through of the adaptation of *Hamlet* she is directing at the Grand Opera House. Alex seemed comfortable, if not a little shy, though I saw him beaming over at me once or twice when Jojo applauded his efforts. Admittedly I hadn't been inside the Grand Opera House for many, many years—my memories were still fresh of when they pulled the shutters down at the height of the Troubles and scheduled the beautiful building for demolition. Jojo remembered this, too. "It's one of the reasons I pushed so hard for this project," she explained during a brief tour of the auditorium and the stage. A teenage kid was attempting to reposition a light overhead, and although Jojo assured me that he was trained and equipped to be hanging precariously from a height of some thirty feet above, the clanks and creaks made me look up anxiously.

I followed Jojo down small narrow steps from the Grand Circle to the front of the stage. A young girl with a long pink wig and a shell suit—Bonnie, Jojo told me, who was cast as Ophelia—ran up to Jojo and asked for change for the vending machine. Jojo sighed, then dug her hand deep into her enormous jacket.

"There you go," she told Bonnie, who wrinkled her nose as she smiled. "Don't tell the others, mind."

"You give the kids money?" I asked once Bonnie had gone out of earshot.

Jojo gave another dramatic sigh. "I can't help it, they've started to feel more like family than kids I've picked to work on the project." She stopped and looked up at the ornate ceiling above us. "None of these kids recall anything beyond the Stormont Agreement in '07, and most of their home lives are so troubled that the outside world is alien and insignificant. They aren't in touch with their heritage."

I sensed there was a little more to her drive for the project than heritage—the power that lies in handing people their dreams, for example. "What about Alex?" I asked. "Why did you pick him for this project?"

"Talent is a difficult thing to put into words," she said. "But Alex is gifted. He has a way of seeing right into the human soul, though I don't even think he knows he's doing it."

"How so?"

She laced her fingers. "Despite his age, Alex somehow has this uncanny ability to perceive the angelic and the demonic in a human being. He sees the good and the bad and he understands a lot more than your average ten-year-old."

"Can you expand on that a little?" I asked.

She contemplated this. "Like most of the kids here, Alex has been exposed to a lot of things no child should have to deal with, you know?" She fell silent. I shifted tack.

"How has he taken to working as part of this group? Have there been any fights? Outbursts?"

She looked at me knowingly. "We had a team of social workers here for the first few weeks. You've met Michael, I presume?"

"Of course."

"He usually comes to check up on Alex, make sure he's hunky-dory. And the parents are always welcome." She glanced at a handful of men and women seated at the top of the auditorium. "Alex's mother has never showed up, though. And to answer your question, Alex has been the most affable and easygoing of the bunch. I was very concerned when I found his mother in that state, of course. I didn't even realize he had a problem until . . ." She looked down. "Until your email."

I could see my email had unsettled her. Suddenly her plan to pluck the city's diamonds from the rough and put them into the spotlight had revealed a flaw: What if one of them cracked on opening night?

At that moment, Alex appeared on stage directly under the spotlight, which was ominously starting to sound as if it was going to fall off any minute. Jojo shielded her eyes and looked up at the boy in the rafters.

"Everything okay up there?"

A voice shouted down. "Fixed it!"

"One more thing," I said quickly. She trained a pair of silver eyes on me. "Could I get a copy of the script?"

"Absolutely." She jogged backstage and came back a minute later with a scrolled-up bundle of paper. "Here you go." She paused, nervous for the first time during our meeting. "You think you can fix it?"

"Fix what?"

She fluttered her fingers as if *it* was an ethereal concept. "Whatever it is . . . that's bothering Alex?"

I nodded and held up the script she'd given me. "This is wonderful, thank you very much."

Alex looked down at Jojo intently. "Are we ready to start again?"

She threw me a smile. "See? He was *born* for the stage." Then she clapped her hands together and shouted: "Everyone back for the third act!"

I thanked her for her time and waved up at Alex. He didn't acknowledge me. He stood stock-still in the center of the stage, lit up by the spotlight, his eyes fixed ahead.


I spent the rest of the evening reading Jojo's script. From my limited memory of the original play—about a young prince who's devastated by his father's death and his mother's hasty remarriage—I was able to pick out those parts that Jojo had retained intact and those she had tweaked to comment on contemporary Belfast. Some of the heavier-handed alterations—"to riot, or not to riot," Hamlet says at one point—made me wince, though parts of the retained original made me wonder whether Alex's participation in the play was doing him as much harm as it was doing him good. He was confident and believable on stage, no doubt about that. His joke even made me chuckle.

But there was a scene in there that made me wonder, a scene that could easily confuse a young boy's sense of reality and fantasy: When Hamlet and Horatio see the looming ghost of the dead king, Horatio cries out, "It harrows me with fear and wonder," comparing the specter to a demon. "I swear," Horatio adds in Jojo's version, "I wouldn't believe that I could see this demon without the sensible and true guarantee of my own eyes."

The reasons for Ruin's presence in Alex's life are becoming clearer. But the steps toward his eradication are not yet in focus.

So today's task is to go to Alex's home and meet his aunt Beverly, and also to scope out Alex's immediate surroundings. I am never satisfied with the picture of a patient that a general evaluation gives me; Poppy was so much more than the individual she portrayed in psychiatric interviews. Alive in the Scottish Highlands, confident and thoughtful at Arthur's Seat, she was a product of her environment. In a way, I find myself considering Michael's push for Alex to stay at home, in a place where he obviously feels safe and more at ease. But I have learned there are ways to make the transition from home to residential unit much smoother, if one takes the time to understand exactly where a person has come from.

I put on my talisman and head toward the city on foot. I make it as far as Saint George's Market close to the Belfast Waterfront before my phone rings. It is Michael. I consider ignoring the call. I feel awkward about speaking to him again, given our conflict over Alex. I stare at my phone for a moment, then press ANSWER.

"Man, you walk fast," Michael says on the other end. He's panting and I can hear the drone of traffic in the background.

"Where are you?"

"Can you wait where you are for a sec? I'm almost there."

I look around. A tall, blond-haired figure in a billowing black rain-coat waves from the other side of the road. It's Michael. I frown and wave back. When the traffic lights turn green he jogs toward me, smil-ing. A far cry from our encounter at the hospital. As he draws closer his smile fades into concern, then into a look of apology. He sticks out his hand, and when I shake it he pulls me gently toward him, pecking my cheek.

"How are you? Better than last time I saw you?"

I nod. "Much."

His eyes are searching. "Look, I'm sorry about . . . well, getting so tense the other day."

I feel myself soften at his apology. "I know this case is important to you. And I should probably reassure you that I have only Alex's interests at heart."

He nods. "I know things probably seemed a lot simpler in Edin-burgh. But it's different here. None of the kids I've seen being sepa-rated from their families has fared well . . ."

We have started walking now, his voice drowned out by the hustle and bustle inside the market. We take a side street toward the city hall where a man is begging. Michael stops to throw some change into the small red cap on the ground in front of him. Suddenly, he rises two notches in my estimation.

"Maybe you didn't believe me when I said I had no interest in separating Alex and Cindy," I say lightly. "But I meant it. A spell at MacNeice House would ensure that Alex receives the correct treat-ment . . ."

Michael looks ahead, his hands deep in his pockets. "Once bitten, twice shy, I guess," he says.

"What do you mean?"

He hesitates. "There was a guy who worked there a few years ago, same position as you. Manson. One of my cases was a twelve-year-old girl. Nina. Cute little blond thing. Suffered from Asperger's, and also this rare disease called Cigarette Burns. Her dad even confessed to abusing her. Mother kicked him out, pleaded with us to let Nina stay with her. But as soon as Manson finished Nina's treatment he sent her off to a foster family."

We have reached the end of the side street, the blare of the city traffic inching closer. I stop to let him finish.

"Was she reunited with her mother?"

"Yes, but there was a lot of unnecessary heartache caused. And I guess I'm just a skeptic anyhow. I think a lot of these kids make things up to get attention."

It's at this point that my heart sinks. The team involved in assessing Alex's needs consists of a jocular, doughnut-obsessed occupational therapist, Howard Dungar, who remains mostly in the sidelines as a signature on the report; Ursula, whose presence in the case is surprisingly in the form of a stony silence of disapproval at meetings, her head firmly turned toward the date of her retirement; and Michael the skeptic, who doesn't believe in what I do.

"So what are you out here for, anyway?" he asks, visibly forcing a smile.

I step out toward the road, waiting for a break in oncoming traffic. "Sightseeing."

"Sightseeing? I thought you grew up here?"

"Demon hunting, then," I say lightly. "I'm investigating Alex's environment."

Just then, he steps toward the road, thrusts an arm out, and a few seconds later we're both bundling into a taxi.

"Just up the road, please," he tells the driver.

"Where're we going?" I ask Michael.

His green eyes are serious, unsmiling. "You said you wanted to hunt demons. We're hunting demons."

The taxi pulls around the front of the city hall and carries us out of the city, taking us along a sprawling, congested street that has large murals on either side, some of them spreading across three or four walls. Michael leans across me, studying the rows of shops and houses.

"Alex's old school is around here," he says.

"We're going to Alex's old school?"

He shakes his head. I catch a whiff of aftershave as he leans close.

There's tobacco, too, lingering in his clothes. It is oddly reassuring. "This is the route he used to take to walk there. Look."

He taps the taxi driver on the shoulder and asks him to pull over. Outside, he jogs across the road toward one of the biggest murals. This one has an enormous oval in the middle in which are painted the words UVF FOR GOD AND ULSTER. There are five named faces of terrorists above and four gun-wielding figures at the bottom, all faceless, all dressed completely in black. Here, too, we find murals of famous Belfast folk, a thirty-foot stretch of wall dedicated to C. S. Lewis, the side of a house commemorating the *Titanic*.

But one mural makes me freeze. It is a demon holding a gun, snarling at the viewer and stalking across the graves of dead Republicans.

"You've never seen this before?"

"There's murals all over the city. I've seen dozens like this."

"But not with demons in it?"

I stare at the image above me. What kind of impact would seeing this image daily have on an impressionable boy?

"There's more." Michael taps my arm and heads back to the taxi. Inside the cab he leans forward to the driver and gives directions. The driver does a sharp U-turn and pulls us through streets that reveal a city in the process of being rebuilt; old, graffitied buildings en route to demolition, spewing the contents of interior rooms as if a giant ax has chopped them in half; beside them, smaller, newer buildings with silver siding and artwork on the exterior. I can't decide if this is a good thing or not.

Finally, we pull up alongside a pub on a busy road, prompting some angry car horns behind us.

"Come with me," Michael says, jumping out of the car and racing around to the other side to help me out. Despite myself, I'm warmed by his chivalry.

"What do you think?" he asks, nodding at the wall in front of us.

Another mural. This time, it's a wall-sized portrait of Margaret Thatcher. Only, she has red eyes and blood trickling from the corners of her mouth. Another demon.

● ● ●

"So, can I ask a personal question?"

Michael reaches for the sugar pourer. We are at a café on the Waterfront overlooking the River Lagan and the usual clouds of starlings looping around the Victoria Bridge. An early-evening coffee is the farthest distance I will travel in a professional relationship.

I stir my coffee and watch, amazed, as Michael dumps sugar into his coffee without abandon. "Ask away."

"What made you want to become a child psychiatrist?"

I take a gulp. The coffee is much too hot and I struggle not to splutter.

"You say it like I'm a lion tamer."

"Not far off, though," he says, grinning. He sets down the sugar pourer.

"That's the common assumption, isn't it? That we psychiatrists are all trying to tame the wild imaginings of damaged kids . . ."

"No, it's just I . . ." He loosens his tie with a flick of his thumb under the green knot at his throat.

"My parents sent me to a shrink when I was little. Made me nervous about the profession ever since." The admission makes him clear his throat and cross his legs.

"Nervous in the sense that you don't believe I can help Alex?"

He throws me a look. "No, I do. It's just . . . well, my stance on treatment is a little more grounded in the theory that medication only works on a short-term basis. In the long run, if we're to ensure Alex has a future in society, I believe we need to work with him and Cindy. And his auntie Bev. I believe Bev is going to play an important role in his life now."

"Doesn't she have to return to Cork?"

He looks past me. "You didn't answer my question."

I retrace my train of thought. "Oh. Long story. The short version is that I got a scholarship to medical school, then further funding to study child psychiatry."

"Two scholarships?"

"Three, actually." Usually I am self-deprecating, but not about my scholarships.

"Three?"

"I grew up in Tiger's Bay."

Michael gives a whistle of surprise and raises his eyebrows. I find myself warmed by his response. *Tiger's Bay* meant nothing to anyone in Edinburgh. To a Belfast boy, it means something akin to the Bronx in New York City, or South Central in Los Angeles. It means that, in all likelihood, I should have ended up at the other end of the social scale. The truth is, my childhood has earned me an invaluable amount of self-respect. Or rather, what it took to climb out of there has.

"How . . . on earth . . . does a girl from Tiger's Bay end up a child psychiatrist?"

"The government was keen to give kids from single-parent families in the north Belfast area a head start to grammar school. Scholarship number one. Then a medical degree at Edinburgh University, scholarship number two. Followed by a scholarship to train as a child psychiatrist."

He shakes his head. "If that's the short version, I can't wait to hear the long one."

I rub my scar without realizing. He notices. "Has the long version anything to do with that?" he asks, half jokingly. When I hesitate his smile fades.

"Sorry, that was rude of me."

Before I can reply a waitress approaches, asking if we want anything else. The café is starting to fill with couples on dates, friends meeting for after-work drinks. Michael holds up a hand to the waitress to indicate we're fine with coffee. He looks appalled at himself for the reference to my scar.

I have a very convincing, very rehearsed story for this scar. It is so deep and oddly situated, running from my cheek to my neck, that makeup doesn't cover it fully. The scar is the reason I grew my hair so long, though since turning forty it has started to thin at the ends. More and more I use this lie when my hair fails to conceal it. The lie I concocted—which revolved around an unfortunate coral encounter while snorkeling in Fiji—was to engineer ensuing questions (*Is Fiji beautiful? So you snorkel? What kind of coral?* et cetera) that deflected entirely from the truth and toward a much more pleasant direction of conversation.

Only, right now, I'm not in a lying mood.

"Actually, you're right on the money, Michael," I say breezily. "My daughter has . . . *had* . . . early-onset schizophrenia." I tap my scar. "This was a result of my agreement to put her in an inpatient unit."

Michael nods and presses his fingertips together, his face soft. "I'm sorry." There is a pause as he holds my gaze, fitting the scar to its imagined origin. "It's one thing to treat other people's children. But to see your own child suffering, especially when you understood so intimately . . ." He shakes his head. "I can't even imagine how that must have felt."

I open my mouth to explain how it felt, then find I am lost for words. The fact is, schizophrenia doesn't affect every sufferer the same way. Hallucinations, unshakable delusions, and muddled thoughts are its most striking symptoms. In Poppy's case, her delusions were of a physical, architectural nature. She'd see walls right in front of her that stretched up to the moon. She'd see bridges, vast, swelling rivers, and oceans channeling down Princes Street. This was the cause of her outbursts. And she became increasingly convinced that she was stuck in a hole or being buried alive. Sometimes sitting on our sofa watching television, she'd suddenly begin to scream for dear life, convinced that she was falling into a bottomless pit. "Help me, Mum!" she'd yell, her nails dug deep into the arms of her seat, as if they were the sides of the hole she was sinking into. It took me a long time to understand what was happening when she did this. And when I wouldn't believe her, her reality would shift again: I was trying to kill her. She would become violent.

Michael's stare brings me back into the present. I clear my throat. "She was the reason I trained in child psychiatry. My mother had suffered with what I now believe was schizophrenia. It was never diagnosed, of course. The GPs gave my mother all sorts of prescriptions for depression, told her to chew valerian root . . ."

Michael snorts. "Fobbed her off, you mean . . ."

I nod. "I heard there was a genetic link to schizophrenia. By the time Poppy was three, I had seen things in her behavior that none of the pediatricians could explain. So I changed my course of study. Three years of basic psychiatry, then six months in child psychiatry."

"As a single mother?"

I smile. "Yes. I had a wonderful neighbor who helped out with child care. And I can live on four hours' sleep."

"You must have seen an improvement in her after the treatment," he says. "If you still advocate inpatient units."

"She *did* improve. Before that, she had no life. No friends, no ability to make friends, no hobbies . . . But the problem with schizophrenia is it's unpredictable. Too many riddles for one person to solve."

He lifts his head and looks at me, searching my expression. "Riddles frustrate you. Don't they?"

I blink. "Don't they frustrate *you*?"

He leans back in his chair, crossing an ankle over one knee. "Riddles I can live with. Battered kids, I can't. Man, the stuff I've seen . . . I mean I know you probably deal with the most terrifying psychological nightmares ever . . . But social work—" He grins, though his gaze stretches far into the distance. "Someone shoulda warned me. Someone shoulda warned me." He uncrosses his legs. "I bought a little garden for that reason."

"You bought a garden for *what* reason?"

"To detox," he says, using his hands for emphasis, as if he's brushing an invisible cloud of smoke off his chest. "To free myself from the tangle of all those messed-up families. Nothing like fertilizer and slug repellant to take your mind off a teenager who starved her baby to death because she was out selling crack."

The image makes me shudder, and he sees it. The shadow of a smile returns to his face. "So what do *you* do, then? Swim? Jog?"

I nod. "Both. And I play." I run my fingers up and down the table as if it's a piano.

He raises his eyebrows. "Ah, the merry Joanna? Jazz?"

"Classical. Or post-impressionist, if you want specifics."

"Always."

I feel the conversation slide in a direction that makes me nervous. I change the subject. "I read the notes from the primary consultations with Alex, but I doubt very much that he has attachment disorder," I tell him.

"No?"

"He's not bipolar, either. I won't rule it out, of course, but that's my instinct, and I haven't been wrong in quite some time."

He taps a spoon against a cup. "What about childhood schizophrenia?" I sigh, and he looks up. "What, that's a possibility?"

I am tentative. "From what I've seen, yes. But a proper diagnosis requires admission and observation," I remind him.

His face looks heavier, all of a sudden: his shoulders slump. "If Cindy gets home and finds Alex has been shipped off to some . . . and forgive me, but *nuthouse* . . . I don't think she'll be able to deal with it. I think it might be the final straw."

*The child's interests must come first,* I think. But, clearly, so much is at stake, and I am willing to give Michael's approach a little longer. I look out over the darkening skyline, rush-hour traffic forming a necklace of crimson brake lights across the bridge. The birds swarm and swoop as they settle in for the night. I meet Michael's gaze across the table, wincing at the concern in his eyes.

"For now, I'll evaluate Alex at his home."

9

# INVISIBILITY

ALEX

Dear Diary,

A convict escapes from prison by digging a tunnel that comes up
outside the prison in a school playground. The convict is so happy
when he crawls out of the mucky tunnel that he starts shouting, "I'm
free, I'm free!"

A little girl on the playground walks up to him.

"So what?" she says. "I'm four."


I've been sent back to school, which hasn't been good because all the
other kids seem to have heard about Mum and they're starting to make
up stories, like she's loony and I tried to kill her, or she tried to kill me
and then herself. When Auntie Bev picks me up at the front gates all the
other parents look at me and smile but really they are talking and saying
horrible things about Mum.

Also I'm not speaking to Ruen. When he promised me the special
thing for letting him study me I was happy with it, but the other day I

asked him why he still hadn't given me what he promised and he looked like he had forgotten all about it.

Okay, so I know I said it was a secret but the special thing was a new house for me and Mum. When we first became friends and he asked me to let him study me and told me I could have anything I wanted, I thought of asking for a new bike. I remember Mum was in my bedroom, which was unusual, and Ruen was the Old Man and he was standing over me with his arms behind his back as usual and his face in that tight fishy frown. I could see the bike I wanted in my head—it would be black and say KILLER on the side and the tires would be thick and the seat would be a silver skull. Mum was scrubbing the windowsills with a liquid that smelled just like Ruen.

"You could grow mushrooms on these sills," she said, and even though she was scrubbing hard enough to make her T-shirt all wet the black stuff wasn't coming off. The windows always looked like liquid, even when it wasn't raining.

"The council puts people like us in places like this and forgets about them," Mum said, and her voice rattled because she was now on her knees rubbing the metal brush up and down and I hated the sound. I drew a picture with my fingertip in the wet glass of the window. Mum stopped to press the towel closer to the bottom of the wall to catch the drips. "I mean it's not like I want Buckingham Palace. A place that's not likely to kill us both from live wires might be nice." She wiped her forehead with the back of her hand. "Punishment, that's what it is."

"Punishment for what?"

She tucked one of the long pink threads in her hair behind her ear. Some of the foam sat on the top of her ear like a cloud.

"For not being a perfect citizen. For living off benefits. For reminding the establishment of how it failed."

"Who's the establishment, Mum?"

She nodded at me. "Exactly." She bent down to drip the metal brush in the bucket, then wiped the other side of her face and another little cloud of foam sat on her other ear. I tried not to laugh.

"That reminds me," she said. "I saw Fatty Matthews talking to you at the corner shop last night."

I thought back to it. I didn't even know who Fatty Matthews was.

I'd been buying milk and some big bald fat guy came up to me and starting asking about school.

". . . you tell me, okay?" Mum was saying. "Because that powdery stuff isn't talc. Not even if he offers you lots of money."

I nodded and finished my drawing on the window. After a few minutes Mum leaned back and stared at it and her face looked confused.

"What's that, Alex?"

"What's what?"

She stood up and the metal brush splatted foam on the floor. "Your picture. What is it?"

I looked at it and thought, *Crap, Mum doesn't know who Ruen is* and then I tried to think of a lie but Mum was staring at me.

"It's a man."

"I can see that. Why did you draw it?"

I opened my mouth for a long time and said "because I was bored" but she was wiping her face now and knelt down in front of me.

"Alex, is there something you want to talk to me about?"

I shook my head, then thought better of it. "I'm hungry."

She tightened her hands on my arms. "You know, what Dad did—it wasn't anything to do with you."

I was thinking of asking Ruen for a burger now. Forget the bike. I'd seen someone eat a burger through the window of a shop in town, at first I thought it was like a totem pole or something but no. It was a burger, with two fat round brown juicy slabs of burger meat and lettuce and a thick pink strip of bacon and cheese sliding onto the plate and it was so tall someone had stuck a flag in it like Mount Everest.

". . . with chips, too," I said, and Mum stopped whatever she was saying and looked at me with her eyes wide. She looked like me when she did that, because normally her eyes are small and puffy and sad.

"Alex, did you hear what I said?"

My arms were really hurting now. I nodded.

"Repeat it. Repeat what I said."

I tried to think back, though my stomach was growling and I could actually *smell* it now, I could smell that burger. She kept asking me to say what she'd said and so words came rising up in my mind like chips in a deep fat fryer, *police* and *Dad* and *blood* and *got what he deserved*.

"There are some things you're too young to understand," she said, her voice growing softer, and I took a big breath because finally she'd let go of my arms. And then she raised a hand to her mouth and her eyes filled with tears.

"Oh, Alex," she said. "I'm so sorry."

I looked down at my arms and where she'd held me on each arm was a big red mark in the shape of her hand. She tried to rub the mark away with her palms but it didn't go away. So she pulled me close to her and my head was between her jaw and her shoulder and she was rubbing my back. I could smell cigarettes in her hair and also sweat and then Mum's smell, which is really nice. After a long time she leaned back and looked at me and there was a big smile on her face, which didn't happen very often.

"If you could have anything in the whole world, what would it be?"

"A burger with bacon and cheese."

"No, really, Alex. What would it be?"

*For Dad to come back,* I thought, but I didn't say that because I knew it would only upset her.

"What would *you* have?" I asked. She looked shocked and blinked three times. Then she smiled.

"No one's ever asked me, I don't think," she said. She stood up and looked at the windowsill.

"A new house," she said then. "Yeah. A brand-new house. With a garden. And three . . . no, *four* bedrooms, with a guest bedroom and everything. Maybe an exercise room."

She started pacing up and down the room, describing every single room in microscopic detail, right down to the fact that we'd have no crappy attic with mold and a dead person's things all over the place and no mice and no drug-dealing neighbors either.


Later that day I told Ruen that the sort of house we'd like would have a garden at the back that gets some sun during the daytime, a kitchen big enough for two people to move in with an oven that works and hopefully a faucet that doesn't drip, a toilet that flushes, and walls that don't look like the last person living there took a pickax to them.

"Consider it arranged."

"What?"

He narrowed his eyes at me in his Alex Is Stupid look. "I'll take care of it, Alex."

"How will you take care of it?" I asked. "Do you have lots of money?"

He smiled and winked. "I have powers of which you are unaware. A mere house is a trifle, my boy. If you'd asked me for a planet, it might have taken some time. But I could accommodate."

I just laughed. *A planet,* I thought. What would I need a planet for? He's like that, Ruen. A bit of a snob, at least when he's the Old Man. He rolls his eyes when I play football and tells me my drawings of skeletons are *inept,* which means they're crap. According to Ruen, I should be reading something called *Chekhov* and am very *uncultured* for not learning the piano.

But then he tries to do what I see all the other demons doing: He suggests I do something mean, like drop the light in the Opera House on Katie's mum's head. I was too scared to do that. He told me later I was stupid for not doing it because really it would have been Terry dropping the thing and because Katie's mum hits her because she's a drunk and is jealous of Katie. *How can a mum be jealous of her own kid?* I asked him and he gave me The Look again, like I'm stupid.

And then last night Katie only came to rehearsals to tell Jojo she couldn't stay and when I saw her at the door she had a big black bruise on her cheek and her face was swollen and Jojo put her arms around her. Katie gave me a wave and ran off and I looked up at that light and thought *Ruen was right.* Sometimes bad people need bad things to happen to them otherwise the bad things just go on and on and on.


I don't think I've ever done any of the things Ruen tells me to do, so I don't really know why I told Anya who he was when he asked me to. Sometimes his friends will come up to me and ask me to do things, too, like steal from Mum's purse so I can buy her a Mother's Day card, or, once, one of them spent a long time plotting out how I can get back at our neighbors for breaking our window. I told them all to go away and leave me alone. I allowed Ruen to study me, but that doesn't mean I don't have a brain and will just follow what he says like I'm a stupid donkey or something.

Plus, I know what happened to Mum. I don't think Ruen realizes this, and I don't tell him. But sometimes, when she gets sad, I see demons surrounding her and talking to her, and the more they talk to her the sadder she gets. I tell them under my breath to get out. Usually, they just laugh at me.

I am very scared that they'll keep talking to Mum and she'll just keep taking pills and never wake up. I want to tell this to Anya, but I'm not sure what she'll make of it.

Still, when Anya arrives at our front door, I am really pleased. I've made her onions on toast with a glass of milk and set them all on the table like she's a guest. Auntie Bev is really smiley. She wags her finger at me and says:

"He looks like a right wee Charlie Chaplin today, doesn't he?"

Anya looks at my clothes and says, "what a lovely suit, Alex, and the bow tie's a nice touch, too."

"Alex dresses himself," I hear Bev whisper to Anya. "I found a whole closet of stuff left over from the old man who lived here before. I think he's supplementing his clothes with these old suits. I'm taking him shopping tomorrow."

*Him*, I think. It's rude for them to talk about me as if I'm not even there. I look at Auntie Bev's silver shower rail in the doorway and try to pull my head up, but I can hardly reach it. I climb up on the sofa then onto the lamp table beside it. I hold on to the door frame and lift my foot up over the bar to hang like a bat, the way Auntie Bev did.

"Alex?"

I can see Auntie Bev and Anya but they're upside down. Our dinner table looks like it's floating and the blue chair looks like it's stuck to the ceiling and everything looks so different I start to laugh.

Anya steps forward and holds my shoulders. "Careful," she says, slipping my feet off the bar and catching me as I drop a little. Then she turns me the right way up and I feel dizzy.

"Well done!" she says. "That's not easy to do, you know. Though maybe it's best if you warn me next time. Don't want you falling on your noggin." She ruffles my hair and I feel surprised that no one's yelled at me. Anya sits down at the table, waiting for me.

"I'll just be in here while you have your chat, is that okay?" Auntie Bev tells Anya in a loud voice, pointing at the kitchen.

Anya nods. "Sure. Are you making something nice?"

Auntie Bev ducks back out of the kitchen and wrinkles her nose. "I'd love to, but all my sister has in the cupboards is ketchup and"—she glances at me—"what the mice left behind."

"You could make a nice risotto out of that, surely?" says Anya, though her face looks disgusted.

Auntie Bev presses her hand against her forehead and then crosses herself quickly. "We'll go to the grocery store," she tells me, then gives Anya the thumbs-up.

"What's risotto?" I ask Anya.

"Haven't you had risotto before?"

I sit down at the table and shake my head.

"It's like rice," she says.

"Rice?"

She looks at me with her face all blank then says, "you've never had rice, either?"

I shake my head. Mum says she only has sixty quid a week for all the bills, and the way I go through sketch pads and cans of dog food for Woof we're lucky we don't have to live on air.

"Do you know you can buy enough onions for a whole week for less than a quid?" I tell Anya, and her face changes. She says, "that makes sense."

She pulls a notepad from her bag, then a pen, then a fat pencil case and a big sketch pad. She hands the pencil case and sketch pad to me.

"What's this for?" I ask.

"I know you love drawing," she says. "I'd love it if you could draw some pictures for me."

I unzip the pencil case and say "cool!" because there's pastels in there as well as pencils, and I like the pastels because I can lick them and make the colors blurry, which looks cool.

"What do you want a picture of?" I say, though I've already started licking the back of my hand and dabbing a yellow pastel in the spit. Anya doesn't say anything and just watches as I start drawing. I don't even know what I'm drawing but it makes sense to use yellow. I start off by drawing a sun with spirals instead of rays because the rays sometimes look like a spider and spiders are gross.

"Why don't you draw your Mum for me?" Anya says.

I take out a peach color and a brown and start to draw. I begin with Mum's face, which is an egg shape with quite hollow cheeks, and then her legs, which are like sticks. When I finish, Anya tilts her head and points at my drawing.

"Someone's carrying your mum. Who is it?"

I look at the picture and realize I haven't given myself a bow tie. I quickly find a red and draw it in. "*I'm* carrying Mum," I tell Anya. Then I use a dark blue for my eyes and find a light blue for mum's eyes.

"Why are you carrying your mum in this picture?"

I'm not sure. "I think she might have a sore foot. Or maybe she's too tired to walk."

Anya nods and frowns so I pick up a red pastel and dab some bits of blood from Mum's foot to show why I'm carrying her.

"What about Woof? Can you draw him?"

I find some white and black and draw Woof with his head under Mum's feet, because if I *was* carrying Mum like that he would definitely help me.

Anya takes a big breath. "And what about your Dad? Could you draw him?"

I look at my colors. I don't know what color to use for Dad. I can't even remember what color his eyes were and for a minute this scares me. Then Anya says: "Even if you can't draw a picture of your Dad, can you draw something that comes to mind when you think of him? Even if it's just a mark on the page?"

I blink my eyes four times. I pick up the blue pastel again and draw.

"Is that a car?" Anya asks. I nod.

"Did your father drive a blue car?"

I shake my head, and she just nods and I stare at the picture. My hands feel tingly and my heart is pounding.

"I saw him in a blue car once," I tell her.

Anya nods and smiles. "What about Ruen? Or any of the people you see. Could you draw them?"

I blink. I had hoped she had forgotten all about Ruen. I wasn't happy when Ruen asked me to tell her about him but I felt I needed to be honest with her, and she seems like the sort of person I can be honest with. I look around me. There's a demon in the kitchen with Auntie Bev. You wouldn't think she was a demon because she is wearing a white dress tied at the waist and she's small with curly brown hair and looks like she eats a lot of cakes, but when she looks at me her eyes are black and I feel sick.

"Who's that?" Anya says, pointing at the picture.

"I don't know."

"Is that Ruen?" she asks, tapping at the picture I've drawn of Horn Head, though I haven't drawn his red horn properly and it looks squiggly. I shake my head and rub it out with my thumb.

I fiddle with the scratchy corners of my bow tie and say:

"I *would* tell you more about Ruen, but I think you just think I'm crazy and that Ruen is someone in my head."

She looks surprised. "Does Ruen live in your head?"

I shake my head, very slowly. "I'm not sure where he lives. Hell probably. But for a long time he's lived mostly with me."

"How long, would you say?"

I shrug. "Since my Dad died."

She nods and writes something down in her notebook.

"Where does Ruen sleep?" she says, and she says it while she's writing.

"I don't think he sleeps. He comes and goes. Sometimes he disappears and I don't see him."

"How long does he disappear for?"

I shrug. "Sometimes a few hours. I usually see him every day, at least three times. Sometimes he just walks up and down our hall."

"Why does he walk up and down the hall?"

"I think he gets bored."

"What does he get bored of?"

Just as I'm getting sick of answering for Ruen he appears in the corner of the room. So I lean forward and look at him and ask, "what do you get bored of?"

This shocks both Anya and Ruen, who is the Old Man just then. Auntie Bev is still in the kitchen, singing. Ruen looks very weird, like he's managed to crack his scowl into an open cave and his eyes are all droopy, like Woof's.

"Is he here now?" Anya says, her eyes all wide and round.

"He wouldn't dare miss a conversation about him, would you, Ruen?" I jeer at him and he scowls. "What. Do. You. Get. Bored. Of?"

Eventually, he answers.

"Not being seen," he says, and his voice is very croaky like he's been smoking.

I thought so. I tell this to Anya.

"Not being seen?" she says. "You mean, because only you can see him?"

I say yes and then I remember something Ruen told me a while ago. "He says that demons are old-school angels of Hell, which is a culture as old as the earth. Demons have souls but they don't have human bodies. This is like a big deal to them so they get points for stuff they do."

"What sort of things do they do?" she says, and she has to turn over her page because it's filled up with scribbles. I pause for half a minute because there's a demon right above Anya, and he's so fat his skin drips down around his body like a mountain of ice cream. It's like he's lying on her shoulders, trying to get comfortable. He yawns and then he disappears and I take a big breath of relief.

"I thought he was gonna squish you," I say by accident.

"What?"

I shake my head and remember what she asked me. "Ruen says he likes bringing a human to their lowest point. That's when demons get a prize called a human likeness."

"They become human?"

I shake my head. "No, they just *look* like a human. But even then they don't really get seen by anybody, not really. And I think invisibility's a very odd thing to be bored of," I tell Anya. "Being invisible would be so cool!"

I start to tell Anya all the cool stuff I'd do if I turn invisible, and she writes some of it down and then holds her hand up.

"Can I ask Ruen another question?"

I glance at him and feel a bit annoyed. I'm sick of talking about him now and wish I'd never bothered telling Anya about him in the first place because he's getting all the attention. He just stares. "Yeah," I tell Anya.

"Wait, where *is* Ruen?" she asks, looking around the room. I point at the spot he's standing in, which is right next to the window and beside the blue armchair.

"There," I say.

Anya shuffles in her seat so she can see the exact spot. She points. "There?" Ruen looks surprised by all this pointing and for a moment I think he's going to disappear.

"Yeah, there." I get up and stand next to him. He looks down at me, frowning. He doesn't seem to be angry, just in a bit of a daze. I hold my hands out to my side. "Right here."

Anya nods. "Can you hold your hand up, Alex, so it touches Ruen's head? Just so I know how tall he is. Because only you can see him."

I stretch up on my tiptoes to measure Ruen's height. My fingers brush the bald spot on top of his head and it feels cold and smooth.

Anya smiles and writes something down. "Ruen seems tall for a boy," she said. "Didn't you say he was a boy?"

I shake my head. "He's old."

More scribbles in her notebook.

"Can you describe for me what Ruen's wearing?"

I tell her. I could tell her with my eyes shut, when he's the Old Man he never wears anything else. Same dusty brown suit with the same smell of a dead dog. It makes me want to throw up. I don't mention that he's a monster sometimes, and I would never, ever tell her about Horn Head because when he's the Horn Head he freaks me out.

"So you're both wearing suits?" she says, and she laughs. "Is there some wardrobe copying going on here?"

I look from the straggling bits of black thread dangling from the hems of Ruen's suit to the shirt collar so green and crusty it looks like someone gobbed on his neck, and I say: "there's no *way* I dress like that."

Then she asks something weird. "Can you tell me what Ruen is *thinking*?"

I look at him. He looks at me and raises an eyebrow as if he's curious about that, too. I look back at Anya.

"Of course I can't tell you what he's thinking. That would make me a mind reader, wouldn't it?"

She just smiles. Then it occurs to me: She thinks I'm lying. She really does think I'm making all of this up. I feel my cheeks get hot. I clench and unclench my fists. "I don't want to do this anymore," I tell Anya. "Can I see my Mum now, please?"

"Hold on a minute, Alex," she says quickly, setting her pen on her lap. "I was enjoying learning all about Ruen. Maybe you can tell me what his hobbies are?"

And so I look at Ruen again, and he rolls his eyes. "Tell her I quite enjoy genocide," he says, and I start to say it but then remember what *genocide* means and think that she might look at me funny and so I stay quiet. When I don't say anything Auntie Bev comes in from the kitchen with a big smile and bends down in front of me.

"If you tell the nice lady all about the things you can see, we can go see your Mum. Okay, Alex?"

"Today?"

Bev looks at Anya and then nods. "Yep. Today."

And I feel really excited then and tell Anya that I can see all Ruen's friends, too, that some of them are scary and look like dragons, and some of them look like human-looking robots with red eyes. "Like *The Terminator*?" she says and I realize that yes, that's exactly how some of them look. And so I start wondering whether James Cameron who directed the film sees what I see, too, and maybe she could speak to him as well.

I hear Bev whispering something to Anya about "masculinity issues" and Arnold Schwarzenegger and Anya nods and says "potentially."

"Let's talk more about Ruen," Anya says, turning back to me. "What does he like to eat?"

But I've had enough. I just want to see Mum. So I say: "Why do you want to know so much about Ruen, huh? He's a miserable old fart who does nothing but make false promises and whine about how crappy our piano is."

I glance over at Ruen, expecting him to be mad at me for saying this. And he does look really mad, just not at me. He is looking right past me at the doorway. I follow his gaze but I don't see anything.

"Alex?" I hear Anya ask.

"What's wrong?" I say to Ruen, but he doesn't say anything. He is showing his teeth like Woof does when he's angry, his face is turning bright red. Then he changes into a monster right in front of me, his short skinny arms bursting out of his shirt and turning dark and shadowy, and his eyes rolling back in his head. He grows so tall that his head bends against the ceiling and instead of his funny, purplish monster-skin he looks like thick black smoke with eyes and a hole like the middle of a tornado where his mouth should be. And in the middle of that hole are four long fangs. Then he turns and lunges toward me and I shout "Ruen!"

When I look up I see he's thrown himself across the other side of the room in a kind of twist and crashes into the doorway of the living room, and I am screaming.

When he crashes, I feel very strange. There is such a sharp pain in my chest that I fall to the floor.

"Alex!" I hear Anya shout, and Ruen lets out a huge, deep roar and then there is nothing.

# 10
# THE THIN EDGE
# OF BELIEF

## ANYA

At my last session with Alex I met his temporary caregiver, his aunt Beverly, who drove up from Cork on the evening of Cindy's suicide attempt. I am relieved when I meet with her—she is lively, warm, and eager to help Alex in whatever way she can. Beverly is Cindy's elder sister by eleven years and works as an ear, nose, and throat doctor. She has no children of her own and, having had a somewhat intermittent relationship with Alex over the years, is anxious to make up for lost time and be a support for her sister and nephew.

"I wish I'd come home sooner," she tells me over and over, her face twisting as she looks at the broken window in Cindy's kitchen boarded up haphazardly with cardboard and tape, the spots of mold above the sink. She pulls a cigarette from a fresh packet and asks if I mind. I shake my head and she opens the kitchen door, stepping out into the mossy yard.

"I knew Cindy was struggling. I should have come back for good, helped out. I love Alex to bits. Cindy and I haven't always seen eye-to-eye but . . ." She breaks off, taking a deep drag. "We had such different childhoods. I've never understood Cindy. She's always kept things to herself. Our mum did a good job of pulling information out of her, but she never opened up to me."

I glance back at Alex, who is bringing his plate into the kitchen. He sets it on the countertop and smiles at me. Bev waits until he is gone before she continues.

"I only have so much time that I can take off work to care for Alex," she says. "But I'm all he's got until Cindy pulls herself out of this."

"What about Alex's grandparents? Are they living?"

She stubs out her cigarette. "Dad died when I was little," she says quietly. "Mum passed five years ago. She would be horrified by all this."

"And Alex's father?" I ask. "Does he have contact with him?"

She steps inside, shutting the door behind her. It won't close until she kicks it, making a dent in the base. She sighs. "You'd need to talk to Cindy about that. The identity of Alex's father is something she chose to keep from all of us."

I wonder why the decision has been made to hold it secret. I make a note to ask Cindy about it; even if Alex's father needs to remain un-named, I still need more information about their relationship.


My session with Alex ends badly, although it reveals much about his relationship with his mother. When I ask him to draw a picture of her he sketches an image of himself carrying his mother, and I notice that his self-portrait is much larger than his sketch of Cindy. She looks baby-like, vulnerable in his arms, her own arms wrapped tightly around Alex's neck. From this I deduce that Alex has sensed her fragility and instability for a long time, which must have had a huge impact on his sense of security and his role in the family as protector. His drawing of his father is in the form of a blue car, which I believe is a memory from his childhood—most likely his father picked him up in such a car during his visits.

He also tells me numerous things about the spiritual world, about what he can see and hear, and what he makes of it all. Most of it I can peg on the things I have witnessed in his surroundings, and there are connections to be made between his role in *Hamlet* and his interpreta-tion of his home life. I notice his descriptions flit in and out of religious rhetoric—"a dragon with seven horns," which I believe is in Revelation in the Bible—and the language he uses for such descriptions is far beyond his usual ten-year-old vocabulary.

"Ruin is not *bestial*, he says he's a *committed intellectual*," Alex informs me when I query the portraits of some of the beings in the world he describes. His fondness for Ruin is palpable, protective, and I believe there is something of Alex's feeling toward his mother projected onto his imaginary sketch of Ruin, and with good reason: Alex cannot control his mother, but he can control his imaginary beings.

It is common for psychotics to construct a highly fantastical world with clearly defined boundaries and with a system of rules that derives from a system that exists in reality, in this case, the supernatural. Alex never mentions angels, which I find very interesting. No mention of God or any other deity, either. However, he insists there are demons everywhere, all the time, and that when he enters an empty room it is not empty, it is like a pub, with demons grouped in corners, plotting, huddled around any humans who happen to be about, tempting, cajoling, scheming.

When I press him to discuss Ruin in more detail, Alex erupts. His descriptions of Ruin ascend into a screaming fit, and to my horror he passes out in the chair opposite me.

Bev charges across the room and grabs him. He is limp and deathly pale, and for the first time during my treatment of him I feel fear. I feel myself turn over the things he had told me about demons, about spirits—immediately I dismiss the idea, but the fear lingers. On reflection, it astonishes me how frail a thing belief is.

After a few moments Bev shouts, "He's awake! He's awake!" I am in the kitchen getting Alex a glass of water. Then: "He's going to be sick!" I grab the basin out of the sink and race into the living room, just in time to catch a spew of vomit from Alex's mouth.

"That's better, that's better," Bev is saying, thumping him on the back and fumbling in her pocket for her mobile phone.

I kneel down in front of Alex and take his pulse. His heart rate seems fast, his pupils dilated. "How do you feel, Alex?" I ask calmly. He blinks and tries to focus on me. Then he presses a hand against his chest.

"It hurts."

"What hurts?"

"Here."

Bev quickly unbuttons Alex's shirt. She gasps, and I look down to see three red stripes on his chest, as if something had just scorched his skin.

"Did someone at school do this to you?" Bev is shouting, and I try to tell her that these marks must have been made recently—as recent as my visit, in fact. My mind reels with questions, but just then Alex leans forward, his face pale and strained. I yank the basin up to his face, just in time to catch another fountain of puke. Bev dashes into the kitchen to find a cloth. When Alex collapses back in his chair he looks weak, but he gives me a small, faint smile.

"You feel better?" I say. He nods.

"Is Ruin still here?" I ask tentatively. He looks around, then shakes his head.

Bev returns, a tea towel in one hand, Alex's coat in the other. Alex is mumbling something about a diary.

"What should we do?" Bev splutters.

I look him over.

"We need to take him to hospital."

We travel in Bev's car to the hospital, where an examination determines that he is absolutely fine. The doctor can't find any signs of the marks, despite Bev and me confirming that we saw them.

"Could have been from wrapping his own arms around himself too tightly," the doctor suggests. "Maybe leaning against something. In any case, there's no bruising. In fact, no external marks at all."

Bev turns and stalks away in frustration. I thank the doctor for his time and jot down some notes while they're fresh in my mind. I note that his separation from Cindy has intensified his anxiety, so I arrange for Alex to visit his mother as soon as possible. She is in the psychiatric ward of this hospital, and it strikes me as sad that both mother and son are hospitalized. Michael Jones will be beside himself.

Once Alex is settled, I slide a chair close to his bed and pull the curtains around us.

"Where's Bev?" he asks.

"She's getting some fresh air." *She's outside, smoking.*

"Is she okay?" *No, she's hyperventilating.*

"She's absolutely fine, Alex. How are you?"

"I'm okay. I really like Auntie Bev. I haven't seen much of her for a long time but she's really nice." A pause. "Did I scare her?"

"She just wants to know you're safe and well, that's all."

He feels his chest. "Does it hurt?" I ask.

He shakes his head. "Not anymore. It was weird . . ."

"What did it feel like?"

He opens his mouth to describe it but can't seem to find the words. "Like fear," he says eventually.

*"Fear?"*

He nods. "Can I see Mum now?"

I pull my chair closer and look him over. He has a sweetness about him that makes me feel intensely protective. For a moment I hear a B natural note ring across the room from a dropped petri dish. Already my mind is turning to Poppy. Her dark head bending at the piano. *I love you, Mummy.*

I close my eyes and try to focus on what I want to ask next. It is important that I do not let Poppy enter this case. Alex is a patient, not a projection of my daughter. She is not an entity I can revive with another's breath. I open my eyes.

"Alex, I wanted to ask you something."

He stares at me. *"Please* not more stuff about Ruin . . ."

I shake my head. "I'm going to take you to see your Mum very soon. But do you mind if I stay, too?"

His face lights up. "I'm going to see Mum?"

"Not this afternoon. But maybe tomorrow morning, when you're feeling better." His eyes fill with tears. And to my astonishment, he flings his arms around me and sobs into my neck. I feel tears rising in my own throat. His vulnerability is screaming at me, and, with only one exception, I have never felt as helpless in my whole life.

• • •

In the light of Alex's hospitalization, it is crucial that we review the management of Alex's case. I call a meeting at MacNeice House for the next morning and arrange to meet with Michael later that day. I need to preempt him about what I intend to put before the team: that I wish to move Alex into my inpatient unit.

I don't tell Michael why I want to meet, however, and he sounds flattered. "Okay," he says on the other end of the line after a long silence. "I'm on my way back from the Falls Road. What say we meet somewhere less formal than your office?"

"*Your* office, then?"

"How about the Crown Bar?"

"Sure."

Michael arrives late. I see him bobbing through the heavy throng in the same bottle-green sweater, his hair gleaming golden in the bright lights.

"Evening," he says breathlessly, reaching down and kissing me on the cheek. He takes off his jacket and folds it neatly before setting it down beside me.

"G and T?" he asks, still out of breath.

"Orange juice."

He gives me a look. "You driving?"

"I don't drink alcohol."

He cocks his head. "A teetotaling child shrink from Tiger's Bay. That's an anomaly."

I shrug. "I like to take care of myself."

Michael blinks at me. Then he straightens up, heads to the bar, and returns with two glasses of fresh orange juice.

I feel hopelessly stodgy—the Crown Bar is a jewel in a country that has transformed the act of drinking alcohol into a cultural art. "Just because I'm not doesn't mean you can't," I say, then wonder what has caused me to humiliate myself by stating the perfectly obvious.

He slides up next to me. "And how gentlemanly would that be of me?"

His crooked smile is wider tonight, enticing, teasing. In this light it strikes me that, under different circumstances, I would enjoy his company. And I sense it then, that old buttery flutter in my belly. Flirtation. Which I am reciprocating despite my better judgment. I really, really don't want this. I think of Fi, her blue eyes heavy with sincerity and kindness. She would tell me this is a *sign*. Fi is all about signs.

"A sign of *what*?" I once asked her when a wasp stung me on my cheek, of all places.

"A sign that you don't believe you're beautiful," she retorted. She had a point; a garish scar on one's face is a powerful antidote to vanity. And then I think of her sitting at my kitchen table and taking both my hands in hers, saying:

"Repeat after me. 'Poppy's death does *not* mean that I have to abstain forever from life's pleasures.'"

At the time I squeezed her hands and let go. "I can't say it, Fi. I can't."

She reached out and stroked my face. My oldest friend, we've known each other since grammar school. A divorced mother of four, maternal and warmhearted; even at ten years old she was kissing my knee scrapes to make them better.

But even Fi didn't understand why I wanted to stay single. Something changes inside when you lose a child. No, *everything* changes. This kind of loss is far different—I won't say worse—than going bankrupt or losing everything you own in a house fire. Poppy's death was a different kind of agony, a different loss, even, than watching my mother sink beneath the yellow waters of cancer. Add together all the men I ever loved, then multiply that sum by how bad it felt when they all left, one by one . . . you still don't come close to what Poppy's death was like. The only way I can describe it—and I rarely describe it, not even to Fi—is that continuing to live and breathe in a world where my child was eternally robbed of her own opportunities to grow up, fall in love, build a career, and have babies means that I must remain my own personal fortress. I run, don't drink, and watch what I eat so that no one ever has to take care of me. I save 60 percent of everything I earn in a high-interest account so that I never have to depend on anyone. And I will not love again, because I can never, ever experience that degree of loss again.

There is a heavy pause as I realize Michael is staring at me. He has said something that I'm certain requires a response other than a blank stare.

"Sorry, could you repeat that?"

He gives a half smile and finishes his glass of juice. "Actually, I was saying that I had Googled you. Quite an impressive list of awards, Dr. Molokova. The Freud medal for excellence in child psychiatric research, no less. And a Rising Star from the British Association of Child and Adolescent Psychiatry." He gives me a small round of applause. "I should get you to sign this coaster."

I grin, until he presents me with a pen and holds up the coaster. I am laughing now, and the sound feels alien and delicious to me. Eventually, I sign it and he tucks the coaster into his coat pocket.

"What else did Google tell you?"

He lowers his eyes, and I know he has read about Poppy. "Only about your outrageous toothpick fetish, your astonishing passion for bath mats . . ."

I take my chance. "Can I ask *you* a personal question?"

"Yeah."

"Why did your parents send you to a psychiatrist?"

"Wow, that's a curveball down memory lane. Because I had an imaginary friend. Why d'you ask?"

I make a mental note of the "imaginary friend." Seems he and Alex have a lot in common.

"It's just that you portray mental illness units as bad places, Michael. A lot of kids with even the most extreme psychosis can live a relatively normal life when they're properly treated. That's why I'm here."

His smile is fading. He stares at a spot on the table for a long time. When he looks up, his eyes are hard. "You want to move Alex. Don't you?"

I tell him what happened earlier that day, about the marks on his skin. "If he has psychosis, he needs treatment at the proper facility with the requisite medication and medical staff. Just as if he had to have surgery."

"Surgery," he repeats, unconvinced.

"The success rate of MacNeice House is impressive, Michael. Really."

He shakes his head. "To you, maybe. To those of us who've been in Belfast for the last seven years . . . not really."

I try another tactic. "In any case, I'm concerned about his long-term living arrangements. I mean, have you seen the state of his home? Do you know how many health and safety hazards I spotted?"

I tell him about the electrical socket I saw hanging off the wall and occasionally flicking blue sparks, the ancient, leaking radiators, the cracked ceiling, the window at the front of the house covered with tape and cardboard. Conditions that no human being should be forced to live in, and certainly not a mother and a child with mental health issues.

Michael says nothing. Instead, he drains his glass, then says "excuse me" before stalking toward the pub door. For a moment I wonder whether he's figured out what I'm *really* doing, and has responded by simply leaving me here, high and dry. I sip on my juice and check my phone for messages.

Minutes later, I see him threading his way through the crowd toward me.

"Done," he announces with a wide smile, thumping down on the seat beside me. Though, I notice, not as close to me as before.

"*What's* done?"

He slaps his mobile phone on the table in front of him. "I just phoned a friend of mine who works at the housing association, told him everything you told me. He says he'll have Alex and Cindy at the top of the rehousing list first thing tomorrow morning." He raises his eyes to meet mine. "It's your call if you want to put Alex in MacNeice House. But I know what I know."

Then he heads to the bar and brings back another OJ for me and a pint of Guinness for him.

# 11
# STRAWBERRY
# PICKING

## ALEX

Dear Diary,

So there's this man who walks into a doctor's office with a carrot up his nose, a cucumber in one ear, and a banana in the other. "Help!" he says to the doctor. "I don't know what's wrong with me!" The doctor looks at him and says, "clearly, you're not eating properly."

Well, I'm in hospital now, not to see Mum though. I'm in hospital because Ruen went crazy and turned into a monster and attacked something that he said was an angel, though I didn't see any angels. He came last night when everyone had gone home and I could hear the nurses' feet slapping up and down the corridor. I hope I don't have to miss rehearsals tomorrow. Everyone kept asking about the pain in my chest but it's gone now and so is Ruen.

He came just after Anya left. At first I was nervous to see him because he really frightened me before. He was Ghost Boy then and he had a blue table-tennis paddle and a small white ball that he was trying to balance on the bat.

"Pity you're stuck in here," he said. "Otherwise you could come and play a game with me."

He stood by the bed and started bouncing the ball up and down and counting.

"Stop that," I said. "Someone will hear you."

He looked at me with his horrible black eyes. "Are you soft in the head? No one ever sees me."

"But they *feel* you, don't they?"

He stopped bouncing the ball. "What you mean?"

"Don't be stupid, you know what I mean."

He sat down on the bed next to me. I saw the blanket crease under his legs and I tugged it back because I was cold.

"Go ahead, then," he said, smiling and folding his arms. "Since you're the one who can see both worlds, why don't you fill me in? How do people *feel me*, Alex?"

"They just know, okay. They smell you, that's how."

He pouted and I hope I don't look that girlie when I pout. "Why do you always have to be so mean? All I ever do is try and help you."

I went to tell him he was a real baby, always complaining, but then I wondered whether he really was trying to help me. "That's what I was doing before, you know."

"What you mean?"

"Oh, you mean *now* you actually want to hear?"

I sat up and looked around. The other people on the ward were asleep and the light above kept flickering and I could hear the nurses laughing in the corridor. One of them kept snorting and it sounded like a pig. Then another laughed and sounded just like a horse and I realized I'd never been to a farm.

Ruen picked up the ball and balanced it on his head.

"You can't see everything, you know," he said. "You never see angels. They're *so* annoying."

I was thinking about what a farm might look like when I realized he was right, I'd never seen angels. I'd never even thought about it until Anya mentioned it before. *How come you don't see angels?* she'd asked.

*And what about God? And the Devil?* I said God was a man with a white beard and a red suit and a jolly face and the Devil was red, too, and he also smiled but was *inherently evil.*

"Is that what you think you are, Alex?" Anya said, and I asked her what she meant and she said *never mind.* I told her angels had long golden hair and huge white feathery wings and usually lived on top of Christmas trees.

I told Ruen about this and he wrapped an arm around his waist and chuckled. "Oh, you *are* thick, Alex," he said. "Angels don't look like that at all. In fact, angels keep trying to hurt you."

That's the thing with Ruen when he's Ghost Boy. He's always trying to prove he's smarter than me but sometimes he says stuff that makes me think and think. "I thought angels were good and they protected people."

Ruen reeled off the bed and staggered across the floor dragging his feet and holding his stomach and making hacking noises as if my brain-deadedness had stunned him to the point of death. Finally he slumped to the floor and gave a big sigh as if he'd actually died.

"Ruen?" I said, and I felt a sharp pain in my chest in case he'd actually died.

He jumped up to his feet and gave a big stupid grin. "It's *me* that's been protecting you!" He walked up to me and leaned very close. "They know you have a gift to see into our world. And they don't like it."

"Why?"

Ruen looked around again in case someone saw us talking. The nurse that sounded like a pig was still snorting and I started wondering what it would be like if a cow wandered down the corridor. Ruen jumped up and sat on the bed beside me.

"Because everyone thinks angels are beautiful. When in fact they're hideous creatures. And they'd rather everyone believed the opposite."

"So angels are trying to attack me?"

"Haven't you seen the white lights appear every now and then?"

I shrugged with one shoulder, which meant maybe I had but who cared? But really, I had seen white lights. They happened sometimes when I was getting scared or when Ruen was trying to make me do something and they looked like a bit of sunlight had drifted out of the sky and into the room. Ruen picked up his bat and ball and looked like he was going.

"You off, then?" I said, trying not to sound like I could give a rat's backside whether he did or not.

He turned and grinned. "You want me to stay, don't you. You're *scared*."

"Am not," I said, but when he turned and sat back down and put his arm around me, I gave a big sigh of relief.

When I started to fall asleep Ruen said I was boring as an old lady and left. Then I had a dream that was really lovely and really horrible at the same time. It was horrible mostly because I didn't want it to be a dream, and when I woke up I sat with my palms pressed against my eyes and sang the only song I could think of over and over again which was "Away in a Manger."

My dream was about Granny. Granny reminded me of a Doberman, which sounds funny but I mean that she was really snarly and people were scared to say the wrong thing to her but when she liked you she'd protect you and scare bad people off. One time two men called bailiffs knocked on the door of her neighbor Doris because they wanted Doris's sofa. Granny ran out with a broom and whacked the men until they left because she said Doris hadn't done any harm to anybody, though I wonder why they wanted Doris's sofa 'cos it had cat hairs all over it. Granny lived a bus ride and four and three-quarters' minutes of walking away from us and everyone called her *Granny*, like she'd been born with that name. She was short and the skin on her face shook when she laughed and most of her teeth were metal stubs screwed into her gums like a pirate and she smoked so many cigarettes that her voice was deep like a man's. Sometimes she lit one while another one was still making spirals of smoke in her ashtray. She was ill for years and years. I remember she said she'd rather *burn out than fade away* and at the time she was holding a cigarette in each hand.

Granny was very proud of her back garden because not many people we knew actually had back gardens and she'd always grown up with a yard made of concrete. So she decided to grow strawberries, which were red as postboxes and big as fat men's noses. The only time Granny ever told me off was when I ate them because she said she needed them to make jam.

"Jam keeps forever," she used to say, "but strawberries only last a season, or a few minutes once *you* get your mucky paws on them."

So in the dream I was in her kitchen and she told me to go outside to collect strawberries to make jam. Outside it was really sunny, and the clouds looked like balls of wool in the sky. I walked down into the grass, which was really deep. There was a snake in the grass and at first I was really scared and backed away, but when I looked again I saw it wasn't a snake, it was a shadow. Then I noticed that the shadow was really long and I couldn't see what was making the shadow. I followed it all the way through the grass toward the end of the garden and when I looked up I saw Ruen standing in front of me. He was the Old Man. The shadow led right up to a thread hanging down from his suit which I thought was crazy.

"What do you want?" I said. He looked down at the shadow. That's when I saw that it split in two, like a fork. One of the forks led to Ruen, and the other led to me and it was wrapped around my chest.

"What's this?" I asked him.

Ruen just did that thing where he flares his nostrils and wriggles his ears and I could see the tufts of white hair in them. It means he's annoyed but I just stared at him. Then Granny called out the kitchen window.

"He wants to hurt you, Alex."

This was weird to me because Granny had never seen Ruen and in the dream I wondered if maybe they'd met.

I turned around and shouted back to her, "What do you mean?"

She started waving. "Come on inside, Alex. He's no good for you. Leave him alone."

I shook my head. "No, he's okay, Granny. Ruen's my friend."

She gripped the edge of the window ledge and looked very cross. "No he is *not*, Alex. He wants you to think you're nothing. He wants to hurt your soul."

"My *soul*?"

When I turned around again Ruen was gone, and then when I looked back at Granny the kitchen window was closed, though I could see Granny there doing the dishes at the sink, just as I remembered. I turned to the strawberry patch but beneath their green leaves they weren't red and juicy as usual. They were like big fat blobs of shadow and they smelled like poo.

I picked them anyway and brought them inside. I went to set the basket down on the table and tell Granny about the strawberries. I wanted to tell her it wasn't my fault they'd gone bad. But she picked them out of the basket and they were red and beautiful and I thought I'd gone nuts, so I said nothing. Granny was humming and happy and there wasn't even a cigarette in sight.

"Will you stir these, Alex?" she said, plopping the strawberries into a big boiling pan on the stove while she got some sugar from the cupboard. I took a ladle from the jar on the counter and started to stir, and the strawberries bubbled and smelled delicious.

Granny poured in the sugar and said, "memory's a funny thing, Alex. Sometimes it can hurt us without us realizing."

I nodded but I had no clue what she meant. I figured this was what old people said when they were about to lose their marbles.

But then I looked inside the pot I was stirring. The jam had already gone from being a big boiling mass of lumpy goo like something Woof had barfed to a cold stew that Granny could pour into the jars that she'd lined up on the kitchen table.

"Now, Alex," she said. "You have to hold each jar so I don't knock it over as I pour."

I stopped stirring the stuff in the pot and walked over to the table. Granny nodded at the six jars on the tablecloth. "Hold it tight," she said, so I did. Granny went and got the pot and slowly tipped it over the jar I was holding. The jam plopped out into the jar.

Granny said: "You can make jam out of strawberries, but you can't make strawberries out of jam."

I looked at her. "What do you mean?"

She set the pot down and stroked my cheek. "Ruen wants to try to change you into someone you aren't. I want you to remember who you are, Alex. Do you know who you are?"

I nodded.

"How do you know Ruen?" I said. She smiled and the room started to fill with a bright light. The light grew and grew until it squeezed everything out of view.

And then everything changed. When I looked around I wasn't in Granny's kitchen anymore. I was in a street with shops and lots of people. I recognized the street but didn't know how I did. The street was small with a black wet road in the middle with small stone shops at either side and there was a post office on the other side of the road. People were running on the pavement and I was outside a church. I think I might have been singing in a choir because I could hear singing and I knew the words.

In front of me I saw a man in a black mask and a black jacket and jeans. He raised his gun in the air and pointed it right at me. And then it was like time went on hold. There were pigeons flapping in the air and they still had their wings outstretched so I could see the white feathers. Someone's Coke can was floating through the air with Coke pouring out of it like a brown ribbon. A policeman next to me turned his face and his lip curled like he was afraid or angry. His face was blurry.

I turned back to the man in the black mask. I could see his blue eyes through the holes in the mask and they looked right at me. I could see his gun, black and shining and wet. He squeezed the trigger and I heard a deep crack. Beside me, the policeman's knees buckled and his arms flung up in the air like a puppet. As he fell to the ground the man lowered his gun and started to take his mask off. I watched, and my heart was pounding and my mouth was open.

Just before I woke up, I saw his face.

It was me.

# 12

# THE PAINTINGS

## ANYA

My mornings are filled with meetings with other inpatients at MacNeice House. Our youngest resident is a girl, Cara, aged eight years old. Autism spectrum disorder. She is also a gifted artist, and our visiting art therapist Iris seems to have made a lot of headway in developing Cara's social skills and channeling a lot of her aggression through art sessions. Cara brings one of her paintings to show me.

"Look," she says, her gray eyes wide as she shows me a large painting on the wall of her room here at the unit. It is of four stick figures engaged in various activities, gardening, football, and ballet. One of them seems to be fixing a car. "There's me, there's my Mum and Dad, and that's Callum."

"It's beautiful, Cara," I assure her, noticing the colors she's chosen. They are telling: Instead of her usual preference for black, the painting features a mixture of sky blues, pinks, and yellows. Iris also points out that Cara has started drawing circles as complete wholes instead of never-ending spirals—another sign of improvement.

Some of the other kids have more severe problems that refuse to be easily resolved—fifteen-year-old Damon had been on a self-imposed hunger strike for four days before his parents brought him in. When I visit him in his room he refuses to make eye contact, let alone open his mouth to speak, and when he strikes another consultant I am forced to have him restrained and put on a drip. Psychiatric assessments have indicated psychosis, and his medication had seemed to be working. This sudden relapse is quite out of the blue; there are days when I feel the human mind is a jigsaw puzzle that I will never be able to solve.

The morning after Alex's transfer to the hospital, I call the review meeting of Alex's case in the conference room that involves Michael, Ursula, and Howard Dungar, the occupational therapist. I needed to present my findings and to get a variety of expert perspectives on the best program of care for Alex.

Michael is already in the conference room when I arrive, warming his hands on an old radiator by the window.

"How's the garden?" I ask, noticing his posture. He is stiff, frowning, ready for battle.

He turns and leans on the windowsill, thrusting his hands deep into the pockets of his tweed trousers. The corners of his mouth twitch. "My runner beans are four inches long," he says blankly.

"I love it when a man says that to me."

His mouth makes it all the way to a half smile and I blush, hearing the flirtation in my retort.

Ursula arrives, surrounded in her usual cloak of self-importance and wearing jeans for the second day in a row. The day before yesterday an advertisement was posted for a replacement clinical psychologist, so her noticeable distancing from Alex's case is understandable. Howard shows up a minute after the hour, a white ring of sugar around his mouth and his fly undone.

When everyone has taken their seats, I begin the meeting with a brief commentary on my assessment of Alex to date.

"Alex Connolly has witnessed his mother attempt suicide four times that we know of. He's also been exposed to countless episodes of her self-harming. He has indicators of schizophrenia, including high vigilance, mild paranoia, bizarre behavior, and frequent and intense hallucinations. After an initial consultation at the hospital I arranged for him to undergo a series of physical tests to rule out any physical cause for his presentation. His brain MRI and EEG are normal and his blood tests proved fine."

I look up from my notes to check everyone is still with me. Michael has his head raised slightly, his wide palms pressed into the wood of the table. Ursula is studying me through her small reading glasses. Howard is picking at a shaving cut. I continue.

"As we'll all agree, there is a clinical consensus that it is often better to keep the family together, but because of Alex's current state I feel it might be dangerous to let him remain at home. It's my diagnosis that Alex needs constant assessment at MacNeice House. And of course I will do my best to keep the contact between Alex and his mother as regular as possible."

Howard looks up. "Can you explain what you mean by *dangerous*?"

"My interviews with him have revealed that he has frequent perceptual disturbances and delusions, including a strong attachment to an imaginary friend named Ruin. It's this delusion that I'm most interested in, because it tells me a lot about how Alex perceives himself."

Ursula laces her fingers and frowns. "How so?"

"He tells me Ruin is the 'bad' version of Alex."

"So Alex isn't saying *he* is bad?"

"No, but I believe Ruin is Alex's projection of himself. He also claims he can see demons, all the time, everywhere. I want to move him to MacNeice House for a period of at least one month for proper observation and assessment. Transferring Alex to MacNeice House requires his mother's consent. Cindy refuses to give it. She is currently being evaluated to determine whether she is fit to make decisions for Alex as his mother. If she is found not to be, Alex will be moved to MacNeice House at the first opportunity."

Michael leans forward. "I think we ought to consider the fact that she is being treated at the adult psych unit. We're told that she'll be there for another three weeks. Wouldn't it be better to wait until she gets out?"

Ursula turns to him. "Why?"

"Alex and his mother are very close," Michael replies calmly. "If you wait until Cindy is released, she will be able to visit Alex here at MacNeice House. This contact will provide security and reassurance for both mother and son, and will almost certainly make it easier for them to receive treatment—"

"What about the marks on Alex's body?" interjects Howard. "Is the boy being abused?"

"Most likely self-harming," Ursula offers loudly, folding her arms.

"If Alex *is* self-harming," I say, "we need to intervene as soon as possible."

I look across at Michael, noticing his jawline beginning to grow red. I feel sad that I have still failed to convince him I'm on his side.

"Both Alex and Cindy will be distressed about their separation," he insists. Nobody mentions the irony that Cindy's suicide attempts have been efforts to separate the pair for good—Cindy's mental state doesn't perceive it that rationally.

"This is a medical problem," I remind Michael gently. "A medical problem requires medical intervention . . ."

". . . but you haven't given a diagnosis!" he shouts.

Ursula turns back to me. "Didn't the notes mention Alex has ASD?"

I shake my head. "Alex seemed to have been passed around psychiatrists like a guinea pig." I barely conceal the acid in my tone. "One assessment pointed to Alex's enhanced vocabulary and his social difficulties as a possible indicator, but I'm eager to rule it out altogether. Which is precisely why I need him transferred to MacNeice House," I say, but suddenly Howard and Ursula are consulting loudly and I feel my suggestion has gone unheard. For a moment, Michael and I stare at each other across the long table, two forces on opposing sides. I am the first to break off his stare.

I clear my throat. Ursula looks up. "Sorry," she says, her tone brittle. "Howard and I are of the opinion that a holistic approach to this case is the better option. We need an approach that takes in the whole picture. Frankly, the boy's mother is part of that picture."

From the corner of my eye, I see Michael nodding.

Ursula continues. "For my part, I recommend a solution-focused approach to Alex's case. Michael, you've been working with this family for several years now, haven't you?"

He nods.

"Anya, perhaps it's best if you and Michael work closely from this

point toward a program that takes the individual contexts and require-
ments into consideration." She glances at Howard. "We can review
again in a couple of weeks."

I open my mouth to protest her decision, but she is already standing
to leave. Howard smiles awkwardly and follows, pausing to pour himself a cold cup of coffee from the stainless-steel canister in the corner of
the room. Michael stays seated, his eyes lowered, and so do I.

He waits for Howard to slurp from his coffee cup and bustle noisily
down the hall before raising his eyes.

"Anya," he says quietly. "Look . . . I just want to go easy on this
family, okay? I appreciate that you're a mover and a shaker, and we're
all just playing catch-up after years of too much shaking and not enough
moving, you know?"

I feel my cheeks burn. I remind myself that Alex's case is not a battle
of wills between me and my colleagues. I try to reason with myself that,
maybe, waiting until Cindy is released is absolutely fine. But I am furious at being overruled. I am seized with an urgency to resolve this case
and I don't really know why.

Michael stands up, walks around the table and sits down in the chair
beside me.

"Are you okay?" he says, and I realize that he looks worried. I raise
a hand to my cheek and find, to my horror, I have started to cry.

I nod and laugh and try and rein in whatever emotions have slipped
out of my grasp without my noticing.

"Yes," I tell him, looking at my wet fingertips as if they belong to
someone else. "I guess I'm just trying to find my feet in this place. We
just arm-wrestled each other in review meetings in Edinburgh, played
some poker. None of this debate stuff."

He smiles and I seize the opportunity to run a finger under both
eyes, mopping up the inevitable black smudge. Then I pull out the pen
that's holding my hair up. Suddenly I want it down, covering my scar.
Michael stops smiling.

"I don't mean to be a hypocrite," he says carefully, "but I think you
should be careful not to become too involved in this case."

"You think I've become involved?"

"You said before that riddles frustrate you. I'm worried that the *real* riddle that bothers you is Poppy. And that you see much of Poppy in Alex's case."

I frown at him. "I deal with dozens of kids with mental health issues all the time, what makes you think—?"

"Not with Poppy's illness, Anya," he interrupts. "Not like this. You're scared, aren't you? That he's going to hurt himself, like your daughter did?"

I can feel the blood roaring in my veins, and it is difficult to breathe, suddenly. He is angry because I disagreed with him, making wild assertions to get even. I refuse to rise to it.

"I intend to keep interviewing Alex's schoolteachers and his aunt. If I *do* find proof that he's self-harming, I'm sure you'll agree that I have no option but to bring him in."

Michael gives me a curt nod and a smile before striding out of the room.

When I return to my office I find a new message in my inbox. I am relieved when I see it is from Alex's schoolteacher, Karen Holland.

To: A_Molokova@macneicehouse.nhs.uk
From: k.holland@stpaulsprimary.co.uk
Date: 05/12/07 1:44 PM

Dear Anya,

I would be more than happy to speak to you—indeed I remember Alex very well. I had concerns about him when I taught him three years ago and am pleased he seems to be receiving proper treatment at last. I have a couple of slots available for a meeting here at the school—next Thursday at 5 PM, the following Tuesday at 4:30, or perhaps today at 4 PM? Do you need directions?

Sincerely, KH.

I email her immediately to take her up on the offer of an appointment that afternoon. I change my heeled shoes for running shoes and transfer Alex's files from my briefcase to my backpack, then head off on foot, threading through the familiar streets around Queen's University. Among layers of students' advertisements pasted on lampposts and boarded-up buildings I spy a large, dazzling poster for Jojo's company, Really Talented Kids. HAMLET is spelled out in bullet holes, and there are several pictures of nuns holding machine guns and kids making gang signs with several movie-star endorsements beneath. I spy a small image of Alex during one of the rehearsals in his role as Horatio, and I smile at the thought of him attempting to concoct bad jokes for the part. Jojo had whispered to me that bad jokes was exactly what she was aiming for, though it was Alex's confidence that was the real reward—he had transformed from a stage-shy, nervous kid who was barely audible to the front row to a boy who was beginning to command his presence and find his feet on stage. I make a mental note to invite Jojo to MacNeice House.

I cut through the quad of Queen's University, its new buildings gleaming alongside the old red-brick ones. I find myself thinking back to the days I spent as a student on a blanket with friends—it takes me a moment or two to remember their names—a picnic of jam sandwiches and cold tea, Blondie on the radio.

*Was that really a quarter century ago?*

I pass a gleaming new building bearing the sign THE SCHOOL OF MUSIC, its clean, spacious rooms visible through large windows. A couple of students walk past, one of them on a mobile phone, another holding a Starbucks cup. I continue on toward the Botanic Gardens, then stop in front of the dome of the hothouse, where two patches of white tulips have been grown to form the shape of a pair of wings. They are so real, so richly bright, that they almost seem to move, and the petals ruffle distinctly like feathers. I stop walking and spend a long time staring at them, moved by the way they had appeared so different from a distance—shaped in the form of a dove's wings, I realize, fanning outward, the bird's head rendered by a smaller patch, its beak rendered by primroses. The symbol of peace.

• • •

When Poppy was buried, I could not bear the thought of a tombstone. It seemed too final, too grim for my little girl. On her grave plot in Edinburgh, I had a craftsman cut dove's wings into Portland stone—a kind of stone that whitens with time. Each wing was carved with precision, the feathers so lifelike that they appeared to move in the sunlight. I had hoped to bring her peace. It is my own peace that I have never found.

And I don't know how.

I arrived at Saint Paul's Primary School fifteen minutes early. Housed in a converted chapel, the school has a distinctly religious air about it outside that continues inside in the form of child-crafted murals of saints and religious festivals. I studied the scenes of angels and Jesus in the stained-glass windows, their colors and pathos ripe in late-afternoon sun. A sign directed me to reception, where I found a young man typing at a computer.

"I'm here to see Karen Holland," I told him. He nodded and asked me to sign a register before taking me to the staff room.

"Karen's in a meeting." He nodded at the sink and coffeemaker opposite a square of sofas. "Make yourself comfortable."

In the corner of the room stood an old black upright piano, candelabras curved like cactuses in its front panel, lid open. Its keys were yellow and chipped, like the teeth of an old man. I looked up at the doorway to be sure no one was coming, then I slid my fingers over the notes that formed the opening chord of Beethoven's *Sonata Pathétique*. For a moment I was tempted to lean down, sound out the thick, hungry texture of that gorgeous chord, but I stopped short of pressing down on the keys. Slowly I lifted my hands and left the piano to its silence.

When Poppy died, I sold her beloved baby grand for a sliver of its value just to be rid of the sound of it. It seemed that even when the lid was closed the wind would find its way inside, brush across the strings, and Poppy's songs would rise up like ghosts. I had been playing since I was a child, tinkering on the old Yamaha at my school, then offered free piano lessons by a generous teacher. It was important for me to teach Poppy, to give her the same joy I'd felt—but I had not anticipated how deep the sound would dig into my veins after she'd gone. How much loneliness would suddenly infuse the music I had once loved.

"Dr. Molokova?" a voice said. I turned to see a short round woman in a rust-colored dress standing in the doorway, her eyes hidden by tinted glasses. She had a helmet of thick amber-colored hair, a run in her brown tights and hands that felt warm as toast when I returned her handshake. She grinned broadly. "I'm Karen Holland. Would you like to come to my classroom?"

I nodded and followed her out of the room along a corridor lined with papier-mâché mosaics of Africa, self-portraits sketched by thirty eight-year-olds. I searched for Alex's face among them but it wasn't there.

"I dug something out of my archives to show you," Karen told me when we were inside her classroom.

"Archives?"

I looked around. The walls of the classroom were covered in paintings, progress charts, lists of rules. A film about elephants played silently on the whiteboard on the far wall. Karen walked past me to her desk, where a handful of childish paintings had been spread out for me to view.

"What are these?" I asked, unable to make sense of what seemed to be a series of large, misspelled phrases with boxes and small profile pictures in old, cracked black paint.

"I'm glad I kept these, now," Karen said, removing her dark glasses and rubbing her eyes. I could see they were small and intensely blue, narrowed against the soft light from the window.

I turned my head to view the paintings from a different angle. "Are these newspaper headlines?"

She put her glasses back on, sighing at the relief, perhaps of dimming the light in her eyes. "Alex did these for a class project when he was six years old. We were studying how the sinking of the *Titanic* might have been conveyed in headlines . . . As you can see, Alex devi-

ated substantially from the task in a way that always struck me as significant."

I looked over the headlines. MONSTROS CRIME read one. Another bore
a picture that looked like a swaddled baby Jesus and the title, ROT IN
HELL. Then another: RUEND PEEPELS LIVES. I paused at the word *ruend*.

"I've showed these to Alex's doctors. But they didn't see a link,"
Karen said.

I glanced up at her. "Did you ask Alex why he'd done these paintings?"

She nodded. "He didn't seem to know why he'd done them."

"But the lesson was about the tragedy of the *Titanic* . . ."

I scanned the paintings again, tracing my conversations with Alex in
my mind. He must have read the headlines in a newspaper. I glanced
again at the word *ruend*. Could *Ruin* be *Ruen*?

"What was Alex like as a pupil?" I made a note.

Karen raised a hand to touch her thick hair. "He was always polite.
Quiet. An above-average student. No friends, not really. I used to feel
sad when he'd be the only boy in the class without an invitation to so-
and-so's birthday—but it happens, you know? I think it was this sense
of exclusion that contributed to his anger."

I stopped writing. "Anger?"

She nodded, though I sensed some reluctance on her part to admit
this. "Alex had . . . not often of course . . . explosive rages that would
end with him in floods of tears."

I remembered what I'd read in the files. "Alex hit you, didn't he?"

She sighed. "He lashed out, struck me in the chest with his fist. It
was painful, but I really think he was more shocked than I was. Still, I
reported it to Alex's doctor at the time. Alex was growing more and
more tense by the day, I thought it was in his best interest . . ." She
faltered.

"Did he ever hit another student?"

She shook her head. "He never explained *why* he blew up, either. It
was like a tantrum, but much worse. Cursing, shouting, threats."

"Threats?"

"Yes. To me, to the other children. But they were . . . I know this
sounds odd, but they were what I would call *blind* threats. As if he

could hardly see who was there. As if he didn't recognize me or the people around him. As if he'd forgotten who we were." She paused, upset by the memory of it. "He was completely devastated, an utterly different version of the sweet, quiet boy we all knew. When I spoke to his mother about it she seemed distressed, but refused to offer any suggestions." She sighed again. "There's only so much we can do here at school. The buck stops at home. Which is unfortunate in some cases."

When my page was filled with notes I thanked her for her time and began to close up my briefcase.

"He isn't a bad kid," she said, taking off her glasses again. "And there's something I never told the other doctor . . . Alex wrote me a little note after he hit me that time."

"Do you still have it?"

Karen smiled. "Of course I do. It's at home. I kept it, as I do all the gifts I get from my kids. He'd drawn a little picture of me with the word SORRY in big block letters, then signed it with kisses and hugs. Not every kid would do that, you know?"

I smiled at the thought of it.

"Karen, you taught Alex on and off for several years, didn't you? When would you say his behavior changed?"

"December sixteenth, 2001," she said without hesitation, surprising me. She smiled crookedly. "The day Alex's father died. Or so he told me."

# 13

# THE UNBESTED
# FRIEND

## ALEX

Dear Diary,

It's three sleeps till we perform *Hamlet* at the Grand Opera House. I like it loads in there. It's all red and I feel bigger when I'm on stage, like I'm a giant. I bet you could fit three of our house inside there. We had a rehearsal last night for *Hamlet* and for once everyone remembered their lines and Jojo's makeup ran and she hugged Cian, who she doesn't usually like, and then she made us all sit in a circle on the stage and talk about our Fears and Hopes for Opening Night.

Katie raised her hand first. "I'm afraid my Mum will go crazy," she said. Jojo's smile came right off her face. She asked Katie what she meant. Katie just shrugged and wouldn't say anything after that but kept snapping the elastic on her wristband until I told her to stop it.

I put my hand up. "I hope the audience shouts 'encore,'" I said, and Terry and Sean snickered.

"I hope that, too," Jojo said, giving me a wink. "Though I think it's more likely that they'll applaud for a very long time if they like our performance."

Then she held up her two index fingers, which is a sign for everyone to be really quiet. "Now. Who thinks they understand why we're doing this play?"

We all looked at each other. Finally Bonnie Nicholls put her hand up. "Because we're really talented kids?"

Jojo gave her a big smile. "That's definitely one reason, thanks, Bonnie. Anyone else?"

"Because the play is famous?" Liam said. Jojo said yes but she said maybe we needed a hint. "Where is this play set?"

"Belfast," I said.

"Correctamundo!" Jojo said, and I felt proud. Then she looked serious and pressed a finger against her lips. "But where did *Shakespeare* set his play?"

There was a lot of whispering. I saw Terry Google it on his mobile phone. "Denmark," he said.

"Yes!" shouted Jojo, nodding at Terry. "And what does Shakespeare say about Denmark?"

"It's rotten," I said quietly. And she opened her mouth to say *correctamundo* again, but I put my hand up and she tilted her head.

"Are you saying that Belfast is rotten?" I asked.

"It *is* rotten," said Terry, and everyone agreed.

"All of it?" Jojo said in a small voice. "Or just some of it?"

Bonnie stretched her hand up high. "I like Maud's Ice Cream. You can't buy Maud's Ice Cream anywhere but in Northern Ireland which makes me feel sorry for anyone not living in Northern Ireland."

Queen Gertrude—actually her real name is Samantha but she makes us all call her Queen Gertrude—raised her hand next. "I like Helen's Bay." Helen's Bay is a beach three miles from our house that I've never been to but Granny has pictures and it looks nice.

"Good jogging," said Jojo in agreement, pointing at Samantha. "Anyone else?"

"I like it when nobody gets shot," I said, and Jojo turned her head to look at me. For a moment everyone was silent.

"Hear hear," said Liam. Then Bonnie said it, then Katie, then Samantha and Terry and everyone else. Even Jojo.

After a few minutes Jojo put her chin to her chest and folded her hands behind her back the way she does when she's thinking. We all knew to stop talking and the stage went very quiet.

"There's a line at the end of this play that gives a message. A message of hope. Who can tell me what it is?"

*Hamlet* wasn't really about hope as far as I was concerned. It was about a boy whose Dad haunted him and made him kill someone to get back at him but it only made things worse.

"We defy augury," I said quietly, because I wasn't sure but it was the final line of the play and Jojo had told us she chose that line for us all to end on because it meant that just because the future was predicted in one way didn't mean we couldn't choose a different path.

"What was that?" Jojo said, looking over us all.

"He said, 'we defy augury,'" Katie said. "This play is about us saying that we don't care what's happened in the past 'cos we have a say in what happens to the future."

Jojo's face lit up and she started to applaud and we all joined in, too. We clapped and cheered and then started chanting *"Hamlet, Hamlet, Hamlet, Hamlet,"* which gradually turned into *"Belfast, Belfast, Belfast, Belfast."* Jojo waved her hand back and forth like she was conducting us and then finally when Liam and Gareth changed the chant to *Celtic, Celtic, Celtic* she held up her index fingers again. We all got quiet.

"Remember, people. This is an important statement about who you are and where you want to be," Jojo said.

"McDonald's," Liam said under his breath. Some people giggled but Jojo just stared.

"This is more than Shakespeare's play. This is about what it means to rise up from the ashes of Belfast's past. Do yourselves proud."

The other day after lunch I was thinking about the dream I had about Ruen and Granny and I remembered that when Ruen came to the hospital I saw he had a thread hanging down from his black sweater, just like in the dream. I have threads hanging down from my clothes all the time and in the hospital I had a gown on that had a long bit at the back but I could have sworn there was a second when it looked like the thread from Ruen's sweater was linked to the bit at the back. I don't know what this means but it makes me feel weird.

So I decided to tell him that I don't want him to study me anymore. I thought that it might make him mad. I don't care about getting a new house. I mean it would be nice and all but I just care that Mum gets happy again and that she doesn't cry anymore. And I don't know if being someone's friend means that you have to do stuff for each other, either. Anya told me that she has arranged for me to go see Mum again very soon and I hardly slept all night because I was so excited about this and also because I was worried in case Mum died before I got to see her. Sometimes I think of the times she took all those pills and I think she actually knew that she would have died if the doctors didn't fix her. Why would she do that? Why would she *want* to die? And if she did, who would look after me then?

I hardly slept last night because I was scared that if I told Ruen that I don't want him to study me anymore, I wouldn't have a best friend. But I've seen that Mum starts to get worked up when Ruen is around and I think maybe he's the reason she gets upset. I still don't know why he wants to study me. It's stupid actually because I'm just a ten-year-old boy from Belfast not a prime minister or a football player or anything, and also he is starting to scare me lately. He used to be funny and tell me comebacks. Like the time when Eoin Murphy got everyone at school to call me *Azz* instead of *Alex* and kept saying I was a *psycho*. He had the whole class laughing at me and I felt so embarrassed that I couldn't think of anything to say back, not a single word. Then Ruen came up to me and whispered something in my ear. Next time Eoin was getting everyone to start chanting *Azz is a spaz* I turned to him and repeated what Ruen had said.

I said, "Eoin, the zoo just called. The baboons want their bums back, so you'll have to find a new face."

Everyone stopped chanting and Jamie Belsey snickered into his hand. Eoin's face went red. He looked at me and said, "you think you're funny, faggot boy?" Ruen whispered to me again and I repeated what he'd said:

"I heard your parents took you to a dog show and you won." Then everyone laughed and Eoin got really mad.

"You wanna fight?" he said, shoving me backward, but I stood straight and said what Ruen had told me to say: "I would love to beat you up, but I don't like being cruel to dumb animals."

Eoin punched me in the neck then, which hurt but I still felt like I'd won somehow.

Ruen and me have had lots of fun and he's been a really good friend and we laughed about stuff like that for days. When he was the Old Man he was like a grumpy uncle who occasionally ruffled my hair and dared me to do naughty things, like jump off a bus while it was still moving or copy someone's homework or steal Miss White's cigarettes when she'd left her bag on the table. But these days he's scary and angry and I feel weird when he's around. I know he'll be mad at me but maybe he can study someone else.

It makes me so nervous to tell him this that I get up eleven times during the night to pee. My hands and feet are icy cold and when Woof refuses to get into bed with me I get out from under the covers and curl myself around him on the floor.

When I woke up this morning Ruen was already downstairs. He was the Old Man and was sitting in Dad's old blue armchair with his feet up on Granny's coffee table with his hands folded on his potbelly as if he was waiting for me. This surprised me. The second thing that surprised me was that he was very smiley. He looked like he'd just won a prize or something, twiddling with his bow tie and licking his palm to smooth down the strands of white hair that stuck up from his skull like dandelion clocks. When I came into the room he stood up with his hands behind his back and creaked his mouth into a smile that made him look constipated.

"Alex, my boy," he said. "I have some wonderful news."

I didn't really want to hear his news. I was really tired from not sleeping and just wanted to spit out the speech I'd practiced, which I'd cut short to just this: "Ruen, I know we're friends and all but I don't want to be friends anymore."

I knew he wanted me to ask what the news was so I didn't. I stood there staring at him until Auntie Bev came out of the kitchen. She was wearing tight shiny shorts and a small shiny vest that showed the skin on her belly, which meant she was going wall climbing. She put her hands on her hips and sighed at me.

"Do you *really* have to have onions on toast for the fifth morning in a row? That kitchen *stinks*."

"Yes," I said, and turned back to Ruen. Auntie Bev was going on about *a nice omelet or even some porridge* but I ignored her and finally she went back into the kitchen.

Ruen headed for the hallway and waved his hand for me to follow. I yawned and followed. I walked past the coats hanging on the coat stand—all of them Auntie Bev's, she's like a collector of coats—and kicked at the old red rug that's fraying on the floor. Ruen was standing beside Granny's old piano, a big stupid grin on his ugly face.

"Alex," he said. "I've found you a new home."

At this my heart started to beat faster and I felt sorry for thinking how stupid he is. "You have?"

Ruen took a deep breath and his smile grew wider. "Later today Anya is going to tell you that you and your mother will be moving to a brand-new house with a garden and all the things you requested of me."

I just didn't know what to say. "I don't know what to say," I said.

"You can start by thanking me," Ruen said, tilting his head to remind me.

I started to say it, because I was really grateful, but I was still mad at him. He had scared me the other day and I was mad about that.

His smile turned back to his usual scowl. "What is it, Alex?" he said. "I thought you would be really pleased, now that I've given you the thing you wanted most. Don't you think that's a tad ungrateful?"

I looked at the red rug on the ground. It was so old it was just a bunch of threads clumped together, but I kept my eyes stuck to it so I wouldn't have to look at Ruen. I felt scared in case we wouldn't really get the house but then I realized that this was Ruen and that he had helped me so much in the past and hadn't gone back on his word.

"And what is it your mother hates most?" he said, raising his eyes to the ceiling and clicking his tongue.

"People who don't say thank you," I said.

"Exactly."

Auntie Bev called my name from the living room. I looked through the doorway to see her set a plateful of onions and toast on the table.

"You should've been raised in France," she said before turning and walking back into the kitchen. I gave Ruen a look before turning to walk inside. I sat down at the table and looked at the onions. I didn't feel like eating them.

Ruen appeared in the seat opposite me. He looked very concerned.

"Alex," he said, doing that thing with his hands where he makes a triangle with his fingers, only his fingernails are so long that his fingers don't touch. "Is this because of the lady doctor, Alex? She *is* asking a lot of questions, isn't she?" His voice suddenly sounded like he was really concerned for me and I wondered if he really was. "Is it starting to bother you?" he said. "Maybe I can help with that."

I knew Auntie Bev could hear what I said next but I didn't care. I looked at Ruen and said:

"Why are you studying me?"

"What, sweetheart?" Auntie Bev peeked her head around the kitchen door. Ruen glanced from Auntie Bev to me. I felt a warmth around my heart and there was a big fat sob in my throat. I said it again.

"Why are you studying me? I'm not a football player."

Ruen laced his hands, making his triangle collapse, and his eyes grew small and angry.

"I don't like being studied," I said. "Not by you, and not by Anya. I just want my Mum home, okay? And I don't care if she comes home to this house or a fancy house with a fancy garden. So you can *stuff* your house!"

Auntie Bev walked toward me and her face looked worried. She looked around at the window behind her, then at me.

"Are you okay?" she said.

I nodded and told a fib about a bird landing on the windowsill and that's why I was shouting at it but then there was a big lump in my throat and I felt angry and sad all at once. Auntie Bev knelt down in front of me, which made her smaller than me and I could see the freckles on her forehead.

"You're scared, aren't you, Alex?" she said, and I nodded but didn't say what I was scared of. She put her arms around me. She held me for a long long time and at first I wanted her to get off me but then I felt as if I could sleep right in her arms. Then I got hot and needed to scratch so I pushed her away gently and she looked at me and smiled.

"I haven't held you like that since you were a baby," she said, wiping my face, and I realized I had a tear on my cheek. "You were born premature, did you know that?"

I had to think about what *premature* meant.

"You were this big," she said, holding her hands a very very small distance apart. She looked at the small space between her hands for so long that I expected a real baby to appear. Then she looked up at me and her eyes were shiny. "You looked like a little bird. All the doctors said it was amazing that you lived." She lifted a hand to my face and tucked a piece of hair behind my ear. "I had to go back to work the next day but Granny sent me photos, when she could get around to it. I promised I'd come and see you more often but . . . well, you'll know what it's like when you're older." There was a long pause. I wondered if she'd finished but then she took my hands in hers and squeezed them tight. "This I *can* promise, Alex. I'm here for you now."

She was really close to my face and I felt the lump in my throat get bigger and I was afraid I was going to throw up so I pulled my hands free and ran up the stairs.

"Alex?" Auntie Bev was calling after me, but I ran all the way up my bedroom and locked the door by pushing a chair against the handle.

A few seconds later Ruen appeared in the chair and I almost jumped out of my skin. He was Horn Head. I could see the blood all clotted on the barbed wire next to his furry chest and I felt trapped because there was no other way out. He had the metal mace in one hand and the light from the window made the spikes glint.

"Go and study bacteria," I told him.

"You want to know why I study you?" Ruen's voice whispered in my head.

I wiped my eyes and folded my arms but said nothing. My chest felt like someone had scraped the insides out with a metal spoon and I felt angry with myself for pushing Auntie Bev away. Maybe she could get Ruen to leave. Even if I shouted I didn't think she would be able to hear. Mum never did.

"I would have thought you had already worked that one out, Alex," Ruen whispered, and I squeezed my eyes shut. I hated that he had no face. Sometimes parts of his face appeared: a pair of blue eyes, a mouth like mine. But it was just so weird and horrible that I couldn't look at it.

"For whatever reason, we can't seem to tempt you. None of us seems to have much of an effect on you. And we need to know why that is."

I wanted to ask why, but didn't. I kept my eyes shut.

"If you simply told me why this is the case, perhaps I might be able to stop studying you quite so intensively," he continued.

I thought about it. After a while I forced myself to open my eyes and stare at him. I looked at the red horn coming out of his forehead. It looked like liquid floating upward.

"I guess I don't like people telling me what to do."

"Admirable. Commendable," whispered Ruen. Then he turned into the Old Man and I gave a big breath of relief. He stood up and walked to the window, his arms behind his back as usual. I glanced at the door and moved the chair away, but just then Ruen was back in front of me.

"I promise you, Alex, I won't tell you what to do. I already know you can't be tempted, so you have my word. I won't even try to tempt you. You're much too strong-willed, even for the likes of me." He cackled and it turned into a cough. "You will love your new house, Alex. Are we still friends?"

I thought of the new house and felt happier. "Yes, Ruen. We're still friends."

# 14
## MISTS OF
## THE MIND

## ANYA

I met with Cindy yesterday to ask her questions about Alex's home life, about his absent father, and also to ask her permission for Alex to be transferred to MacNeice House for about a month. Usually, a parent is the first port of call when it comes to detecting any abnormalities; patterns of withdrawal, any indications of voices or hallucinations, a sudden slipping away from school and friends. But unfortunately Cindy's own depression has created a veil over anyone's issues but her own. A history of abuse, both as a child and as an adult, has been compounded by the breakdown of her relationship with Alex's father. Since then, repeated suicide attempts have been her method of dealing with it. Her "bracelets," as she calls them, or the many white lines on her wrists from self-harming episodes, aren't easy to conceal. She thinks Alex is receiving counseling to deal with her suicide attempts, which is partly true.

For her own treatment, I am pleased to learn she's in the care of Dr. Trudy Messenger, one of the most experienced psychiatrists in the United Kingdom. She is famous for making her patients feel like human beings after a single consultation. After years of feeling ousted, separate, and vilified by the legions who don't understand mental illness, these patients experience a kind of homecoming in Trudy's office. Trudy has seen to it that Cindy is actively engaged in a variety of daily activities, mostly arts and crafts, and when I arrive she is completing a beautiful needlework of a small white dog.

"It's for Alex," she tells me with a small smile. "Woof. He loves that dog. Thick as thieves, those two. I know boys don't like girlie things but maybe he'll make an exception."

I spend a few minutes talking about the facilities in the hospital before telling her gently that I have some concerns about Alex's mental health. She looks puzzled.

"Alex has seen a psychiatrist before," she says. "But they've never had any worries about him, not really. And he's spoken to Michael. You can hardly expect a kid from his side of town to be tap dancing with joy every day. That's my fault."

"I don't think he's depressed," I say.

"Then what do you mean?"

I tell her there are other possibilities that I'm investigating. I assure her I'm optimistic that Alex can be treated, but that I'm determined to ensure he receives the correct treatment.

"I'd like to know about Alex's father," I ask gently, thinking of my meeting with Karen Holland, Alex's paintings spread across her desk.

Her face darkens. "Why do you want to know about Alex's father?"

My voice is gentle. "A boy's relationship with his father is important in forming his identity and his place in the world."

She sets down her needle and thread and crosses her thin arms tightly. "I haven't told anyone who Alex's real dad is. Well, except my mum."

"I don't need names," I say evenly. "Would you say he was a good father?"

She looks out the window. A hand reaches for the other wrist, making a circle around it with her forefinger and thumb.

"He saw Alex once in a while. Maybe a handful of days every month. Sometimes he'd stay with us for a week. Then we wouldn't see him for two months." She raises her eyes. "I named Alex after him."

I nod. "He was never abusive with Alex?"

She looks disgusted. "No, never! He wasn't exactly overjoyed when I told him I was pregnant but he still provided for us. It was the reason he . . ." She falls silent.

"It was the reason he what?" I ask.

She takes a breath. "He'd take Alex to play table tennis sometimes, said it was good for his hand–eye coordination. He was thoughtful like that. He'd buy him toy cars. Alex hated cars."

"When did Alex stop seeing him?"

She is lifting a hand to cover her eyes, lowering her head. I must tread carefully.

"If it's okay for me to ask, what were the circumstances surrounding his departure from Alex's life?"

She shakes her head, her hand pressed to her forehead. I crouch down beside her.

"Cindy," I say, lightly touching her hand. "I promise you, I'm only asking these things so I can help Alex."

She lowers her hand and fixes me with angry, burning eyes. "You think he's insane."

"I don't," I assure her. "But he has mentioned some things he can see that appear to be harming him."

Her eyes widen. "Someone's hurting Alex? Is it someone at that theater?"

I shake my head. "Alex claims he has a best friend called Ruin. Several times now Alex has gotten quite aggressive during our sessions and claims that Ruin got angry. Have you ever come across any marks on his body, any unexplained injuries?"

She narrows her eyes. "I'm not abusing him, if that's what you're getting at."

"I think it's possible that *Alex* is hurting Alex," I say softly.

She gasps and searches my face. "Why would you say a terrible thing like that? Why would you say my baby's hurting *himself*?"

I hesitate. I'm confounded by the fact that her own arms bear hundreds of scars from her own efforts to hurt herself and yet she cannot conceive of Alex doing the same. And as if she knows what I'm thinking, she reaches one hand across her forearm where sunlight is making silvery rivers of her scars.

"What if he's telling the truth?" she demands, her lip trembling. "I mean, Alex wouldn't do that. Would he? He's so talented and smart and braver than me." She looks up at me. "He would never do that."

"If Alex has seen you self-harm, chances are he'll do it, too."

My words smash around the room. Cindy's face crumples and she lets out a long, loose cry. It takes me a moment or two to realize why she is crying: She has never, ever considered the impact of her own illness on her child.

I walk across the room to retrieve a box of tissues. She plucks one out with a trembling hand and holds it to her eyes.

"I want to see him," she says.


Alex was brought to the hospital later that afternoon. I asked Cindy if it would be okay for me to stay and observe their time together. I expected her to ask why, but it seemed my comment about Alex's potential self-harming had knocked the fight out of her. I wanted to ensure that I gathered the information I needed to answer these pressing questions: Is there a link between Ruin and Cindy? Or between Ruin and Alex's father? Is Alex's hallucination—and indeed, his condition—linked to an incident in the past?

The adult psychiatric unit is close to MacNeice House and is surrounded by a sprawling green lawn dotted with patches of bright flowers, fenced off from the outside world by tall fir trees and an array of greenhouses. One of the nurses suggested Alex and Cindy take a walk outside—hinting at me to provide the necessary medical supervision—and so I carried three coats and an umbrella, in case the fat gray awnings of cloud toppled their load, and ushered us all outside. Cindy was eager to show Alex the result of her horticulture therapy workshop, and so we headed toward the greenhouses.

I let Alex and Cindy walk ahead of me, noticing the way Alex linked his arm around Cindy's. There was genuine affection between the two, and playfulness; on several occasions Alex made Cindy giggle, tickling her until the giggle became a substantial laugh, at which she thumped him over the head, visibly careful not to hit him too hard. They were almost the same height, mother and son, although Cindy's frame was starkly bird-like beside his, the bones of her ankles and wrists jutting out like white buttons on her arms. I noticed that they had the same walk.

We reached one of the greenhouses, which was crammed with tomato plants and hanging baskets exploding with lobelias. Alex and Cindy huddled around a toilet bowl outside that someone had filled with bright yellow daffodils. Cindy waved to me and asked me to join them.

"I won a prize," she told me, her thin face alight. "My first ever."

"Where did you get the toilet, Mum?" Alex was inspecting the broken back of it and utterly perplexed by its incongruity beside the other plant pots.

"Never mind that, Alex," Cindy said. She looked up at me again. I saw she was eager to share an achievement. "*You're* smart, aren't you?" she said to me. "Can't you figure out what I was doing?"

I looked over the arrangement, at the rather haphazard way the daffodils had been planted into the compost, though their fat trumpets indicated they were healthy and being taken care of. A good sign. I noticed she'd painted the word HOPE on the bulge of the toilet.

"Well, you're making a statement, aren't you?" I said, winking at Alex. "Even when you're in the gutter you can become something beautiful."

Cindy gave a big cheer. "See, Alex? Told you she was smart. Daffodils mean hope. I thought that sticking them in a toilet bowl would be poetic, sort of. Plus they were throwing this out and I thought it would be a waste."

Alex looked disgusted. "But it's a *toilet*, Mum. That's *gross*."

As we headed back to the ward, Cindy put her arm around Alex's shoulders and leaned her chin on his head, and Alex wrapped his arms tightly around her waist. Both of them had slowed down their pace considerably, until I was forced to stop behind them and pretend to remove a stone from my shoe.

Just as the side entrance came into view, the sky turned from cloudy blue to wet slate. In a matter of seconds, the wind had started to move so fast that all the small white flowers I'd collected from the tall grass flew out of my grasp as if someone had slapped them from my hands. I was about to shout to Cindy and Alex that it was time to go inside when I noticed something very strange. Both of them were gone. In fact, the hospital entrance was no longer in view; nor were the trees, the greenhouses, even the grass that had been at my feet only moments before. Stunned, I stood dumbly in a dark vacuum for a few seconds, rolling through a rapid list of possibilities: fog? a blackout?

Without warning, my surroundings had changed. It was as though I'd been transported into another realm. Instead of being outside I was in a hospital ward sitting in bed, the walls around me blank and white, the only sound a steady *bleep* from a heart monitor. I started to call out, but instantly I was back outside, Alex and Cindy ahead, ambling toward the entrance. The sky was feathered with white clouds, and all around me was green lawn and bowing trees.

Shaken, I quickly said good-bye. All the way back to MacNeice House I felt on edge, raw with shock.

I canceled a meeting with Harold, Ursula, and Michael, went straight to my apartment, and slept for nine hours straight.

## 15
## THE GREATEST
## DREAM OF ALL TIME

ALEX

Dear Diary,

A sandwich walks into a bar and says, "a pint of Guinness, mate." The barman replies, "sorry, we don't serve food here."

I have to write really fast 'cos I have a dress rehearsal for *Hamlet* and Jojo is going crazy about people who turn up late. Good stuff and bad stuff has happened. The good stuff is so good, though, that I'm not even sure I can call the bad stuff bad, it's just not even important anymore. The first cool thing that happened was that Anya came and told me I could see Mum. I thought it would be a while before I could see her because she's chilling out and getting her strength back, according to Auntie Bev. But when I saw Mum I couldn't believe how much better she looked. Her hair had been washed and was shiny and soft and not like pasta that's been in the fridge for a week. Her cheeks were pink and her eyes didn't have dark bits under them and she was wearing a long white T-shirt that almost covered all the marks on her arms. It made me feel happy.

"Alex!" Mum said when I walked in, and her voice was normal and she hugged me so hard I coughed. "How have you been?"

Then, before I could tell her about Auntie Bev throwing out all the onions and about the play and how I would love her to come she said: "You know what's weird? I had this dream about Granny last night and she told me I needed to give you a big hug."

"Did she tell you to crack my ribs, too?" I said, rubbing my sides from her big bear hug and she laughed but I was serious.

Anya said she'd wait outside and Mum nodded and when Anya had gone she asked me if Anya was asking me anything that bothered me. I thought about Ruen but I didn't want to say anything to upset her.

"Has Anya asked *you* anything that bothered you?" I asked her instead.

"No. But my therapist keeps asking about my childhood. All she wanted to know about was my favorite doll." She made a clicking noise with her tongue then put on a voice as if she was imitating someone. " 'Why did you call her *Ugly*? Why did you dress her in a black dress? Why did you put her facedown when your foster dad came in?' "

"Why *did* you put the doll facedown when your foster dad came in?"

She looked at me funny. "Sorry, Alex," she said, looking down. "I shouldn't have let my mouth run off. Sometimes I forget you're not an old man, you know? How are *you*, sweetheart?"

I shrugged. "When are you coming home?"

She bit her lip and ran her fingers through her hair. It was starting to go black again at the roots and I was about to tell her that if she came home I could help her put the sky-blue stuff in it to turn the roots yellow but she said:

"I don't know."

"Woof misses you."

"*Woof* misses me?"

I nodded. She leaned forward and looked at me very closely and I touched my face in case I had a black mark on it or something.

"You've never . . . hurt yourself, have you, honey?"

I felt my cheeks turn hot. "Why do you ask that?"

"I just wondered if what I'd . . . I mean, you're different from me, aren't you? You're Alexander the Great, aren't you?"

Just then I had a flash in my brain of someone else saying the words *Alexander the Great,* and I could see our living room but from way up high. For a second I remembered my Dad saying *Alexander the Great!* and I was on his shoulders and he was bouncing me up and down, and then the memory was gone.

Mum started to say something but then a nurse knocked loudly on the door and came into the room.

"Sorry for interrupting," she said though she didn't look sorry. "Trudy thinks you should get out today, Cindy. Maybe take Alex here to the greenhouse, show him what you did with the horticulturalist?"

Mum nodded. "Okey dokey. Come on, sweetie, let me show you what you can do with a toilet."


I didn't see Ruen all day after that. I remembered he said that Anya would tell me that we'd be moving house by the end of the day, but she didn't and I thought *I'm definitely, definitely going to tell him I don't want to be friends next time I see him.* But he didn't turn up, which was nice because I got to go back home that night and Woof licked my face and whined as if he'd really missed me and slept on my bed all night.

And then Anya came to see me this morning instead of the afternoon because it's Saturday. She couldn't stop smiling. I asked her what was wrong and she told me to sit down at the table, which I did, and she started taking lots of things out of her briefcase and spreading them across the table.

"This," she said, "is your new home."

*I could not believe it.* I watched her arrange photographs of our new house in front of me and Auntie Bev came in and asked all the questions I wanted to ask but couldn't, like *does Cindy know? How did this happen? Where is it? When can they move in? Is this for real?*

Anya kept smiling and bouncing on the balls of her feet like she was moving, too. I think it was because she was just really happy for this to happen even though she didn't even know that it was my Greatest Dream of All Time. Auntie Bev said things like, "well thank the elephant in the sky for that, then, this place is falling apart," and "is it seriously a council property? Looks stunning."

"And there's more," Anya said. "The reason that some of the photographs look as though the rooms aren't finished is because this is a brand-new property."

"Brand new?" I said, and I tried to think of the last time I had something that was brand new.

"Yes," Anya said. "No one else has ever lived there before."

". . . my pencil case," I said, because it was brand new. Anya was still talking about how it meant I could have a bedroom that no one would have had before and so there would be no old clothes or rubbish for me to have to throw out.

"You can even choose your own wallpaper," she said, her smile growing wider. "And the front door can be whatever color you want it to be. The council are keen to ensure their residents have proprietorship over their accommodation."

"What?" I said, because this made no sense.

Anya laughed. The sound was like bells and made me laugh even though nothing was funny. She turned to Auntie Bev, who was smiling and kept folding and unfolding her arms as if she didn't know what to do with them.

"They're calling the street *Peace Street,*" Anya said to Auntie Bev, and they both found this really funny and laughed for about a decade. Apparently the politicians had knocked down one of the old streets where they used to barricade people in their houses and have riots so they bulldozed the whole area and hired a poet to rename all the new streets and write a poem that would be carved onto a wall instead of a mural with gunmen.

"Which poem?" Auntie Bev asked.

"It's called 'Belfast Confetti,'" Anya said and she pulled out a page and read it out loud.

*Suddenly as the riot squad moved in, it was raining exclamation marks,*

*Nuts, bolts, nails, car-keys. A fount of broken type. And the
explosion.*

*Itself—an asterisk on the map. This hyphenated line, a burst
of rapid fire . . .*

*I was trying to complete a sentence in my head but it kept
stuttering,*

*All the alleyways and side streets blocked with stops and
colons.*

*I know this labyrinth so well—Balaclava, Raglan, Inkerman,
Odessa Street—*

*Why can't I escape? Every move is punctuated. Crimea
Street. Dead end again.*

*A Saracen, Kremlin-2 mesh. Makrolon face-shields. Walkie-
talkies. What is*

*My name? Where am I coming from? Where am I going? A
fusillade of question-marks.*

"It's by a poet named Ciaran Carson," Anya said. "And they're carv-
ing it in letters that will be three feet tall."

I looked at the pictures for ages and ages as Auntie Bev and Anya
talked. The house was big at the front and didn't have other houses at
either side and it had a garden. It had a big kitchen, which I knew
would make Mum happy. There was a driveway at the front in case we
ever got a car and didn't want to leave it on the street in case someone
slashed the tires. I thought of what it would be like if we got a car and
all the places we could go to, like Helen's Bay and Portrush and the
Giant's Causeway. My mind filled with so many thoughts and wishes
that I got a headache.

"Well, Alex," Anya said to me at last. "What do you think?"

I didn't say anything, not because I wasn't thinking anything but
because I was thinking too much, and I thought that if I opened my
mouth all the words would just explode out like streamers from a party
popper.

"You don't seem very excited, Alex," said Auntie Bev, and I saw
Anya reach out and touch her arm as if she shouldn't have said that.
Auntie Bev said "sorry" with her mouth but no noise and then turned

to say something else to me, but I stood up, still looking down at the pictures.

"There's something very important I have to do," I said. I walked out of the room, which I knew worried Anya and Auntie Bev because they looked at each other. When I reached the stairs I remembered something and went back into the room.

"Thank you," I said to Anya, and then she asked me loads more questions about Ruen and about demons and whether I could see angels.

"There are demons everywhere," I said.

"Are there any here now?" she asked. I looked at the fat man who'd appeared above her again. Sometimes I could only see a bit of him, like his toe or his belly with the belly button I could probably fit my head in. His eyes were black and when he grinned at me I saw his teeth were, too.

"Alex?"

I pointed up at him 'cos I could see all of him now. "He's fat," I said.

She looked puzzled. "Who is?"

"Your demon."

She laughed. "I have a demon?"

He was stretching his arms out now like he'd had a really long nap, and the blanket that was covering up his penis almost slipped off. I looked away.

"Can you tell me what his name is?" Anya was saying. I looked back at him but he was disappearing.

I shrugged. So she asked me what demons looked like and why I thought I could see them and I was still so excited about the house that I can't even remember what I said. It was like there was a film of the house in my head and I could see every room really clearly and it was beautiful, just beautiful. Then she asked me something crazy that made the film stop suddenly and I was back in my own living room.

"Alex, have you ever been involved in a terrorist attack?"

I asked her what she meant.

"Like a bomb scare? Or a shooting? Did you ever get hurt in a riot, maybe?"

I thought about it. Granny's first husband died in a bomb and last year someone set a car on fire and rolled it down our street. So I told her that.

Anya nodded and wrote all this down. "What about a policeman, Alex? Did you ever see a policeman get hurt?"

I felt sick and shook my head.

She looked at me very closely. "Are you sure?"

I saw the policeman's face in my head, his mouth curling in a funny way as his head snapped toward me. I opened my mouth to say something but then I felt my hands make fists and I knew it was wrong to say anything, it was wrong, wrong, wrong.

"Deep breath," Anya was saying, and when I opened my eyes I had both arms wrapped around me very tightly. When I felt normal again I said, "I saw people on TV at a policeman's funeral. They were crying."

She nodded. "Did you feel bad for those people?"

I started to cry. Anya reached out and touched my arm. "It's okay," she said. "Did you see what happened to the policeman? Did he get hurt?"

I nodded and wiped my eyes.

"Alex, was your Daddy a policeman?"

"I want to go lie down now," I said.

"Did you see something on TV, Alex? About a policeman?"

Her voice was starting to sound very far away. I stood up and my legs felt like they were made of melting ice cubes.

"We'll talk later," Anya called after me, and I hoped she would just forget everything she had asked.

I ran upstairs to my bedroom. For some reason I knew Ruen would be there. As soon as I opened the door Woof ran out barking, then hid behind my legs and whimpered. I leaned down and stroked his head and I could feel he was shaking. I stood up and walked into my room.

"Hello, Ruen," I said. He was Ghost Boy and was sitting in the chair by the closet as usual, his arms folded tightly like he was in a right huff.

I sat down on the bed and waved at Woof to come in, but he stood in the doorway looking at Ruen and growling. After a bit, he whimpered and ran downstairs. I thought of the photos Anya had showed me.

I looked at Ruen. "I want to tell you something."

He looked up. He actually looked a bit nervous, like I was going to tell him to go away. The knot that Anya had made in my stomach started to get smaller and I smiled at him.

"I want to say thank you," I whispered.

"You want to thank me?"

"Yes," I said. I stood up then, feeling better by the second. After a few minutes I was bouncing up and down, thinking about our house. "Thank you thank you thank you! Our house is fan-flipping-tastic! How did you do it? Where did you find it?"

His mouth hung open a bit but he didn't answer. I stopped jumping and started to cry again. He looked very confused. I sat down on the floor and held my face. My head felt like it was going to burst.

"I'm really, really sorry," I said. "I didn't mean to be ungrateful or horrible. I just . . ." Really quickly my heart went from feeling ripped up like an old newspaper to feeling really warm, as if someone was hugging it. When I looked up, Ruen had vanished.

"Ruen?"

There was no one in the room but all of a sudden it seemed to fill with light, as if the sun had walked inside, and there was a smell of strawberries. I didn't know what was happening. I just felt happy. And for some reason I thought of Granny, which made me cry again because I hadn't thought about her for ages. This would make Granny happy, too, I decided, Mum and me moving into a new place. I was really, really young when she died but I remember her begging Mum to move into her house because she didn't like the thought of us being alone. She used to shout at our neighbors, too, and they wouldn't even shout back, they were so scared of her.

I must have fallen asleep because the next thing I knew I was in bed with all the blankets over me and it was no longer sunny. I looked over at the chair and saw Ruen sitting there. "Where did you go?" I said, but he didn't answer.

I rolled upright. All the pictures of the house came back into my mind and I started smiling again.

"Ruen, I don't even know enough words to say thank you for this."

"You don't?"

"There aren't even enough words in the whole of the dictionaries in the whole world to tell you how grateful I am. In fact, I'm more grateful than a whole field full of grated cheese!"

He looked at me as I started going on about grated carrots and great big sausages and Alexander the Grateful. He wasn't smiling his Alex Is Stupid smile but I didn't care.

"How about *showing* me how grateful you are?" he said.

I stopped laughing. "Okay. I'm grateful *this much*," I said, stretching out my arms. "No, *this* much," and I ran to one side of the room and slapped the wall and then ran to the other side and slapped the other wall, "times a billion."

Ruen stood up. "Can I make a suggestion?"

I nodded. He looked around. "Find yourself a pen and paper."

I searched my closet for my sketch pads, then eventually found one under my pillow. The pen I found had been chewed up by Woof but after a few minutes I found a felt-tip pen in my sock drawer.

"I'm ready," I said.

Ruen sat down again and made that triangle with his fingers, the way he always does when he's deep in thought.

"I'd like you to write down the following questions. And when I tell you, I'd like you to ask them to Anya."

"Okay," I said, and he started to talk.

# 16

# THE BITTER SIDE
# OF FREEDOM

## ANYA

The weather has taken a turn for the better and I've started spending lunchtimes sitting on the grass in front of the city hall, watching new blood circulating through Belfast's veins. It's still stunning to me to see my homeland so transformed, to see faces from all over the world walking through its streets. The world has remembered Northern Ireland, and for the first time since I moved back I feel assured that my decision was the right one. I considered coming back home to Belfast when Poppy was about to enter primary school in Edinburgh. On the day that I had to decide on which school she was to attend, two car bombs exploded at an army barracks in Lisburn, about ten miles away from Belfast. The second bomb was deliberately targeted at medical staff treating those wounded from the first bomb. Poppy and I stayed in Edinburgh.

Still, my return home this time has coincided with the beginnings of real peace in this land. Better yet, old friendships I thought I had forever crippled by my move to Scotland have proved stronger than ever. My best friend, Fi, insists on crossing the Albert Bridge every lunchtime to catch up with me, determined to make sure I stay put in Belfast this time around.

I arrive at the city hall on the dot of noon after a morning spent talk-ing with a new patient's parents about their son's dissociative identity disorder. A handsome, polite thirteen-year-old, Xavier is heir to his father's multimillion-pound fortune, excelling at private school, and a national chess champion. The problem is, Xavier has twenty-two differ-ent identities—a creation of personas usually developed in the wake of abuse or trauma, or chemical imbalance, and a very disturbing illness for those who are close to the patient. The personalities can be of various ages, genders, temperaments, dialects, and disposition. Xavier's identities are becoming increasingly difficult about coexisting in his mind, and some of them are severely depressed. He has no history of suffering physical or sexual abuse, no drug problem. He has a loving, supportive family, who are heartbroken to learn that their beautiful boy is extremely ill. Cases such as his remind me that the biological factors of mental health are foremost, and that urgent medical intervention is necessary. Michael, of course, would disagree.

I spread my coat on the grass, tuck my legs behind me, and nibble my sushi. Ten minutes later my phone bleeps with a text message.

Meeting with the boss pushed ahead—sorry honey! Meet up tomorrow? Will bring CAKE! Fi xx

Ten minutes later, as I get up to leave, I spy Michael sitting cross-legged on the grass beside the *Titanic* Memorial. He is wearing a white polo shirt instead of his standard bottle-green sweater. He sees me ap-proaching and jumps to his feet, scattering a package of macadamia nuts.

"Dr. Molokova," he exclaims. "Ursula's stretching the leash a bit far today, isn't she?"

"Can I join you?" I say.

He looks around him. "I'm alone, aren't I? Have a seat." Sitting, he pats the space on the grass beside him. I hesitate, recalling the tension between us at the review meeting. Still, I am anxious to ask him about demons and the supernatural dimensions that Alex invokes continually in constructing his fantasies. Michael has mentioned that he trained as a priest, before having a breakdown of conscience and switching to a career in social work. I think there's more to it than that, but I don't ask. I sink down on a spot a little farther from Michael than he had indicated. The grass is warm and soft. For a moment, the sensation is so intense that I want to fall asleep.

"Would you like one?" Michael holds the bag of nuts in my direction.

"Are you trying to kill me?" I hold out my talisman and give it a jiggle.

He rolls his eyes. "Oh yeah. *Allergies.* What, do you break out in a rash?"

"Something like that."

He looks at me intently, carefully folding the plastic bag neatly into eighths, before slipping it into his shirt pocket. "No, seriously. How bad is it?"

I take a breath, recalling the last time I experienced anaphylactic shock. I was newly qualified as a child psychiatrist, attending a symposium at Cambridge for the British Association of Child and Adolescent Psychiatry. I hadn't had a reaction since I was in my teens, and so I'd been careless. The chocolate cake had ground hazelnuts in it, the chef admitted later. No more than a handful. Still, that delicious slice of chocolate cake was enough to start a reaction in just minutes. First the familiar tingling sensation around my gums, then into my teeth. Dizziness. It was the metallic taste in my mouth that made me start to panic. But by the time I tapped the person at the table next to me to tell them to phone a doctor, my airways had swollen so badly I could barely breathe.

I tell all this to Michael. When I'm finished, he unzips his briefcase, takes out a packet of antibacterial wipes, and scrubs his hands. "Just in case," he says.

I laugh. "I wanted to ask you about some of the religious undertones of Alex's descriptions," I say carefully. "Do you have a minute?"

He nods, his eyes lingering on my talisman. "Shoot."

"Okay, so I've treated a handful of kids who've claimed to see demons, angels, what have you, but none of them has ever described the spiritual world with the depth that Alex has. There's a specificity to his descriptions that I need to explore. You're Catholic, aren't you?"

"Recovering," says Michael with a wink. "Doesn't make me an expert but I'll see what I can do. Define *specificity*."

"Alex told me that Ruin is a Harrower."

"A *Harrower*?" Michael repeats, frowning.

I tell him about my meeting with Alex a few days previously.

"You say Ruin is a demon, Alex," I had asked gently. "What does that mean, exactly? Does that mean he's bad? Does he work for Satan?"

Alex had glanced to a spot next to the window, leaning toward it as if he was receiving instructions. "Of course, I've seen a similar kind of attention to imaginary friends before," I tell Michael now. "But it was what he said next that astonished me. I mean, he's *ten*."

"What did he say?"

I reach into my pocket and bring out my mobile phone. "I recorded it," I tell Michael, hitting the PLAY tab on the screen. In seconds, Alex's voice is audible over the blare of city traffic. He speaks slowly, stopping often.

"A Harrower is a job title bestowed upon the kind of demon that's closest to the top of Hell's hierarchy." He pauses to take another attempt at pronouncing *hierarchy*. He continues. "After which is Satan and his advisers. Many demons are tempters, like worker bees, assigned the task of fishing impromptu ideas and suggestions in the rivers of human weakness, hoping someone will take a bite, but the more educated and experienced demons carry out the tasks of developing temptations into hobbies, habits. Into small axes that will eventually fell the whole tree."

There is a pause as I let Alex recover from this wordy description.

"Why a tree?" I say.

Alex pauses, then attempts another metaphor.

"The ultimate goal of a demon is to take away choice. Choice makes for a very messy universe. Kind of like a garden that is left unattended for all the weeds to scatter wherever they want.

Choice leads to all the bad stuff in our world. So we want to stop it."

"We?" I ask.

I remember how Alex had glanced at the spot next to the window again. "Sorry, I was just repeating what Ruin said. Shall I continue?"

I make a note of the *we* and ask him to go on. He coughs loudly.

"We see the removal of choice as a noble purpose. Every demon's existence is dedicated to the fulfillment of his or her role, for which he or she trains for hundreds or even thousands of mortal years. Every demon who has any sort of role in the human realm, even a role as menial as tempting or discouraging, is a scientist, steeped in millennia of knowledge on human frailty. If a demon fails to achieve his or her purpose at any time, the punishment is severe." Alex stops. "That's a bit harsh, isn't it?" he says to the spot by the window.

"What is?" I ask. He turns back to me.

"If a demon fails, he's chained to the bottom of a pit a billion miles beneath the sun for a hundred years, and *then* he has to do his training all over again."

I nod. "I'd say that's harsh." I refer to my notes. "What is a Harrower?" This term clearly has great importance for Alex, and I want to know all the meanings he has attached to it.

Alex looks down, as if listening, then returns his gaze to me.

"What is it, Alex?"

"Ruin wants me to repeat his own words, as if he's talking now. Is that okay?"

I nod and watch him carefully.

" 'I am a Harrower. My job is to go in after the barriers have been broken, after the action has been taken, even after regret has sunk its fangs deep into memory. And then I rake the soul until it is ripe for the seeds of doubt and hopelessness for which no human language has adequate lexicon. I could give you a thousand translations of *anguish* in the various tongues of the human realm, because all of them differ, and yet none of them comes close to capturing its complexity. This is because there is no translation for the kind of work I perform. Nobody needs to be taken to Hell to experience it. We just grow despair inside the soul until it becomes a world in and around a human.'"

Alex takes another breath, his shoulders relaxed, his eyes flitting across the room as if he is bored. Then he continues.

"'Harrowing is an essential part of cultivating the soul to reject the idea of choice. Contrary to popular opinion, the soul is not like smoke on water; it is somewhere between liquid and metal, like the earth's core. When one strokes it, grooves are made, impressions formed. The soul can only be removed by God, that is true; but when the door is opened, when the path is made clear for my entrance, I can mold that slick substance into countless shapes and create hollows that channel through to eternity.

"'There is much waiting around in this job. In order to do my work effectively, I must watch as other demons perform the complex tasks of analyzing, tempting, suggesting, then deftly plucking away the scales of human realization until remorse and horror pave the way for my entrance. It's no joyride. I am virtually alone, and there is no one to applaud the work I achieve. There is only the sight of a human falling deeper and deeper within themselves, toppling through the distances created by my grooves and hollows.'"

When I am sure that Alex has finished, I hit the PAUSE and SAVE buttons on my phone. There is nothing more I want to ask at this point. I need time to process the information that has been given. Suddenly Alex says:

"Now shall I ask her the questions?"

He is speaking to the empty space by the window, not me. Still, I say:

"What questions?"

Alex nods. "Never mind. He doesn't want to ask you just yet."

I smile and thank Alex—and Ruin—for their time.

"Ruin says you are most welcome, my lady," says Alex.

● ● ●

Michael sits in silence for a long time after I've played him the tape, twisting a stalk of grass between his fingers. Finally he says, "Man, that's some serious stuff."

"Is any of this regurgitated from a religious text?" I ask. "Is the concept of a Harrower part of any faith that you're aware of?"

Michael scratches his head. "In ten years of religious studies, I never came across the term *harrower*. I'll look into it and see if there's any passages in the Bible that refer to it. Though, as far as I know, Alex's family wasn't religious."

"We don't know anything about his dad," I remind Michael. "Maybe he was. In which case, most of what Alex is saying could be his working his way through a severely religious upbringing." I pause to reflect on Alex's bewildering comments. "What about that whole thing about choice?"

"*Butter and honey shall he eat, that he may know to refuse the evil, and choose the good.* Old Testament, Isaiah chapter seven, verse sixteen. No, fifteen. Free will underscores most of Christian belief."

"And you never found out about Alex's father?"

He drops the mangled twist of grass, shaking his head. "Cindy refused to talk about him. The most Alex ever said was that his dad was dead and gone to Hell."

*"Hell?"* I say quickly. "Not Heaven?"

"No. Hell. He was, as you say, quite specific about that."

I sigh. "This kind of religious, intellectual thinking is *not* that of a ten-year-old." I pick up my phone and look down at it for moment before putting it back in my pocket. "What do you make of the questions Alex said Ruin wanted to ask me? Has he ever wanted to ask you questions?"

"No, I don't think so. Look," he says, and there is something different about his tone, the look in his eyes. He leans forward and strokes my arm. I pull it back, a sudden reflex, and he looks alarmed. "What? I washed my hands."

"No, it's not that," I say.

"So what is it?"

*You are forty-three years old,* I remind myself. *You are quite capable of setting professional boundaries.* Still, I feel bashful when I tell him what *it* is.

"I'd rather we be colleagues. And nothing more."

He stares at me as if I've lost my mind, and I feel my cheeks burn. Still, in the past I've let men wander way past the iron gates of friendship, then watched their faces fall when I refused to reciprocate. I'd rather be up front about it. I don't want anything to get in the way of Alex's treatment.

"Well that's a pity," Michael says lightly. "I don't go to the Opera House with any of my colleagues, and here I was thinking we could share a taxi to Alex's performance of *Hamlet* tonight."

I breathe a sigh of relief. "I don't mind sharing a taxi."

He looks visibly pleased. "Good. I'll be at your house around seven. Okay?"

I open my mouth to say, *Actually, I'll meet you there,* but he has moved on, telling me about his garden, his brussels sprouts. How we should share a bottle of his homemade tomato juice sometime.

It is only when I try to find an outfit suitable for a visit to the Grand Opera House that I realize how much Alex's case has eaten into my personal time over the last week or two—my apartment is still only partially furnished and filled with boxes, meaning that I have no cutlery, plates, chairs, and only a small rack of clothes. I dig deep into a box marked CLOTHES and pull a dozen outfits on to the red Mexican tiles of my living room. Each is black, and each is a variation of knee-length skirt or three-quarter-length shirt. Once I've assembled a row of possibilities along the floor, my mind turns to Poppy. The memory is sharp: She is standing in our Morningside flat, shaking her head as I pull garments out of my closet. While I have absolutely no fashion sense, Poppy had an innate sense of style before she could talk. I remember her fumbling in the laundry basket, picking out the colors and textures she liked before draping them around her head and shoulders, then staggering around our little flat in a pair of my high heels.

"What about this one?" I recalled myself saying, holding another black dress up. She rolled her eyes and groaned.

"Everything you own is black," she complained, fishing through my closet. "Why not anything red? Or orange or even yellow?"

"Are those my colors?"

She flicked her beautiful eyes at me. "Your skin is olive, your hair and eyes are dark brown."

"I'll take that as a yes."

She found a white dress lurking in my shoe rack. "Aha! Here we go."

There's a price tag still hanging from the dress. A Stella McCartney, bought on a whim. Back then, my motto was *If you can live without it, live without it—unless it's Stella*. Poppy thrust the dress against me.

"*This* is it," she insisted.

I shook my head. "It's far too tight!"

More eye rolling. "Mother, you're skinny. Flaunt it, okay?"

And now, as her precocious words chimed in my ears, I spied something at the bottom of the box. Something I hadn't even remembered packing. A white puddle. I reached in and pulled it out, noticing the label. It was the same dress. I hadn't worn it the night that she insisted upon it. Stella or not, it wasn't *me*, I'd argued, to her annoyance.

Now, I strip down to my underwear and slip the dress over my head. Cut elegantly below the knee, one-sleeved, with a modestly straight neckline just under my collarbone and a discreet gold zipper on the seam, the dress still fit perfectly. And it still isn't me.

At seven o'clock a car horn sounds. I grab my briefcase and talisman and run outside to find Michael standing beside a taxi. He is wearing a navy suit and a white shirt without a tie, his hair combed back.

"Evening," he says, holding the door open.

I pause, utterly certain that I chose the wrong clothing.

"You look lovely, Dr. Molokova," he says, giving me a small bow. It's as if he's read my mind.

I smile back at him and slide into the backseat.

At the Grand Opera House I tell Michael to go ahead and find our seats while I search for a staff member to take me backstage. I want to be certain that Alex is all right. I spot Jojo's red head bobbing among the hordes in the lobby and call her name. She turns at the sound, and I wave.

"Is everything okay?" I ask once we find a quiet corner close to the stairwell. "With Alex, I mean."

"Absolutely fine with *Alex*," she tells me. Her face looks strained. "But we're a man down. Well, a girl, really. Katie, who plays Hamlet? I mean, thank the Lord we've an understudy to fill her shoes, but can you imagine? On opening night?"

"What happened?"

She dusts down her dress, a strapless cerise number made of swimsuit fabric, a garish orange feather boa draped around her shoulders. Her gray eyes show that she's tired and anxious. "Had an accident, poor thing. Broke her leg in six places falling down a flight of steps. Anyway, we're fine now. *And* there's a casting director from London here tonight. Roz Mardell, have you heard of her?"

I shake my head. She *tsks* in disapproval.

"Roz is casting for the new Tarantino *Hamlet,* can you imagine?" She fans herself. "I think Alex has an excellent chance."

"You do?" I felt a sudden mixture of excitement and dread. Excitement at the opportunity this would afford Alex, but dread at what impact it might have on his fragile emotions.

"You know his aunt is here?" Jojo asks me. "She's upstairs in a box if you want to say hello."

A teenage boy in a black T-shirt bearing the REALLY TALENTED KIDS logo waves at Jojo from the other side of the foyer.

"I better go," she says. "You look beautiful in that dress, by the way."

"Thanks." I watch her squeeze her way to the other side of the foyer before heading up the stairs to my seat in the Grand Circle.

Along the crescent of filled seats I spot Michael's blond head. I inch my way across handbags and legs just as the lights begin to dim and take my seat next to him.

"Everything all right?" he whispers, leaning toward me. I catch his smell—the lime tang of aftershave, turf, and macadamia nuts—and forget why he should be asking me if everything is all right. I smile and nod, tugging the hem of my skirt self-consciously across my knees.

The curtain rises to the thrum of a drumbeat from the orchestra pit. A soft mist wafts across the stage, where a figure holding a gun is wandering.

"Who's there?" a boy's voice calls fearfully. Another figure backs his way across the stage in the direction of the boy, a hand resting on the holster at its waist. The figures collide.

"Francisco?"

"Bernardo?"

"What are you *doing* out here in the dead of night?"

"Taking over guard duty from you, you jackass. It's past midnight."

"It is?"

Another figure crosses the stage, a boy I recognize instantly as Alex. Dressed in a camouflage suit, his brown hair slicked into an old-fashioned side part, and his feet in heavy black boots, he no longer resembles the nervous, timid boy whom I've been treating. Instead, he walks with an air of authority, and when he speaks, his voice is deeper, shot through with command. A wind whips the mist up around him, the sound of strings rising up from the orchestra pit.

"Francisco—where are you off to?"

A moment's banter. "Bernardo's on guard duty. Good night."

A second figure appears behind Alex, thumping his hand heavily on his shoulder to make him jump.

"Marcellus!" Alex shouts. "Speak first next time!"

Marcellus raises his gun to indicate he is armed, then nods at Bernardo. "You're more on edge than usual, Bernardo. Has the ghost been spotted?"

Bernardo shakes his head. "Not tonight."

Marcellus turns to Alex. "Horatio says he won't believe what we've seen till he's seen it himself. Isn't that right, Horatio?"

Alex pulls the strap of a rifle over his head and sets the weapon down in foliage by his feet. He settles down as if to sleep. "No such thing as ghosts, you idiots."

"There *is,*" Bernardo insists, crouching to gather leaves and twigs together before creating a fire—or in this case, a strip of red material blown upward by a small wind machine, lit up from behind with a light. "We saw it last night, just before one. Looks just like the king."

Marcellus crouches down. "It *is* the king."

From the corner of my eye I see Michael turning to me. Half of his face is in darkness, the other illuminated by the spotlight on stage. He throws me a smile in praise of Alex, which I return. The worry that had tugged at my heart—this is Alex's first public performance, at a time when his private life is anything but calm—is easing now, and at the sound of a slow melody rung out by a piano in the orchestra pit a familiar song rises up in my head. Poppy's song, the one she was composing the night she died. My mouth goes dry. The events on the stage before me vanish as Poppy's face rises back into my mind.

But instead of recalling her by my side, instructing me on the rules of fashion and laughing at my decision to wear *that* blouse with *those* shoes, I feel her absence so keenly I have to choke back a sob.

*"There it is!"* I hear Alex shout. *"A ghost! Oh, it harrows me with fear and wonder."*

My thoughts enter a territory of my memories that is fenced off with rolling barbed wire, with armed guards at various posts keeping trespassers at a considerable distance. I ignore them, crossing beyond the familiar plains of my memories with Poppy to the day I learned I was pregnant. Poppy's father was an acquaintance from medical school. Daniel Shearsman, an American researcher spending a semester at University College London. We were never involved, at least not beyond a memorable weekend in Switzerland that started off in the lobby of a ratty convention center for a postdoctoral conference and ended up in a minimalist hotel overlooking Lake Geneva. Daniel never knew about Poppy. I was eleven weeks' pregnant before I found out, and when I did, I kept her to myself like a guilty secret.

*"This ghost,"* Alex shouts onstage, his voice trembling. *"This ghost is an omen. A sign that something is not right in our nation. Something troubles it."*

I walk on past the guards of that territory of my past, recalling months of sleeping on friends' spare mattresses throughout my pregnancy in case my mother—in the thick of her own psychosis—harmed the baby; then the birth; Poppy's small, creamy face presented to me in the nurse's arms, eyes squinted as if she was closing them against bright sunlight; bringing her home to my student flat, both of us curling up each night in a narrow bed against the window; Edith, the eccentric old spinster downstairs who offered to look after Poppy while I finished my studies; the first day I noticed something was wrong with Poppy. Not wrong—*different*. It was the day Edith told me she couldn't look after Poppy anymore.

"Why?" I asked at the time, bewildered.

Edith's gray eyes had always sparkled when I dropped Poppy off at her apartment, but lately her expression at the door had grown troubled. "She killed my fish," Edith stuttered, blinking back tears of disbelief. I thought of the large tropical fish tank Edith kept in her tiny sitting room, in which swirled a large purple ribbon that Edith had proudly informed me was a Japanese fighting fish.

"Swiped him clean out of the tank, like a cat," Edith continued, her lips trembling. "She just stood there and watched him gasp for air on the sideboard."

"I am *so* sorry," I said, horrified. I turned to Poppy. She was standing by my side, so easily bored that she was already doing a little dance and tugging at my arm to leave. I bent and cupped her small chin, turning her face up to mine. I could see Daniel's face in hers, that high forehead, the dark curls bouncing off her shoulders.

"Poppy, tell Edith you are very sorry and we will buy her a new fish."

Poppy rolled her eyes away from mine and continued to dance and bounce. Edith shook her head at me. "There've been other things," she said gravely. "Little things, but strange . . ." Her eyes darted down at Poppy, as if she was something unclean.

"She's only three years old," I reasoned, pulling Poppy away from Edith's legs. She was pretending to claw at her now, snarling and laughing.

"I'm sorry." Edith had stepped backward into the darkness of her hallway, closing her door for good.

And I remembered, all these years later, that Poppy had never apologized.

*"That it should come to this . . ."*

I glance at Alex on stage, noticing that he has managed to keep his body facing the audience while addressing his fellow actors. His dialogue is crisp and clear. I look down at the white hem of my dress bunched tightly in my fists, realizing that now, in my forties, I am finally living a normal life. A life without excuses for Poppy's behavior. A life without apologies to the parents of Poppy's classmate who sobbed after she lashed out, without pleas to countless GPs to find the right treatment, without rejection after rejection to potential lovers because my daughter needed a stability that a new relationship would rupture. I'm living a normal life. A life without Poppy.

And, to my horror, a part of me is relieved.

When the first scene ends, a sudden burst of applause startles me out of the past. I give a small start, holding my hands up as if I'd just landed in my seat. Michael turns to me.

"Are you all right?"

The stage clears, the orchestra picking up the theme tune as the wedding procession of Claudius and Gertrude begins to roll from the wings. I get to my feet. "I think I just need some fresh air . . ."

I stumble past the handbags and bent legs toward the exit, pushing through the doors to the stairwell, taking the steps two at a time to the lobby downstairs. I ignore staff who ask if I wanted to buy snacks and souvenirs, pushing past a queue bristling at the ticket desk toward the front doors. Outside, I take off my shoes, relieved by the feel of the cold, wet pavement, the indifference of loud, busy traffic. I walk a little distance away from the doors and lean my head against the cool wall.

"Anya?"

I turn to see Michael at the entrance, his suit jacket blowing open in the wind. He strides toward me.

"Are you sure you're all right?" His face is creased in concern. I turn away, anxious for him to leave. I don't want to have to explain myself, and lying makes me miserable.

"I'm fine," I say. "I just felt a little hot, that's all."

He nods, but the worry in his eyes doesn't fade. There is a moment when he should get the hint and go back inside. He doesn't.

"Alex was great, wasn't he?" He grins, plucking at the thin straws of conversation. I try to return his enthusiasm, but before I can speak I feel a sob form in my throat and my eyes well up. I raise a hand to my eyes, embarrassed.

"I'm fine," I mutter. "Really. Go on, you're missing the show."

I glance out at the traffic, shivering a little in the sweep of cold air thrown up by the stream of cars, watching the lights of the Opera House dance on each new shining vehicle. Michael is still standing there, hands at his sides, watching me. I can see the lines under his eyes, the slight fuzz of gray stubble around his jaw. I want to say *please, leave me alone,* but he steps forward. I stiffen, startled by the look of pain in his eyes. Without a word, he lifts a hand to my cheek. His thumb gently and deliberately rests across the scar inflicted by Poppy. I search his eyes, wondering what he is doing. It is as if he has ventured as close to the line I have drawn between our professional relationship and an intimate relationship as he possibly can. He doesn't move forward to kiss me, doesn't speak. He simply holds his hand there, his eyes intense, burning into mine.

After a few moments he lowers his hand and walks back inside.

# 17
## "REMEMBER ME"

ALEX

Dear Diary,

I did NOT do this to myself, but everyone here thinks I did and I am really fed up. I don't know what happened. I feel so muddled and weird. Ruen wasn't around at the time and all Bonnie did was scream. An ambulance came and carried me out in a stretcher. There were lots of people in the street but also lots of demons, too.

All the doctors at the hospital kept asking me "Alex, did you do this to yourself? Did you throw yourself up against the wall? Did you punch yourself in the face?" and then when I wouldn't answer they asked me *why* I did it.

But something even weirder happened tonight, right when I was on stage.

I'll start at the beginning.

It was like the craziest day all day in rehearsals, or I guess not all day but for about three hours before the curtain was going to come up and Jojo was getting sweaty and swearing a lot and everyone kept forgetting their lines. Katie didn't show up and everyone was worried and finally

Jojo told us Katie had had an accident and Aoife would be playing Hamlet. I thought about what Ruen had asked me to do to Katie's mum and felt bad. He was right. And if I had've done what he said, Katie would have been okay.

Then Jojo found out that a casting director was coming, which made her even more stressed out. "Her name is Roz Mardell," she kept saying, in case we met her and didn't call her by the right name which would be embarrassing, Jojo said. "If she comes up to you, you shake her hand and compliment her on her outfit and mention that you would love to do an audition." She fanned herself as if she might pass out. "One of you could end up in a film!"

*How amazingly cool would that be?* I thought, and I decided right then that I totally *would* act in films like all Jojo's famous friends and when I was really famous I would come back to Belfast and run a theater company for kids, just like Jojo. But then I had a sinking feeling, as if a pit of quicksand had landed on my chest. There was no way I could ever end up in a film. I was just Alex with a crazy Mum.

Jojo made us all sit in a circle on the stage with our legs crossed and our hands on our knees and chant "Um," which made me forget the sinking feeling and I started to giggle. Then Liam changed the chant to "dumb" and someone else said "rum" and then it became "bum," and everyone laughed.

Jojo said she'd hired professional makeup artists and technicians for opening night, which really made it all feel real, and then when the orchestra turned up I felt sick with excitement. I know there was over twenty of us in the play but somehow I couldn't get it into my head that I was a part of something so cool. I had this feeling as if a warm wave of seawater had just passed over me, as if everything was going to be all right.

And then a second later it was as if another wave washed over me but it was icy cold and I had a thought in my head: *what if it all goes wrong?*

It was just after that thought that I saw Ruen. He was the Old Man, strutting around the front of the auditorium looking over a big black piano that someone had just wheeled in. I could tell he really loved this one because he kept looking inside it at the strings and running his horrible hands up and down the keys.

When the curtain went up all the nervousness left me. I closed my eyes and told myself *I am Horatio,* and then I forgot about all the stuff that had happened before. I lowered my voice and thought of the way Jojo said Horatio would speak and how important he was at the end in continuing Hamlet's story.

The orchestra stopped tuning their instruments and all the people who were chatting in the audience went so quiet you would have thought they'd all gone home. But I knew they were there. The lights came on but just slightly. Everyone backstage went tense and nervous.

There were footsteps and shouts on stage. I heard Liam give his line.

*Taking over guard duty from you, you jackass. It's past midnight.*

It was my turn to go on. I looked down at my costume, which was a soldier's costume with shiny lace-up boots and a combat jumpsuit with medals from where I was meant to have done something brave. I had black marks smeared on my face and a big fake gun on my back. I took a deep breath. I stepped out into the spotlight.

"Francisco—where are you off to?" I said loudly. I turned my head to the audience but I couldn't see a single person, even though I knew they were all there. The spotlight was so bright that it seemed there was only me and Liam on stage. The projection of Jojo's friend appeared on the wall opposite. The projection always reminded me of Ruen because it looked like a real person but you could see the wall behind him. The orchestra started playing and it was loud, like scratchy, screaming violins. I gave my line: *Now I see it with my own eyes, I believe you. It is real.* But when I looked at the projection again it didn't look the same. The man was wearing a black balaclava now and a black jacket. I wondered if someone had changed the reel in the projector. He was just standing there, holding a gun.

Aoife came on stage as Hamlet, and she looked at the ghost and reached to touch it. *He is my father,* she said. *He is my father! O Hamlet, progenitor, warmest father, namesake—tell me why you're here.*

The ghost turned and faced Aoife. The voice of Jojo's famous friend filled the auditorium.

*I was murdered by that same traitor who has married your mother . . .*

Aoife stared as the ghost talked to her, telling her to avenge his death. She looked really scared and clung on to me, and I felt numb.

*Remember me, Hamlet.*

I looked at the ghost and he held up his gun. And then it was like the stage and the smoke and the projection of Jojo's famous friend as the ghost and the audience all disappeared. And I wasn't even Horatio anymore.

*Remember me . . .*

Aoife was no longer standing beside me. The stage had disappeared and instead of a black sea of faces, I was standing on a country road. There was a row of small stone shops behind me and a church and a post office. Some women were pushing prams along the narrow pavement and a little girl in a yellow dress was standing in a shop doorway eating a packet of chips and throwing some for the pigeons. The road was black and shiny as if it had been raining. There were two policemen at either side of the road, one old, one young. A police car was parked on the side of the road just past me. *It's a police checkpoint,* I thought. I could see the camera in the back of it pointed at the patrol.

A blue car came up the road toward the checkpoint. *Enjoy them while they're young,* the policeman on the opposite side of the road said. *Not long before they start borrowing your car and bleeding you dry.* The young policeman spotted the car coming toward them and he walked into the center of the road with his hand up.

The blue car came closer and I could see two men in the front. The man behind the driver's wheel was so small I could hardly see his face over the steering wheel, but as he got closer I saw he was old and bald with a white tuft of hair at the back. The other man's face was hidden behind a black balaclava. I could feel my breaths getting faster and my heart galloping because I knew who he was.

He was my Dad.

The policeman in the middle of the road shouted something to the older policeman who took out his radio and started talking into it. The policeman in the middle of the road reached for the gun in his holster at his waist and when the blue car stopped my Dad jumped out of the car and pointed a gun at him.

It happened so fast I thought I must have missed something. There was a woman pushing a pram nearby and she screamed and ran into the post office and someone came out and grabbed the little girl who was feeding the pigeons and slammed the shop door. Another man just froze, as if he had turned to ice. The young policeman raised his hands.

"Don't shoot!" he said, and his voice was full of warning not fear but I was close enough to see his face, which was sweaty and strained. The older policeman had his gun pointed at my Dad and I was very scared.

But my Dad wasn't. He kept his gaze on the policeman in the middle of the road.

"There's another patrol nearby," the older policeman said, still pointing his gun at my Dad. "It's not worth it, pal. You won't get far."

My Dad turned his head back to the driver, as if he needed to ask him something, and in that split second the older policeman shot at him but the shot missed my Dad and cracked the windscreen of the blue car. My Dad spun around and aimed his gun and the younger policeman pulled out his gun but my Dad shot him first.

I saw it like it happened slowly.

The man who had froze like ice dropped his can of Coke.

The pigeons flapped up into the air.

The sky bounced off the wet road.

The policeman's head spun around to me. His mouth was curled in a weird way and his face was a blur. Blood shot out of his forehead like a red horn.

My Dad turned and I heard another shot. It was a crack, like a firecracker only much louder and with a kind of thud behind it that made me feel sick. The second policeman's arms flung forward and his knees crumpled and he fell forward. And when I looked back at my Dad he was already in the blue car and the old man behind the wheel made the tires spin and they drove away.

When I looked up again I wasn't at the police checkpoint or on stage. I was in my dressing room in front of a mirror and I wasn't wearing my combat suit anymore, just my boxer shorts and my black boots. My face was wet and my mouth was red and I was shaking all over. I lifted my arm up to see the marks on it and it was shaking but I could see I was bleeding. Someone was behind me. It was Bonnie Nicholls.

"Alex," she whispered. "Alex, what happened?"

I looked around the dressing room and for some reason it looked like it had been burgled. The dressing table was turned over with all four legs sticking up. One of the big photographs on the far wall was shattered and my locker was open with all the contents on the ground.

"What happened, Bonnie?" I said, but before she could answer my legs turned to jelly and I heard her scream and everything went black.

When I woke up I was in a hospital bed in different clothes and my body hurt like I'd been trampled by a herd of dinosaurs. The nurses gave me some medicine, which has pushed most of the pain into the distance. I had a huge black shiner and my nose was so swollen that every time I said "I didn't do it" it came out like "I nin't noo it." After the nurses came a doctor came in and all he wanted to know is why I like drawing skeletons. I got so angry that I started to cry and I saw him write *anger issues* on his notepad.

Anya and Michael and Auntie Bev came later on. I was so relieved to see them that I burst out laughing. This surprised Auntie Bev but made her laugh, too, even though her eyes still looked upset.

"You look like a queen," I said to Anya, though I just meant to say she looked nice. She was wearing a clean white dress with no marks on it and her hair was up, which made her neck look long, and she had makeup on.

"What happened, Alex?" she said. "Did Ruen do this?"

Anya looked at some papers the doctors had written about me and then she started asking me more questions, but I felt sleepy and I just wanted some onions and toast with a cup of tea.

"Do *you* know what happened?" I asked Anya.

"We were hoping *you* would tell *us* what happened, Alex," she said.

I pressed the balls of my palms into my eyes and took deep breaths. I felt so confused. I thought, *maybe I really am going crazy.*

When I moved my hands from my eyes I noticed that I'd said this out loud. Both Michael and Anya were looking at me really strangely. "Were you upset about your mum tonight, Alex? Did something happen earlier in rehearsals?" Anya said.

I opened my mouth to tell her about the policeman and the shooting and that I had seen my Dad, but even though I tried no words came out, just sobs and I started crying so badly that my whole body shook and my back started to ache.

Auntie Bev sat on the bed beside me and took my hand. Then she put her arms around me and held me for a long time.

"Was this an accident?" she said when she let go, and her voice was very small. "Or did you do it to yourself? You can tell me, you know. I won't be upset. We all just want to help you."

Just then, Ruen appeared as Ghost Boy. I must have jumped with fright because right away Anya asked me what was wrong. Ruen stood at the end of the bed, staring at me. He was giving me the Alex Is Stupid look.

"I'm not stupid!" I yelled at him.

"It's okay, Alex," Anya said, but I shook my head because I didn't mean her. I hated Ruen's eyes right then, it was like they were bigger than normal, like *bulging,* and even though they were black as two lumps of coal they could see right through me.

"Tell them you did it," he said, nodding his head and smiling.

The way he said it made it sound like he was offering more of a helpful suggestion than a command, like he knew something I didn't and that it would be a good idea to do as he said. He said it again. "It's okay, Alex. Just tell them."

I took a deep breath. "I did it," I said.

Auntie Bev let go of me and Anya and Michael looked at each other and I was really sorry I'd said it. I wanted Auntie Bev to hold me again. I wanted to ask Ruen why he said I should say that so I just said, "Can we talk about this more in the morning? I'm really tired now."

Anya crouched down so she could look me in the eye. "You did this, Alex? Or Ruen did it?"

Ruen looked angry then. I remembered the police checkpoint.

"My dad did something very, very wrong." I said it very carefully, and Anya's face changed as if she'd seen something she hadn't seen before.

"Did he hurt you, Alex?"

I shook my head.

"Did he hurt your Mum?"

I shook my head.

"Can you tell me what your dad did?"

For a moment I was going to. But then I felt a new feeling. I felt really, really ashamed, which didn't make sense because it wasn't my fault. But I still felt like she would be disappointed in me.

"Maybe after a sleep you can tell me," Anya said, and I felt so glad of that because I was so tired and sore and my brain felt like mud. I nodded and lay back and closed my eyes.

When I was sure they'd left, I said to Ruen, "why did you tell me to say that?"

He was just staring out the window as if he was looking for someone. He didn't answer so I asked him again. I was starting to get really mad at him.

"Why would you tell me to lie?" I asked him.

He turned and pressed his face really close to mine. His breath smelled like a butcher's shop on a sunny day. I turned my face.

"But you *did* do this to yourself, Alex," he whispered. And then he didn't look angry anymore, but like he pitied me. "Poor Alex," he said, picking up the ball and batting it off the wall opposite. "You don't realize it, do you?"

"Realize what?"

"That you *did* do this."

"And *how* did I do this?" I said loudly, though it hurt my chest to yell. "How would I lift myself up and fling myself into the wall?"

"Weren't you asleep at the time?"

"I was not! I was getting ready for the third scene . . ."

He stopped batting and tilted his head as if he'd just thought of something that I hadn't. "Or were you *dreaming* that you were getting ready for the third scene?"

My head felt like hamburger meat now. I just wanted to sleep.

"I have to sleep now, Ruen," I told him.

He nodded. "I promise not to tell your mum about this."

I thought to myself, *but Mum doesn't even know you exist,* but I said nothing because if I really did do this to myself I certainly didn't want Mum finding out. It would make her sicker. And I felt glad then that Ruen was going to keep it a secret.

"Do you think Mum is okay?" I said.

"Oh, I'm sure she's fine. Would you like me to make sure she's okay, Alex?"

I nodded and felt so relieved. "Yes, please. I would love that."

Ruen smiled and leaned over me. "Can I ask you to do something for me?"

I nodded.

"Tomorrow morning I'd like you to ask Anya those questions I gave you. Can you do that for me, Alex? I would be extremely grateful."

"Okay."

And then I don't remember anything else because I fell asleep and dreamed of Granny all night.

## ANYA

Alex's latest predicament is a shock, to say the least.

I had returned to my seat in the auditorium just as Alex was on stage consoling Hamlet about the hasty marriage between his widowed mother and uncle. I looked over the other members of the audience— many sat forward in their seats, eager to hear this young man's advice to Hamlet. I felt a swell of pride for Alex. And I wondered if he had crossed a bridge of sorts. I glanced at Michael and thought about Alex's treatment. *Should he receive treatment at home? Should I sidestep the furor that will be caused by having Cindy deemed unfit to act as Alex's mother and admit him to MacNeice House, a place she believes to be for lunatics? Is Alex demonstrating psychotic symptoms, or are these just symptoms of post-traumatic stress?*

But something happened during the intermission. When the curtain went down and the audience were rising from their seats I spotted Jojo elbowing her way across the auditorium, pushing through the crowd. I saw her signal a staff member, then turn to the auditorium, scanning the pews as if she was looking for someone. I waved, but she didn't see me. Her expression frightened me.

"Something's wrong," I said to Michael.

"What do you mean?" He followed my gaze to the front of the auditorium, where two boys in REALLY TALENTED KIDS T-shirts were running to the door that Jojo had just exited. "We have to go," I told Michael.

When we arrived at the dressing room, Michael pushed past a crew member and we saw the state of the place—someone had trashed it. The furniture was overturned and the mirror was shattered, the pieces catching my reflection in a million glinting shards. Worse, a case of stage makeup had spilled across the black floor, giving the initial impression of blood. Bonnie, the girl who played Ophelia, said she had heard a lot of noise coming from the dressing room. When she entered, she saw Alex throw himself against the wall, then fall. He was unconscious for a few moments—she thought he was dead, Bonnie told us, sobbing.

I found Alex's aunt and told her that Alex had had an accident, though I still wasn't sure what had happened. The Red Cross team had already taken Alex to the emergency room, a cast member told us, though he seemed more anxious about finding an understudy to continue the performance than answering questions. Beverly, Michael, and I took a taxi and arrived at the city hospital a short while later, where a nurse led us to a side room in the pediatric unit.

Alex looked terrible. Both eyes were bloodshot and his nose was bruised and swollen. A nurse informed me that he had bruising around his lower back that suggested that Alex had deliberately flung himself against the wall. The force that caused the bruising was unusual in the case of self-harm; it looked like a much larger person must have lifted Alex up and thrown him a distance of approximately ten feet. Of course, this was impossible. Alex was alone. I can only hypothesize that the strain of performing had been too much for him. When I read through Shakespeare's original and Jojo's adaptation, I had noticed that the relationship between Hamlet and his father is underlined by a corrosive sense of debt, of the need to carry out revenge on his father's behalf. Alex's relationship with his own father is clearly something I need to investigate more, and I made a note to push Alex a little to talk about it. But I need to wait until he recovers physically.

Michael and I shared a taxi, making the journey together in silence. My mind was racing with *hows* and *whys*, circling the issue of the play's themes like a vulture. The truth was, I had already located my answer, but I wanted to pick the bones of it out of guilt. I should never have allowed Alex to perform in the play. I should have known the kinds of pressures a public performance would have placed on him at such an intensely vulnerable period in his life. And I should have insisted, *insisted,* that Alex be transferred to MacNeice House.

When the taxi pulled up outside my flat, I turned to Michael.

"As soon as Alex leaves hospital, I am moving him to MacNeice House."

He chewed his cheek, keeping his eyes on the space of seat between us. "I know," he said quietly. For a moment his eyes met mine—filled with a startling amount of want. He turned away as I got out and the taxi pulled away.


When I went to see Alex the next day he was dressed and waiting. His aunt had already visited, a nurse told me. She had brought Alex's clothing. He winced as he sat upright, but had taken care in getting dressed, red bow tie, brown-and-white-striped shirt. He had something in his shirt pocket, which he revealed to be one of the photos of the new council house. He was keeping it close to his heart, he said. I was delighted that something I had done had made him so happy.

"Where's Michael?" he wanted to know.

"In his office, I expect," I told him. "Did you want to see him?"

Alex shook his head. His dressings had been changed but the silvery morning light revealed the bruising around his face to be traveling through the blue hues of deep impact. I recognized this was a very serious self-harm episode, completely undermining how happy he appeared on the surface.

"How are you feeling now?" I asked.

He seemed suddenly hesitant to meet my eyes. He rubbed his bicep and said, "Sore."

"I bet."

I pulled up a chair at the table, mulling over the best way to broach the subject of Alex's father. It was important that I ease him into the subject gently, establishing that whatever it was his father had done was not going to land Alex in trouble. On the table was a tray of food left over from breakfast—a dilapidated fruit salad, a tub of warm Greek yogurt, and porridge sprinkled with pine nuts. I lifted it out of the way and set it on the floor close to the door, handing Alex a cup of water.

"You can have some if you want." He gestured at the food. "I'm not hungry."

"Thank you, Alex," I said with a smile. "That's very kind. But I'm allergic to nuts, remember?"

"Nuts?"

I nodded. "These are pine nuts," I say, glancing at the porridge.

"Oh yeah," he said. "Nuts make you sleep, don't they?"

I remembered my lie. "Yes," I said.

"They don't even look like nuts. They look like bullets."

There was a depth to his tone that I recognized instantly. Some of the children I have treated have witnessed the violence here in Northern Ireland firsthand. One girl, Shay, was blinded during a riot in Drumcree several years ago. She is being treated for clinical depression. A fifteen-year-old boy from Carrickfergus had been shot at point-blank range in the knee—*kneecapped,* they call it here—as punishment for his father's defection from a terrorist organization. The trauma of that event has made him suicidal. Michael insists that Cindy and Alex have not suffered by the conflict in Northern Ireland, but I am uncertain. *The Troubles* is a term most significant to those at a distance from the violence—to children who have grown up in the thick of it, the Troubles are simply a part of life.

"Have you ever seen a bullet, Alex? Or a gun?"

"You mean in real life?" he asked, keeping his eyes on the floor.

"Yes."

He nodded.

"Can you tell me where?"

He shook his head.

"Did a policeman come to arrest your dad?"

He stiffened at the mention of the word *policeman,* then shook his head again briskly. Then he squeezed his eyes together tightly, his face scrunched up in concentration. Both hands formed fists. I waited for him to relax. A minute passed. I laid a hand on Alex's shoulder.

"I promise you won't get into trouble if you tell me what happened."

He opened his eyes and seemed to look past me. "Ruin wants me to ask you some questions. Is that okay?"

"Why does Ruin want to ask me some questions?" I asked gently.

"I think he just wants to know more about you," he said, after a moment. "Maybe because he and I are friends . . . sort of . . . and he wants to be your friend, too."

"What sort of questions does Ruin want to ask me?"

"Um . . . I'm not sure. Grown-up stuff, I think. Ruin's really weir—" He stopped short of saying *weird*, flicked his eyes to the right, then clapped his hand over his mouth and laughed.

"If you answer my questions, I'll answer yours, is that okay?"

"About Ruin?"

"No, Alex. About your father."

He blinked, then gave a small nod.

"All right, if I'm going to be interviewed, let's do it properly." I said it lightly, taking my mobile phone out of my pocket and finding the Voice Record app. "We'll record it, shall we? Like a proper interview."

Alex shrugged. "I don't care, they're not my questions." He slid a crumpled piece of paper out of his trouser pocket. I leaned forward and saw what appeared to be a list, scrawled in black marker.

He cleared his throat. "Number one. Was your daughter called Poppy?"

I tilted my head, surprised. I guess I had been expecting questions of the *Do you like jazz?* variety. Although it is important that the patient–therapist relationship is a close one, I am strict about not sharing personal details. I drummed my fingers on the table next to my phone, watching the RECORD button pulse its red light.

Eventually, I said: "Why do you ask, Alex?"

"Not me! *Ruin*."

"Why does Ruin care about my daughter?"

He paused. "I'm not sure."

"Okay," I said, gathering my composure. "Next question."

"Did your daughter die four years ago?"

This time I felt my heart pound, and I felt overwhelmed with confusion. We had reached a critical point in Alex's treatment. He was at long last revealing clues to Ruin. I counted to ten in my head and breathed slowly in an attempt to check my emotions. I needed to stay focused on the real reason why Alex might be asking such questions. When I opened my eyes I saw that Alex was visibly uncomfortable.

"I'm really sorry," he said quietly. "It's just . . . I promised Ruin I would ask you these questions. I don't mean to upset you."

"Can you ask Ruin why he wants to know about Poppy so badly?"

Alex turned and repeated my query to Ruin, who was purportedly standing behind him. After a few seconds' silence he turned back to me. "Ruin says he really likes you and admires that you can play the piano."

"I love the piano. Shall we move on to the next question?"

Alex squirmed in his seat and looked down at his list. "Number three. Do you believe in God?"

"The jury's still out on that one, Alex," I said, before correcting myself. "Sorry, *Ruin*." I decided to play into the charade of Ruin's presence in the room, noticing the way it instilled a confidence in Alex. His posture was straighter, his eyes held mine.

"That answers number four, then," Alex told me.

"Which is?"

He didn't break off his stare. "Do you believe in Satan, the Prince of Hell?"

My heart started clanging in my chest again. For some reason I detected a tone in his voice that suggested a link between this question and the one about Poppy, and it made the very hairs on the back of my arms stand on end. After a long silence I said, weakly: "What's the next question?"

He consulted the sheet of paper. "If you could have anything you wanted, what would it be?"

*Poppy,* I thought, *alive and well,* and just then I caught sight of the hospital-issue painting on the wall, a field of red flowers. Poppies. I smile.

"It's okay," Alex told me. "Ruin says you've already given your answer."

"Can you tell me why Ruin wants to know these things, Alex?"

Again, he seemed to be seeking guidance from his invisible friend. Finally, he nodded and turned to me.

"I only have one more question," he said firmly.

I felt a pang of disappointment. He was continuing to evade direct questions. I nodded and thought of ways to retrace our conversation about his father.

"Go on."

He took a deep breath. "Do you love Michael?"

That surprised a laugh out of me. Alex lowered his eyes to the table, as if he felt ashamed.

"Do I love Michael?" I repeated. Alex nodded, still not looking at me. Why on earth did he want to know this?

"Next question," I said.

"There isn't another . . ."

*"Next question,"* I said, with an insistence that surprised us both. Alex's lip began to tremble. He looked fearfully to his right, then turned to me again.

"It's okay," he said, softly. "Ruin says he already knows the answer."

I watched him fold away the piece of paper. "Can we talk some more about your dad?" I asked him, keeping my voice even to appear more at ease. "What did he look like? What can you remember about him?"

He nodded.

"Was he kind to you?"

He thought about it. "Yes, I think so. He died when I was very little, you see, so I only remember a few things about when he was alive."

"What do you remember? Can you tell me?"

"About when he was alive?"

"Yes."

"I remember he liked buying me toy cars. And we'd go swimming sometimes and he always brought bags full of food when he came to stay."

"So he came to stay with you and your mum? Did you ever stay at his house?"

He shook his head. "Dad lived in lots of different places. I think he lived in America for a while. And Dublin and Donegal. One time he said he was living in a barn."

"A *barn?*"

"He said it was really smelly and uncomfortable."

"I bet it was. Do you know why he was staying in a barn?"

He seemed lost in the memory now, his legs—usually swinging above the floor of his chair—still, his gaze distant. "He'd bring bags of food when he came sometimes and he'd spend all day in the kitchen cooking weird food that Mum didn't really like but she ate it anyway 'cos she was hungry."

"What sort of food?"

"I don't remember. It smelled weird and sometimes it made my eyes water." A pause. "He had tattoos on his arms."

"Tattoos?"

"Yeah. There was an Irish flag here"—he clapped a hand around his left bicep—"and words here." He touched his right forearm.

"What were the words?"

"Not words. Letters. They stood for something. I don't know what."

I held my breath, anxious not to push him too far. "And when your dad died, Alex—how did that feel?"

He stared ahead. "Lonely. Until Mum bought me Woof and then it was okay. She cried and cried."

"Your mother cried when your dad died?"

"Yes, but she was angry, too. And really scared. She tried to throw our piano out but Ruin said we musn't."

"Where is Ruin now, Alex?"

He looked around. "He was here a minute ago. Don't know where he's gone."

"Did Ruin hurt you last night, Alex? Or did he tell you to hurt yourself?"

A sudden terror flickered in his eyes. "The policeman . . . ," he said. And then he started to cry and I wrapped my arms around him, but he would say no more.

I left the hospital with instructions for the nurses to contact me as soon as Alex was able to be discharged. In the meantime, I contacted Cindy's therapist to find out whether she had given her permission for her son to be treated as an inpatient.

"No, she hasn't." Trudy sighed on the end of the line. "But I've diagnosed her as unfit to act in the capacity of Alex's mother. His aunt has agreed to make this decision."

There was a stretch of silence as both of us reflected on this sorry state of affairs. If Cindy had refused to grant permission for Alex to be institutionalized, the news of her own sister going against her wishes would certainly be hard to take. I had failed to persuade Cindy that treatment at MacNeice House would be in Alex's best interests—no doubt she perceived the move as another step toward breaking up her family. Still, I remained determined to treat Alex accordingly. It was, quite literally, his only hope.

The severity of Alex's hallucinations and the length of time they had been active indicated that his condition was deteriorating. Poppy was the same. If his condition was left untreated, there was every chance that soon Alex would pose the same level of danger to himself or others as Poppy did. I can't let that happen to another child, another mother. In consultation with Iris and Michael and with Beverly's permission, I prescribed a small daily dose of risperidone, a medication used to treat schizophrenia, schizoaffective disorder, and the mixed and manic states associated with bipolar disorder. The effects would be monitored over several weeks, and I would continue to evaluate Alex daily.

I returned to my office to write up my notes and compile a group email to Michael, Howard, and Ursula.

> To: U_Hepworth@macneicehouse.gov.uk; H_Dungar@
> macneicehouse.gov.uk; Michael_Jones@lea.govnhs.uk
> CC: Trudy_Messenger@nicamhs.gov.uk
> From: A_Molokova@macneicehouse.nhs.uk
> Date: 05/16/07 5:03 PM
>
> Dear all,
>    I am writing to inform you that I have arranged for Alex to be transferred to MacNeice House, where he will stay as an inpatient for approximately two months. I am treating him for early-

onset schizophrenia. I am happy to brief you further on my interviews with him and the program of treatment, which I am currently compiling. Our next meeting is on May 30 at 2:30 PM— I look forward to seeing you then.

Best,
Anya

I had barely hit the SEND button when an email pinged back.

To: A_Molokov@macneicehouse.nhs.uk
From: Michael_Jones@lea.govnhs.uk
Date: 05/16/07 5:03 PM
     You do realize this will mean Alex is placed in foster care?
Sent from my BlackBerry

I stared at Michael's email, re-reading it, feeling my heart pound. I felt his hand on my face.

And suddenly I questioned everything.

*The ghost I have seen*
*May be the devil: and the devil hath power*
*To assume a pleasing shape; yea, and perhaps*
*Out of my weakness and my melancholy,*
*As he is very potent with such spirits,*
*Abuses me to damn me.*

—William Shakespeare, *Hamlet*

# 19
# ESCAPE

## ALEX

Dear Diary,

There's two fish in a tank. One turns to the other and says, "do you know how to drive this?"

I guess I don't need to write jokes anymore as I won't be playing Horatio again because I'm in hospital and the doctors say there's *absolutely no way* I can get out to perform in the shows for the rest of the week. Though Auntie Bev told me something this morning that made me feel a little bit better. She showed up wearing a blue headband and a thin blue T-shirt with a Superman logo on the front, which I thought was weird for a girl to wear. Her face was pink and sweaty and she was drinking from a lime-green water bottle.

"Have you been wall climbing?" I asked. She gave me a look that said she felt guilty.

"Sorry, Alex," she said, and she sat so close to me I could smell sweat. "I know you'd love to go. I'll take you once you get out." She looked at the clock. "Do you want to come and have lunch with me?"

"They're letting me go?" I said excitedly.

"I'm afraid not," she said, getting up to look for my shoes under the bed. "But we can go to the cafeteria just down the corridor. Would you like that?"

I said I would and stood up. I still felt wobbly on my feet but she grabbed my elbow and helped me put my shoes on.

"I met the casting director before the show started," Auntie Bev said as we walked slowly to the canteen. *"Roz,"* she said. "That's her name. Turns out Roz has very bad sinusitis." I looked up and saw Auntie Bev make a face like she had something really cool to tell me.

"What's sinusitis?"

"It's this horrible yucky illness that makes you feel like you've been punched in the face for about a week."

"You punched Roz in the face?"

Auntie Bev made that hooting sound that meant she was laughing.

*"No,"* she said, pushing a square silver button that made the doors open into the cafeteria. "It means that she has an illness that falls into my area of expertise."

We stood in the doorway, looking over the empty tables and chairs. I was glad it was really empty and the food on the shelves of the open fridge looked a lot nicer than the food the nurses brought me on a tray. Auntie Bev took my arm and walked me to a table in a corner beneath a big clock with a picture of an ice cream on it.

"I told Roz all about you, you know," she told me. "I said you're a star in the making. That Quentin Tara-whatever-his-name-is would be glad to have you." She sat down in the steel chair across from me and clicked her tongue. "And that I'd send her a sinus irrigator free of charge."

She winked. I didn't really get it but the way she was smiling made my heart beat really fast. I felt like I could breathe deeper than I ever had before. She flipped open the plastic menu.

"What do you feel like, Alex? Baked potato with beans and cheese? What about a nice omelet? You can get it with bacon and peppers."

I shook my head. "Onions on toast, please."

Auntie Bev lowered the menu and stared at me as if she felt sick. "Really, Alex?"

I nodded and she looked sad.

"I know you and your mum don't have much money, but while I'm here let me spoil you. I love you, honey. Honest, I'll get you anything you want on this menu."

"Onions on toast," I said, nodding. "It's the best thing ever." And just then my stomach gave a huge growl.

Auntie Bev's smile came back. "Well, maybe I'm missing out, then," she said. "I'll have that, too."

She got up then to tell the lady behind the counter what we wanted and I felt glad that Auntie Bev was going to eat the same as me. When she sat back down she smiled and said, "good thing I keep breath mints in my bag."

When she left I felt good for a while but then I started to feel bad. I think I've upset Anya and I don't really know how or why. I tried to explain to her that the questions were Ruen's but I was stupid to expect that she would believe me when *no one* believes me at all. I don't even know why I ever told anyone about him in the first place. I don't know why Ruen told me that I hurt myself when I didn't. When all the doctors and nurses talk to me now they speak to me like I'm either really stupid or like I'm carrying a knife or something. When I ask about Mum they don't look at my eyes and say things like, "oh, don't you worry about your mother," and "Now, Alex, just be patient while your mum pulls herself together. Why don't you get some sleep?" I just want to get out of here and check that she's okay.

I'm not going back to my old school for a while and when I leave the hospital I am going to a new school at a place called MacNeice House, just for a while, and then Mum and I will move into our amazing new house. I've been given homework until then but I feel like someone's attached a vacuum cleaner to my skin and sucked out all the energy. When I sit up it feels like the whole room wobbles and my head feels like an enormous cannonball so that I have to keep putting my hands around my cheeks to hold it in place.

When the nurse brings me lunch she asks me what I'm doing.

I look up and say, "my head is going to fall off."

I thought she was going to laugh but instead she runs out of the room leaving my food tray too far away for me to reach and I hear her shoes clacking all the way down the hall. When I look down, my bed is covered in vomit and my nails have blood under them from where I was scratching my neck. I don't remember being sick or scratching myself.

I'm starting to feel very strange, not like me at all.


When I wake up again my bed is clean and I am dressed differently. I can see my shirt and trousers hanging in the open locker in the corner. It's raining cats and dogs outside, auntie Bev would say, and I imagine what it would be like if it really was raining kittens and rottweilers. Someone comes into the room. I think it's a nurse and am afraid to say anything in case she gets scared again, but then I look up and see it's Ruen. He's Ghost Boy. He glances out of the door into the hallway and holds a finger to his lips to tell me "sshh." I nod and about a second later a doctor comes in. He is holding a clipboard.

"How you feeling, Alex?" he says.

"Fine," I say. He puts two fingers against my wrist and looks at his watch and says nothing for a while. Then he puts a stethoscope under my robe. It makes me shiver.

"Any breathing problems?" he asks. I shake my head.

A nurse comes in and wraps a piece of material around my arm then squeezes a small black ball until the material gets really tight. "One twenty over eighty," she tells the doctor, and he writes it down, too. He nods and asks, "temperature?" The nurse says something I can't really hear but the doctor writes it down, too.

"Okay," the doctor says again.

"Can I go now?" I ask.

This is apparently REALLY funny.

"No," the doctor says, handing me a cup with pills in it. "You have to take two of these twice a day for a while. We need you to stay here to make sure they're doing their job."

I look down at the round white tablets in the cup. "What are they for?" I ask.

The doctor looks down at me through his glasses before walking out of the room. The nurse says, "to help you sleep better, Alex."

"But I sleep fine," I tell her.

The nurse smiles and hands me a cup with some water. I hold both cups in my hands and stare up at the nurse and doctor. Finally, the nurse says: "Dr. Molokova says you have to take them."

She says it like I should already know this. "Who's Dr. Molokova?"

She looks confused, like I'm being stupid, then she says, "Anya?"

"Oh."

I put the pills in my mouth and they taste very bitter so I drink the whole cup of water in one go. The nurse hands me a tray of food. It looks like Woof threw up on my plate.

"What is it?" I ask.

"Corned beef hash," the nurse says. "You want peanuts or chopped apple for your snack?"

"Peanuts," Ruen says loudly, and I jump. I ask her for the peanuts and she looks at me funny.

The nurse nods and slides a tub on the tray. "Dessert is either custard or rice pudding."

I glance at Ruen. He doesn't need to say anything. "Rice pudding, please."

The nurse slides the tray onto the table next to me and walks out, humming.

"I don't want to stay here," I tell Ruen.

"I don't blame you," he says, still looking out the window.

I glare at him. "I'm not your friend, by the way."

He looks quite shocked. "Whyever not?"

My face is very hot all of a sudden and my hands are shaking. When I blink everything looks blurred for a second. "Because you made me ask Anya those questions and she got very upset. I didn't want to make her upset and it's your fault."

He smiles. "It is not my fault that she was emotional. I merely needed to discover a little more about her, that is all."

Eventually my face goes cold again and my hands go still. That's what happened last time I took the pills but then it went away after a few seconds. So I swing my legs around and put my feet on the floor.

"Then why didn't *you* ask her the questions, huh?"

"She's trying to get rid of me, Alex," he says and his voice is full of hate. "She's trying to convince you that I'm not real."

But I've heard it before. And I decide he's got a big problem with being a demon and not being able to be seen. Which, I think, is *his* problem, because if I can see him surely other people can, too.

"Why do you keep hiding from everybody?" I say.

And then one second he is scowling at me from the other side of the room and the next he is crouching down beneath me, his face close to mine, snarling with little bubbles in the corners of his mouth.

"I *don't* hide," he says. "Do you think I *want* to be invisible, you stupid boy? Do you think it's *fun* not being seen for what you are or what you can do? How do you think . . . *Max Payne* would feel if all his heroic deeds went unnoticed, eh? Or Batman?"

He stands up and walks away. I frown at him.

"Batman wears a costume," I say.

He turns. "What?"

"Batman wears a costume. All the superheroes do, to hide their real identity. It's part of why they're superheroes. They don't want the glory for all the stuff they do. They just want to do good things for people." *Unlike you,* I think.

Ruen stares at me so long and with such wide eyes that I wonder if he's actually died right there on the spot and is about to fall over.

"Ruen?" I say, a little nervous.

He starts to grin. Then he starts to clap. And then—this is what really shocks me—he walks toward me rubbing his hands, reaches out, and ruffles my hair.

"What a clever boy," he says, which is insane really because at that moment he's a boy, too. Then he points at me and starts to laugh.

"Why does everyone think I'm so funny today?" I say. But Ruen is laughing so hard he can't speak. He walks up to the mirror above the sink and looks at himself. He straightens his back and looks tickled pink with himself.

"A costume," he says. "Or a proxy."

"What's a proxy?"

He turns to face me, still grinning like an idiot.

"You're no good to me in here, are you?"

"What?"

He shakes his head. "Never mind. How badly do you want to get out of here?"

"*Very* badly," I say.

"Okay then," Ruen says, and claps his hands together. "Follow me."

I get out of bed and immediately feel like I am on a ship. "Steady now," Ruen says, and I close my eyes and count the number of bones in an adult rib cage in my head and then I open my eyes and feel better.

"Grab your clothes," Ruen tells me. I wobble to the locker and pull on my shirt, trousers, shoes, and jacket.

"Ready," I say.

"You might be needing your cap," Ruen says. "And your scarf. You'd catch your death outside. And then what would I do?" He starts to laugh again.

Everybody else on the ward is asleep. At the end of the corridor Ruen holds a finger to his lips and I stop dead, then hide behind a door as a nurse wheels a boy in a wheelchair past us. Ruen gives a slight wave with his hand and I tiptoe after him. Ahead, I see the EXIT sign. I point at it. He shakes his head and tells me to follow him through a yellow door marked STAFF ONLY. When we get through that door there is a kitchen to my left and a fire exit to my right.

"Push," Ruen says.

I lean against the bar across the door and push. And easy peasy, I am outside. It is pitch black. The rain is so thick I can hardly see through it. This kind of rain is like chain metal, I decide. From here I can see the building that Mum is in, a tall white building with a thin bit at the top that occasionally flashes a blue light. It's about a ten-minute walk to Mum's building and already I am soaked right through my clothes. I decide to run. I run through the parking lot and then I see a lady in a long white coat walking toward me, so I duck behind a hedge and take a shortcut through a really muddy patch of grass. I keep the blue light in sight. Then, when the wind makes the rain come down sideways, I take off my jacket and hold it around my head.

When I get to the front entrance I am panting like a dog. Ruen appears beside the door.

"You'll never get past the front desk looking like that," he tells me. "Besides, visiting hours are over."

I frown. I am cold and tired and feel like if I fell over I'd probably stay there until someone stood on me.

"So what should I do?"

Ruen shrugs and folds his arms like he couldn't care less. "There is one thing," he says finally, inspecting his fingernails like they're really interesting. "But you have to promise to do something for me first."

I am shivering now and my hair is dripping into my eyes and I can hardly speak. I am so angry with him for telling me to escape and then making me promise to do something else for him.

"Is it something to do with Anya?" I ask.

Ruen looks up from his fingernails and nods.

I feel a big wave of anger roll over me and I wrap my arms around my chest to keep warm. I'm shaking like I'm being electrocuted. "Get stuffed, loser," I say under my breath, because I'm so not impressed with him and I turn around and start to walk through the curtains of rain toward my building. Then Ruen appears right in front of me and I stop. My face is dripping wet and when I look up my eyes feel like someone is pouring a jug of water into them. He's Horn Head now, and I've never been this close to him when he's Horn Head. The red horn doesn't really look like a horn this close, it looks like its liquid and I feel sick.

"It won't upset Anya," he whispers in my head. "It's a gift to her."

"A *gift*?" I shout. "Can't you see, you moron—I haven't got any money! I'm only TEN!" I keep my eyes on the ground and walk around him.

"Your mother needs you, Alex," Ruen says in my head.

I feel a pain in my heart but I keep walking.

But just then, flashes of Mum rise up in my head: There's a picture of the last time I found her, curled up in her own vomit on our bathroom floor, her head really limp and her tongue hanging out like a dog. The time before that, when I walked into the kitchen and saw her at the sink, and I wondered why she was crying and chopping carrots, but she wasn't chopping carrots and the sink was full of blood. And the time before that, when I was dying to use the toilet and she wouldn't answer the door and then I opened it and she was in the tub, unconscious, her head about to go under the water.

And then I remember her watching me in the kitchen as I tried to make something called *gorgonzola and caramelized onion bruschetta* and then gave up and made onions on toast.

"You're so like him," she had said.

"Like who?"

"Your dad."

And then I think of coming out of the church that day when we were supposed to be practicing for the school Christmas concert. We were singing "Away in a Manger" and I remember I felt all hot and fed up from standing so long and a teacher let me go to the toilet, but when I got there a big wind was coming through an open door and so I went outside.

On the street outside the church there were lots of shops and people walking along the pavement. I saw a little girl eating potato chips across the road and I thought maybe she'd give me some, but then I saw the policemen and I felt scared and then I saw the blue car. I had just wandered outside, right at the moment my Dad arrived, like we were attached by a rubber band and turned up at the same time at the same place. I never told anyone I had seen him, not even Mum. I don't even think Dad knew I was there. I remember what people said at the policemen's funeral, that the man who killed them was evil and someone said he should burn in Hell and the policemen's wives were so sad and the little girl would grow up without a Daddy.

And then something else rises up in my head, and when it does I know it's been buried in my brain for a long time, like a needle that's been stuck in a chair for ages and poking people in the ass all that time but they didn't know what was hurting them.

It's my Dad. He's shaking something heavy out of a black shiny bag and putting it inside the piano where there should be strings. I remember he was wearing a blue T-shirt and I can see his tattoo on his arm, the one with just letters. I couldn't read then because I had just started school so I asked him what the letters said. He told me and I said "what?"

He smiled. "It's a group, Alex. It's a group of men who believe in freedom."

"And killing," Mum said from the kitchen. I was puzzled.

"Are you in that group?"

My Dad put the last thing in the piano and shut the lid. "Yep," he said. "And my dad was, and his dad, and his dad before that."

In my head there was a big line forming of men I was linked to. Now, that link reaches to me, only it's not something I'm sure I want anymore, and it's like the link has split into two and it feels like I'm splitting down the middle.

I drop to my knees in the mud and start to cry. I cry so hard and the wind is so loud that I am able to scream out all the pain from way down in my belly and I know no one can hear me.

When I open my eyes, Ruen is still there, but he's back to being the Old Man. I sigh in relief.

"What sort of gift?" I ask, wiping my eyes.

"Follow me," he says.

Ruen leads me to a side door at the back of the building. Another fire exit. I jiggle the door handle but it is locked.

"Be patient," Ruen says, and steps back. I take a few steps back, too. A few minutes later, two nurses come outside. As the door swings shut I run forward and catch it. Then I slip inside.

I spot a toilet to my left and go inside, pee, then use lots of paper towels to dry my hair and clothes. By the time I finish I see that Ruen isn't there. I open the door and look outside.

"Ruen?" I hiss.

There's no answer.

I step into the hallway. Still no sign of him. My fingers wriggle like worms at each other and I feel my neck and cheeks get hot. How am I supposed to find Mum now?

I walk down the corridor, digging my squirmy hands in my pockets and keeping my head down. Nobody seems to be around. My heart is racing and I feel sick.

At the end of the corridor is a list of signs. I read down the list and feel very confused. Where is Mum? Then I see the word PSYCHIATRY and it looks familiar so I follow the arrow.

The arrow takes me down another long corridor, at the end of which are women's voices. I stop at the corner and wait until I hear the voices stop, then walk very, very quickly around the corner.

"Can I help you?"

I *freeze*. There is a long reception desk right there with the sign PSYCHIATRY hanging above and a blond fat woman in a nurse's uniform sitting behind it.

"Uh," I say. I look around for Ruen.

"Are you lost?" the woman says. I nod. "You shouldn't be here," she tuts. She starts to get up from her seat to come around the desk to me.

I see my chance. I know Mum is just down the ward in a room to the right, about four doors down, so I run past the fat woman and she yells "Hey!" but I keep going until I reach the room. I push against the door but it is locked, so I stand on my tiptoes and look in through the small glass window.

I can see Mum inside. Her yellow hair is spread across the pillow and her face looks thin and she is fast asleep. I pound the door with my fists and yell "Mum!" but she doesn't wake up. "Mum!" I yell again. *Mum! Mum! Mum! Mum!*

Then all of a sudden there are two men beside me grabbing me by the arms and I yell "Mum! I love you!" and I see her open her eyes and look around but she doesn't see me.


I don't remember much after that. I know I cried and I begged and begged them to let me see Mum and I bit one of the men on the side of his hand and then I ran but they caught me again and threatened to hit me if I did it again.

They took me to another area where a guard in a uniform was wait-ing and he asked for my address. I told him, but instead of taking me back home to Auntie Bev he took me all the way back to the building I'd come from.

This time, when they put me in my room, they locked the door.

I got into bed, pulled the sheets around me, and shivered and stared for ages.

A long time later, Ruen showed up. He was still the Old Man.

"Alex," he said, smiling as if he'd really missed me or something. I ignored him. He sat down by my feet and looked at me.

"How was your mother?"

I said nothing.

"Alex, do you remember that I organized a beautiful home for you and your mother to move into once you both recuperate?"

I thought of the pictures of the house Anya had brought me, the big garden in back and the kitchen. I felt excited at the thought of it but didn't want him to see, so I just nodded.

"And you said you would do something for me if I helped you find your mother this evening?"

I looked at him and glared. He could take a big hike off the tallest cliff.

"Well, I already told you that the something would be a gift to Anya. But there's something else now. For your mum."

"Don't you *dare* talk about my Mum!" I snapped. "I didn't get to see her. The door was locked. Now they'll *never* let me see her!"

He swiped the air with his hand. "Oh, they will. You'll see. Just wait until tomorrow morning, Anya will ensure that you get your visit. This is why we need to give her the gift." He paused. "And if you give her this gift from me, I'll do something else for you, too."

"What *gift?*"

He stood up, glanced at the sketch pad in my locker, and said, "have you got a ruler?"

I nodded.

"And a pencil?"

"Yeah?"

He turned to face me, his face all serious. "I have composed for Anya a piece of music. She loves music so this will undoubtedly be a delight for her. It is composed in precisely the sort of style she prefers.

When Beethoven and Mozart composed their opuses they always dedicated them to their friends, like Prince Karl von Lichnowsky and, on one occasion, Napoleon. I believe Anya should be pleased to possess a piece of music that is not only dedicated to her, but written especially for her. What I require from you is to write it out for me exactly as I dictate."

I stared at him. "Whatever. What about the thing you'll do for my Mum?"

He sat down, coughed, and lowered his eyes.

"Has your mother ever mentioned your father, Alex? I mean, since he died?"

"No. But she was really upset about it, that's what landed her here in the first place. So if you think I'm going to bring that up . . ."

Ruen held up a hand. "No, no. What I was going to suggest was . . . Well, you may as well know."

"Know what?"

He looked away and sighed very deeply. "Your father is in Hell."

I felt like I'd just walked into a wall.

"In *Hell*?"

"In the worst part of it, I'm afraid."

My mouth opened and I went to speak but no sound came out.

"What's wrong, Alex?" Ruen asked, and I shook my head because I couldn't talk right then because my head was too full of memories about Dad.

And then I thought of the black mask and the blue car and the policeman. And I remembered what had happened after that. I remembered that Mum had cried and cried the day after and I knew that Dad had died. His face was in the newspapers and Mum warned me not to tell *a single soul* that he was my Dad because then we'd be split up as a family and the headlines called him a *monster* and *evil* and said he should *rot in hell*.

"Dad's really in Hell, isn't he?" I said to Ruen.

He gave me a long look that told me that I was right.

I thought I was going to throw up. Mum would be very, very upset if she knew this. I pulled the sheet around my face.

"Oh, worry not," Ruen groaned. "You write this piece for me as a gift to Anya, and I'll release your father from Hell."

I let go of the sheet. "You can do that?"

He looked very offended. "Of course I can. Don't you think that would make your mother very happy, knowing he isn't in Hell? And I'm most certain your father would be grateful, too."

"So he'll go to Heaven?"

Ruen grinned so wide I thought his face might crack.

Then I had a thought. "Why did you write music for Anya?"

Ruen narrowed his eyes. "The title is 'Love Song for Anya,' my boy. Doesn't that give you a clue?"

"But you don't love Anya," I said. "You don't love anybody. You're a *demon*."

Ruen sniffed. "Penetrating as always, Alex. The simple truth is that reality lurks in the senses. If we are to prevent Anya from separating you and I then we must make her question what she believes to be real. Your questions have already begun that process, but what she *hears* when she plays this piece of music will surely finalize her self-questioning."

"What the heck does *that* mean?" I said.

"Do we have a deal?" Ruen said.

I chewed my nails. I thought of Mum lying in that room, all by herself. She looked so small in the bed. I wouldn't be able to tell her what Ruen had done for Dad, as she'd probably be very freaked out. But maybe, in a few years, I could. And she would be over the moon.

I nodded. "Deal," I said.

## ANYA

I grab a coffee on my way to the city hospital. I go into the interview room and look over my notes on Alex and the update from the hospital. Observations during administration of risperidone seemed fine, except for one, tiny, microscopic detail:

Last night, Alex ran away.

He made it all the way out of the hospital, across the courtyard, and into the adult unit, where he pounded on his mother's door and sank his teeth into a security guard.

I close my eyes and try to fill my head with the sights and sounds of the Caribbean. This is bad, bad news. It not only suggests problems with the security in this place, but it also underscores Alex's mental instability and a whole swath of negative reactions to his treatment. It will also look very bad on my report.

I look up to find Dr. Hargreaves, a cognitive behavior therapy specialist who works at MacNeice House two days a week, standing in the office doorway.

"Alex is your patient, isn't he?" Dr. Hargreaves asks, glancing up over his spectacles. We've spoken only a handful of times, and from the direction of our previous conversations I'm aware that he thinks I'm a psychotic disorder fascist.

"Yes, he is," I answer.

He nods. "And you *do* know one of the side effects of risperidone is akathisia?" Akathisia is extreme restlessness. It's entirely doubtful that akathisia would have made Alex go to such lengths, but the possibility of it makes me feel dizzy. Dr. Hargreaves sees my reaction and smiles thinly.

I head to the interview room. Alex is seated in a daffodil-yellow armchair beside the shatterproof coffee table. His ankles are crossed and his hands are pressed inside his thighs. He looks very on edge.

"Hello, Alex," I say cheerily. "Sorry I'm a little late this morning. Did you sleep okay?"

He shakes his head.

"No? Is that why you went for a walk?"

He shakes his head, still looking down.

"Why *did* you go for a walk? And at three in the morning, I might add. Were you just tired of being in hospital?"

He looks up at me. His eyes are hollow and tired. "I want to tell you something." He ignores my questions.

"Okay," I say, following his lead. I take out my notepad. He looks at it silently.

"Is my notebook bothering you, Alex?"

"I don't care if you write it down or not. I just want you to listen."

I set my pen down. He takes a deep breath.

"I know that you think I'm a danger to myself. But Ruin is real. And I have proof."

He hands me a sheet of paper. It is a piece of music. The title "Love Song for Anya" is written at the top. The lines, notes, and clefs are very awkwardly drawn, with evidence of much erasing and rewriting. But there is precision in this composition. There are accurate phrase marks, a time signature and octave sign, and at two points Italian terms are used: *andantino* and *appassionato*. A quick scan through the score indicates that it isn't a love song in the ballad sense.

But there is something else that causes my mouth to go dry and my heart to race before I tell myself that it's nothing more than a coincidence: the opening melody is identical to the one Poppy composed on the night she died. A high B for three beats; a trilled A, G, A, each of them a quarter note before another B for three beats; A, G, A, then a G for three beats, A for three, B again; a simple melody, and one that I've heard time after time endlessly over the last four years, as if it held the secret to what happened the night she died.

"Where did you get this?" I ask Alex.

"Ruin told me that he composed it for you because you like music. He told me to write it down for you as a gift."

"As a gift?"

He nods. "He said it's only a short piece because I couldn't manage to score a whole symphony, not yet."

Alex's voice is less animated than usual, and there is a firmness to his tone and manner that makes him seem to have aged several years since our last meeting. He seems reluctant, not excited, to show me what he's written. I stare at the fragment of music. Alex leans forward.

"You ask my mum," he whispers. "I don't know how to play music, never mind *write* it. I can't play any instrument at all. I can't even sing. So how would I be able to write that then, huh?"

I put our interview on hold until after his schooling session with a private tutor. I run outside, dial Michael's number, and leave a message to call me as soon as possible. He needs to know about Alex's escape attempt.

Moments later, my phone rings. It is Michael.

"Why is Alex on risperidone?" are his first words. Aggressive and worried at the same time.

"Do you know he tried to run away last night?"

"Of course I do," he snaps. "The hospital told me to come in immediately. I'm worried that we're being overly zealous with the medication, Anya. The last kid I saw with a risperidone prescription was eighteen and stoned out of his mind—"

"Alex's condition requires medical intervention," I say levelly, interrupting him. "Cindy shows no sign of getting out of the psych unit anytime soon. Would you wait a week before treating a broken leg?"

"Well, you should know that Cindy isn't doing so well," he replies stiffly. "Not since she heard she'd been found incapable of acting as Alex's mother."

*That's not my fault,* I think, then immediately feel guilty. I have had less than ten hours' sleep over the last three nights—a combination of stress and playing catch-up with my other cases. I would do anything right now for a long, hot bath and a comfortable bed. "I'm going to speak to Cindy later this afternoon," I tell Michael. "And there's something else—"

"What?"

I mention Ruin's "gift." I tell him about the piece of music, although I don't mention anything about Poppy. "It's quite an accomplished piece of music for a ten-year-old boy. I'm wondering what he's up to . . . Has Alex ever had piano lessons?"

"Not that I'm aware of. Why?"

I tell him that, as a pianist, I am staggered by the piece's complexity. Even if Alex *has* had some musical training, this is quite amazing. More important, the piece makes me wonder if Ruin is more than a projection—if he is a living person with whom Alex is having regular contact, and an adult who is genuinely threatening the boy's safety and well-being.

"Where are you?" Michael says when I finish.

"Still at the adult unit."

"Stay where you are."


Ten minutes later, he's striding toward me across the parking lot. I expect him to follow me inside the adult psych unit and grab a coffee or something while we kill time until I can speak to Cindy, but after inspecting the sheet of music he tells me to get into his car.

"Where are we going?" I ask.

"I've arranged for us to speak to someone at the School of Music over at Queen's University." His voice is low and uneasy, his eyes resting on the musical score.

"Why?"

"You said you wanted to prove whether Alex could have written it. Didn't you?"

"No, I . . ." I trail off and glance at his car, parked crookedly on the curb. "What was all that about the other night, Michael?"

"You mean Alex?"

"*No.* You. Stroking my face." I'm embarrassed to bring it up, but I hate ignoring what must be confronted.

"Aye, there's the rub," he says with a crooked grin. "Look, I was just worried about you, okay?"

"*Worried?* I said I was just getting some fresh air . . ."

I let him find the words he is searching for on the ground. When he looks up, his expression is troubled. "It won't happen again," he says softly. "I promise."


We head in Michael's car to the School of Music at the university, directly behind the Botanic Gardens.

"How's the running?" Michael asks.

I think of the fresh blisters on my soles from new track shoes, the suspicious bulge of fluid in my knee that suggests another steroid injection will be necessary this year. "Not nearly as exciting as gardening," I say evasively.

I notice a flash of color in his cheeks at the mention of his garden. He proceeds to tell me how his Green Windsor broad beans got black-fly and a rogue rooster from a neighboring patch took umbrage at his beetroot, how he's taken up horse riding just so he can collect manure and take it home afterward ("Couldn't you just ask if you can clean out the stables?" I suggest, to which he responds with "I'm too polite to take it without paying *something*"), how his new potatoes were in his stomach an hour after being in the soil.

I find my thoughts turning to my paternal grandmother, Mei, whose English was limited to the phrase she used often: my *yin and yang,* the balance of my life. She would say Michael is my yang, my opposite. The one who has been sent to teach me, and vice versa. Listening to him describe his Sundays spent up to his knees in compost, I feel the habits of my own life—a supermarket cart filled with plastic-wrapped, pre-washed organic vegetables, a rented apartment, the ability to untether myself from the artificial wall of twenty-first-century life and drop into another at any moment—lose their appeal. The other night I dreamed I woke up in a solar-powered, wind-turbined house built entirely of wood, mud, and straw on an island in the Hebrides, my plate filled with produce from my own garden. Five years ago this would have been a nightmare. Now, to my astonishment, it feels like the kind of life I would embrace.

Michael's friend is a beautiful blond Californian lecturer in musical composition with a PhD in Bach's fugues and performance diplomas in oboe, tuba, piano, and kettle drums. She has so many letters after her name that it reads like a sentence. She tells me to call her Melinda, and we follow her into her office.

Michael hands her Alex's piece of music. She puts on her glasses and studies it, then looks up.

"Gee, did you say this was written by a ten-year-old?"

I fumble for the right explanation. "Well, sort of," I tell her. "He insists he wrote it on behalf of . . . an imaginary friend."

Melinda raises her eyebrows. "Wow-ee, some imaginary friend, huh?" She glances at Michael. "Well, it certainly isn't anything I've ever seen before. Some influences, here."

She uses a short but immaculately manicured fingernail to point these out. "A little Chopin here. Maybe some Mozart in the closing bars. Of course, influence is highly subjective."

She stands up, music in hand, and walks from behind her desk to an upright Yamaha piano against the far wall.

"You play it," Michael says, nudging me. "It's *your* song, after all."

Melinda turns. "Oh, you play? Be my guest." She pulls out the piano seat and gestures for me to sit down.

"I'm a bit rusty . . ."

"Come on . . ." Melinda urges, smiling and patting the seat. "Don't be shy. Let's hear this masterpiece!"

The truth is, I feel extremely nervous about playing the piece. I've already heard the melody in my head by cold-reading the notes, but I'm not sure how I will feel when I play those eight bars out loud. Poppy's song. No, that's surely only my imagination.

I take a seat in front of the piano, slide my fingers up the smooth white keys, and begin to play. I hold my breath as I chime out the open-

ing melody, gritting my teeth against memories of Poppy's dark head
bent over the keys as she played the same tune. When I get to the second section, I allow myself to breathe. I focus on the technique of the
piece. There is a simplicity and an impishness to it that grips me as I play
it. The melody of the second half is technically demanding, lyrical, passionate. I sneak a glance at the title. "Love Song for Anya." Then I note
the smaller text beneath it: "Ruen." *Ruen*. I had always thought the
name of Alex's so-called demon was *Ruin*.

When I finish, Melinda and Michael applaud me.

"I liked that!" Michael says.

"A very talented performer," Melinda winks. She walks over to the
piano and bends down to have another look at it. "Kid isn't terrific with
annotation, though. Needs a little practice with his treble clefs . . ." She
turns to Michael. "You want me to run this through our software,
check to see if it's plagiarized?"

Michael nods. "Definitely."

As I raise my hands from the keys, I see that they are trembling.


Outside the School of Music, we hesitate.

"You want a lift back to see Cindy?"

"It's not far. I'll walk." I start toward the Botanic Gardens and, to
my surprise, Michael follows.

"I'm parked this way anyway."

"Of course. Thanks for contacting Melinda," I say awkwardly. "She
certainly was helpful."

He searches my face. "Something about that music bothers you,
doesn't it."

It isn't a question. "I don't think you know me well enough to . . ."

". . . is it because you suspect Ruen actually wrote it?"

I watch a car trying to park in a space close to us. It backs so close
to the car behind that its reflection pours across the hood. We walk on.

"I wonder if Ruen is Alex's father?" I ask.

"A *demon*?"

"No, I mean, if Alex is actually visiting with his dad. If the physical
violence he experienced was at the hands of . . ." I stop. The thought

that Alex's father is not dead at all but has been meeting with the boy on the sly is ludicrous. But I have run out of answers. The music, the attack, the way he asked about my scar the first time we'd met . . . And then I think of Ursula. How she had urged me to abandon preconceptions.

We are at the foot of the Botanic Gardens now. A woman is jogging; two Dalmatians trot beside her. Michael sidesteps behind me so that he is between me and the dogs.

"Okay," he says, pushing his hands in his pockets and grinning. "So let's consider the possibility. *Is* Alex seeing demons?"

I turn to read his face. He is serious. This is a side of Michael I haven't yet seen. How could this intelligent, perceptive man even consider that there is such a thing as demons, that there is even the slightest possibility that someone could see them?

"You're kidding?"

We are close to the hothouses. I can smell the thick, warm air surrounding them. Students are inside, bent over the hothouse plants that flourish there.

Michael takes a step in front of me, tilting his head slightly to draw my attention away from the students. "When I studied for the priesthood, Anya, I did a lot of research into belief narratives. I read a lot of things by people who claimed they'd seen the unbelievable—angels, demons, God, what have you. People who swore they'd seen demons with forked tails, then realized that these tails were links that gradually grew fatter, binding them to the demon, destroying them." He shook his head. "Crazy stuff."

"What made you so interested in that?"

He takes his hands out of his pockets and gestures toward a bench facing the green lawns of the university. We sit. He takes a breath and combs his hair with his hand.

"When I was little I saw my sister. My parents have never spoken about her. I only found out she even existed last year. My grandmother let slip that there'd been complications during my birth because of the other dead baby inside my mother." He seems to shudder, leans closer to me. I sense that he is revealing something that has made him feel lonely for years.

"I grew up knowing that I had a sister named Lisa," he continues. "That she looked just like me, only she was a girl, and that only I could see her. My parents took me to psychologist after psychologist. And then when I was about eight and they were getting really sick of it, my dad threatened to put me through a glass window if I mentioned Lisa again. He said she wasn't real. After that, I stopped seeing her." He chews his bottom lip. "But I know she was real. She was."

I nod, keenly aware that I am probably the only person he has ever told about this, and wondering why. I don't ask—instead, I choose a response that fits within the boundaries of our professional relationship.

"Is that why you studied psychiatry?"

"Sort of. Probably. I just . . ." He pauses to clarify his thoughts. "I suppose I needed to understand what the difference was between seeing things of a spiritual nature and having a mental health issue. Does that make any sense?"

"You needed to explore whether you had a dissociative disorder as a child or were playing with the ghost of your twin."

"Bingo. And here's the thing: I'm an atheist."

"Yet you were going to be a priest?" I am surprised.

"There's a whole difference between the religious and cultural motivations behind that career path. Few of the guys I met on that route were convinced of the great gig in the sky."

"I guess both career paths are about believing in the unseen."

"I know I saw my sister," he insists. "Mentally ill or not . . . you say 'tomato.' I say 'tomayto.'" He grins uneasily, his wariness returning. "I think there's just some things you can't explain away by science."

"You think Alex is *really seeing something*?"

"Did *Hamlet* see the ghost of his father?"

"*Hamlet* is a *play*, Michael . . ."

He reaches out to touch my arm. "I'm not saying he's channeling the dead, Anya. There's got to be a reason why Alex has latched on to such a specific identity. What did Poppy claim to see?"

I think back to the moment that Poppy had tried so desperately to describe to me what it was like to be her. We were in a restaurant close to the Golden Mile in the center of Edinburgh, her favorite place for steak. I wanted to break the news to her gently, in an environment where she felt comfortable and happy: She was going to spend two months at the Cherrytree Haven Child and Adolescent Inpatient Facility.

"The doctors say that you'll have your own room there, Poppy," I'd told her. "You'll be home weekends. There's a swimming pool, a park outside, and lots of other kids there . . ."

I faltered. Despite training as a child psychiatrist, my professional expertise only got me so far when it was my *own* twelve-year-old daughter on the receiving end of treatment. The thought of putting my little girl in a psychiatric unit for eight weeks was breaking my heart, but I had absolutely no reservations that it was in her best interests.

But she had started to sob. Her face had gone bone white and she was gripping the arms of her chair.

"I'm falling, Mum . . . ," she said.

A waitress approached with two plates in either hand. "Who's got the medium-rare?"

I looked helplessly from the waitress to Poppy. "I'm *falling*, Mum," my daughter insisted, her voice rising to a shriek. "Why aren't you helping me?"

*I should have listened. I should have taken more time to understand . . .*

People were starting to stare. "Is everything okay?" the waitress whispered, and I nodded, bundling my wallet and phone into my handbag and searching for a quick way to get Poppy out of there without more noise.

"You don't understand what it's like!" she'd shouted. "What this *feels* like, Mum! Have you ever even *asked* what this feels like?"

*No, my love. Tell me now.*

"Poppy, it's time to go home," I whispered.

*"No."* Her voice was firm, threatening.

The waitress stared, the plates in her hand like cymbals.

"Come on, Poppy," I said, a little firmer this time.

And that's when she grabbed a steak knife from the table and plunged it into my cheek.

It could have been worse; later she told me she was aiming for my throat.

• • •

It takes a moment to untangle myself from the memory's dark tentacles. Poppy's absence is a continual ringing in my ears of all the things I should have said to her, all the things I should have done.

Michael has said something to me. I raise my eyes to his, and he repeats it.

"I said I'm worried that you see Poppy in Alex," he says. "I know what it's like when a case hits close to the bone. At times like that you have to be sure you're keeping the right amount of distance. It's only human to get involved."

Ironically, he says *the right amount of distance* just as he moves closer to me, reaching out to touch my arm. I look down at his hand, and he draws it back as if his fingertips have brushed something hot.

"Sorry," he mumbles, but for some reason my mind is churning, returning to my past. I am in the kitchen of our Morningside flat, ironing Poppy's school shirt. "Keep your distance," I tell her.

"What did you say?" I ask Michael distractedly, my voice a whisper. He has moved back now, unsure of what to do with his hands.

"When? About Alex?"

"When you asked about the reason he claims to see Ruen."

He blinks. "I said he was channeling the dead."

"You said he *wasn't* channeling the dead."

He looks on, his face full of confusion.

*My darling, I'm sorry. I'm sorry . . .*

Words I can never tell her now. Unless . . .

I smile at Michael and start to walk away. A thought has snagged itself on my heart. A thought that violates every ethical and professional standard I pride myself on.

*What I wouldn't give to tell you I'm sorry.*

Not a thought.

A temptation.

ALEX

Dear Diary,

What do you call a boy with sticky-out ears, a big fat nose, and no chin?
Names.

I started at my new school on Monday. It's a bit crap, just like that joke. I have to sleep at MacNeice House and even though my new bedroom is bigger than the one at Mum's house, I don't like it. Everything is white and the windows don't open and someone said the doors are built so that if you try and hang yourself they'll fall down. I run through all the doorways now just in case they fall over, which makes the other kids laugh.

My bedroom in the new house will be cool, though, so I suppose it's okay in the meantime. Most of the teachers here aren't very friendly, though I like one of them. She's called Miss Falls, and she smells like a used-book store though she seems nice. She's my personal tutor and she meets with me after school every day in my bedroom for one hour. I get to go to her if I have any problems and we talk about stuff like math and 2B pencils and *Hamlet*. Our classes only have ten other kids in them, which is cool because it's quiet and no one makes fun of me. But nobody talks to each other and some of the other kids are psycho. One of the girls is a year older than me and she says we're actually in a zoo and that there's a tiger on the desk and stuff like that. Yesterday she said I couldn't sit on the seat behind her 'cos there was a giraffe on it and I looked at Ruen to check there wasn't and he just rolled his eyes and yawned.

I'm really glad to have Ruen around because I miss so many things now, not just Mum. I miss waking up in the middle of the night and finding Woof asleep on my head. I miss onions on toast. I miss the way our faucet drips all night and sounds like a heartbeat. I miss Auntie Bev and Jojo and the theater. I miss the way Mum wiggles her toenails on the footstool when she's drinking tea and watching *Coronation Street*. I miss Mum even when she's sad. I miss our house, even though there are no broken windows in this place and it's clean and warm.

I asked Ruen if Mum and I are going to lose the new house since Bev has gone home and there's no sign of Mum getting out soon, and he said that it was up to Anya now because she'd put me in here and even though Ruen could help me escape, I'd have nowhere else to go. For a moment, I thought, *why don't I just go home and you can look after me?* But then I remembered that Ruen is a demon and he can't really do normal things, like cook and clean. Which is a pity.

But I'm all excited and freaked out and curious about my dad. What was it like getting freed out of Hell? Is he really really happy? Is he grateful? Is he in Heaven? Or somewhere else? I really don't understand the afterlife, and when I ask Ruen about it he doesn't like to talk about it too much, particularly Heaven. He says it is "overly conceptualized" and "idealized" and that Hell is *"pejoratively dismissed"* and gets *"bad press."*

Every time I ask about death he just looks at me like I'm stupid.

"It's the *end,* dear boy," he says, tutting. "No more body. No more chocolate cake. There are some advantages, but it depends where you end up." And then I ask about where I might "end up" and he starts going on about the *idealization* of Heaven and the *denigration* of Hell.

Tonight, however, I want to ask him about my dad. I've never really found out much about how or why my dad died. I didn't go to his funeral and Mum has never taken me to his grave, and she has no pictures of him in the house. I'm not to tell anyone about him, she said. Only his name, because it's also my name. Alex. When I think of whether Dad is happy to be out of Hell I have a memory of me and Dad and Mum. We are sitting at our table in the living room and Mum brings in some rolls on a plate. Dad takes two of them and sticks his fork through one and his knife through the other and starts bouncing them up and down the table as if they're feet doing a little dance. I remember the way the sunlight was strong and lit up the side of his face and the lines at the side of his eyes when he laughed. I remember Mum flicking him with a kitchen towel, laughing and telling him to stop. Mum used to laugh loads back then.

When I think of this it makes me sad, but more confused than sad. I'm confused because when I think of him making the rolls dance and then I think of what I saw that day, of dad shooting those policemen—it just doesn't make sense. Aren't evil people evil all the time? Aren't funny kind people who bring toy cars for their little boy funny and kind all the time?

I was sad for a long time when I learned Dad had died. He just vanished one day, right after what happened at the checkpoint. I never asked Mum if he fell down a mine shaft or got run over or got the disease that Granny had; she was too upset all the time. She just cried and cried one morning and said "your Dad's gone," and I said "for how long?" and she said, "for life."

And then she went upstairs and didn't come down, which I thought was weird because I needed her to walk with me to school because I was only five. So I waited for hours, then went upstairs, checked the bathroom, then Mum and Dad's bedroom, and she was in bed. I gave her a push and shouted *Wake up!* But she didn't move. So I pulled all the covers off and stomped my feet and clapped my hands and tickled her feet. And then I noticed some boxes under the duvet covers. I knew what they were for because I was with Mum when she picked them up from the doctors. All the pills were gone and I felt funny, like scared. Then Mum started coughing and I felt my heart pound because I was glad she made a noise. "Are you awake now?" I said, but she just leaned over and puked all over my feet.

I remember I ran downstairs and opened the front door by standing on the piano stool and then I ran all the way to Granny's. I told Granny that Mum was sick and there were white boxes in the bedsheets and that I was really hungry. Granny's face went shocked and her eyes were sad and wide and she told me to go make myself some toast and she made a phone call, and then she walked quickly with me back to our house but instead of letting me go inside she said *go to school, go to school.* I went to school but I had a knot in my stomach the whole way which got tighter and tighter. And that was the day I first saw Ruen.

"Ruen," I say when I'm sure that no one is around to hear me, which isn't very often. He is sitting on my bed and I am sitting on the floor of my room doing math homework. When he's the Old Man he is starting to sit more and more, like he's tired. When he walks he sort of drags his feet now and his scowl is becoming so pronounced that it's like his face is melting. After a few minutes he looks up.

"What?"

"So did you get my dad out of Hell yet?"

He grunts.

"Is that a yes?"

He grunts, and then starts to cough. He thumps his chest. " 'Course I did."

I sit upright. "You did?" My heart is knocking in my chest and I feel like I need to pee. "So what happened? Did you have to, like, break him out of there? Was there a big fight?"

He coughs again. "Yes, yes, all of that."

My thoughts are racing now. I see Hell in my mind, a red, fiery place with loads of people. There is lots of screaming, and it's a city, only the city walls are pouring with orange lava and mega-blasts of flame keep shooting out of windows, and there are creatures there like the demons I see all the time, only worse; these are like zombies with their flesh

THE BOY WHO COULD SEE DEMONS 203

ripped off and blood pouring down their faces. Dragons are circling in the red sky and there's big black clouds of smoke there, too. I see Ruen striding toward a big black building with fire pits burning around the front door. There are big mean security guards outside holding long spears and wearing full-body armor. Their helmets have horns sticking up out of the top like a rhino, and their armor is studded with spikes. When Ruen approaches they cross their spears to prevent him from entering. He stares at them, and his eyes are red. He tells them he's a Harrower. They fall to their knees, shaking in front of him. He lifts his leg and kicks the door open.

Inside the building it looks like the biggest cathedral you've ever seen, all naked stone and gargoyles and a ceiling so high you almost fall over when you look all the way up at it. There are horrible creatures with vampire fangs shrieking and hiding and swiping at him with their claws, but Ruen calmly goes toward the place where he knows my dad is being kept: the room at the very top of the tallest tower. He has to duck and dodge past loads of foul creatures but eventually he gets there, and my dad is so grateful, and when Ruen tells him "your son sent me," Dad cries. And then Ruen fights his way out of there with my dad close behind, only at this point Ruen is starting to sound German and is wearing a leather jacket. Outside is a Harley-Davidson motorcycle. He and Dad jump on the back and ride off to Heaven.

"Whoa!" I say to Ruen. "That's just like *Terminator*!"

He looks at me very confused.

"Wait . . . did you fight Satan, too?" I say, standing up. "Was he riding a dragon and did giant hailstones of hot coal come falling out of the sky?"

"What are you talking about?"

"Saving my dad!" I shout.

I hear footsteps walking quickly down the hall so I lower my voice. "Was he really grateful? Did you tell him about me?"

Ruen looks down as if he's thinking about it. Eventually he stands and smiles. "Your father was released from Hell yesterday, on my command, of course. He was extremely grateful to me and told me he would remain indebted to me for the rest of eternity. In fact, he said he hoped his son—you, Alex—would attempt to pay some of that debt by remaining faithful to me and assisting in my research."

I stare at him. I haven't a clue what he's just said. I'm still really buzzed that he's done what he said he would do. And I think about Katie then, of what her Mum did. That Ruen was right all along.

"Will you, Alex?"

"What?"

"Will you remain faithful to me and assist in my research, just as your father requested?"

"Yeah. Yeah, sure. So did my dad seem happy, then? Did he like Heaven? And did he ask about Mum and were there angels in Heaven?"

Ruen grunts.

Then something occurs to me. Something I should have told Ruen to tell my dad.

"Did you tell my dad that I love him?"

Ruen's face looks like a knot. "Did you wish me to?"

I nod and suddenly my buzz wilts a little, like a goal I almost scored but didn't. "Maybe he already knows. Do you think he knows I love him?"

He shrugs. "How would I know?"

"Did you . . . just get a sense that he knew that I loved him? You know, because I sent you to get him out of Hell? Did it show in his face?"

Ruen's face tightens even more. You could probably hide stuff in between the folds of skin. When I think of this I remember the time I hid a fiver behind the radiator in my room and I wonder if it's still there. Ruen snorts and flares his nostrils.

"My dear boy, love is a very *human* thing. I know nothing of love. And if I did, I should be very, very angry."

I sweep my hand over my head to show that everything he's just said is a bit psycho. He looks at the door. For a minute I think he's going to leave and I suddenly feel like pleading with him not to. But he just grunts and sits back down.

"You know, Ruen," I tell him. "In a way, you're like my dad, too. I don't mean that I don't love my dad, it's just . . ." Suddenly I don't even know what I mean. "I'm just glad you're here."

Ruen raises one of his fuzzy white eyebrows and snorts. I climb into my bed and pull the covers around me. Just as I do this all the lights shut off and it is pitch black. They do this every night, even though I *HATE* the dark.

The dark makes me even more glad that Ruen is here.

# 22

# THE COMPOSER

## ANYA

Yesterday I went to the adult psych unit to talk to Cindy about Alex's piece of music. She was reluctant to see me. I overheard her conversation with the nurse through Cindy's open door.

> *There's a lady here to see you, Cindy. Dr. Anya . . .*
> A sigh. *Tell her I'm not well.*
> *. . . she says it's about your little boy. Alex?*
> *Why does* she *keep coming here?*

After a few moments the nurse emerged from Cindy's room. She told me I could go inside.

Cindy was seated beside the window, glancing out at the rain. Her hair was unwashed, her nails bitten to stumps. I waited at the threshold of the door, waiting for her permission to enter.

"Hello, Cindy," I said warmly. "May I come in?"

"Please yourself," she muttered.

I lifted a chair by the bed and set it down close to her, though not too close. "I know you have an art session," I said. I started to take off my raincoat, then thought better of it. "I won't keep you long."

She flicked her eyes at me. "I'm not going to no stupid art session."

I paused. "No?"

She bit her nails in response and locked her gaze on the window, drawing one bony knee up to her chest. "So what you here for?"

I kept my voice light. "I wanted to ask if Alex ever had piano lessons."

"*That's* why you're here?"

I nodded.

She sighed again. "Not to my knowledge. Couldn't afford stuff like that, ya know?"

"You have a piano at home, don't you? Do either of you play it?"

"No. It was a family heirloom. Hadn't played a note in years."

"What about at school? Does Alex take music classes?"

"He's much more into building models of castles, stuff like that. *Boy* stuff."

"So he couldn't have written this, then?" Tentatively, I held out the music. Cindy took it from me and glanced at it.

"No," she said. "He's never written music." She tapped the writing at the top of the page with her finger. "That looks like his writing, though. Can I have a closer look?"

"Take your time," I said. She pulled the page closer to the gray light from the window and leaned in.

"Actually I'd say this *is* Alex's writing." She looked up at me. "Imagine that! My kid, a composer. Not that I'm surprised."

"Why doesn't it surprise you?"

She shrugged and changed legs, drawing the left knee up to her chin. "Alex has always done things beyond his age. Stuff I never taught him, he just picked up somehow. You'd never think he was my son."

I nodded. "Alex says someone else wrote this."

"No, it's definitely his writing . . ."

"I know. Alex said he wrote the music down, but someone else composed the music and told him to write it."

She looked puzzled, then gave a shrug. "Well, if that's what Alex says, I'd believe him."

"Even if Alex says that person was a demon?"

"What's wrong with him copying some music out? Just because he didn't actually compose it doesn't mean he isn't clever . . ."

"I didn't say that . . ."

She thrust the music back at me, her face angry and scared. "Here," she said. "Stop asking about our damn piano, okay? It's none of your business."

I took the music and put it back into my briefcase. She watched me intently, her hands still restless.

"They don't let you smoke in here, do they?" I asked.

Her face softened. "No, they don't," she said, shaking her head. "I'd give you a kidney for a cigarette right now."

I smiled and pushed at the diversion of her frustration from me to *they*. "If I had one, you'd be welcome to it."

"Thanks," she said, smiling weakly. Whatever emotion had been triggered by my questions was visibly lessening its grip. I bent to retrieve my briefcase.

"Still, you'll be out of here soon enough."

She glanced at me. Something in her gaze made me stop mid-rise. "Won't you?"

She was back to chewing her nails. I sat back down in my chair, sensing she had something left to say. After a few moments, she leaned forward, her eyes furtive.

"You have kids, don't you?" she said.

"What makes you ask?"

She scratched her head. "Trudy doesn't have any kids, so I don't think she understands. But you know what I mean, don't you?"

"About what?"

She pulled her chair closer. "That sometimes it feels like *they're* the parent and *you're* the child. You know? Like they have more answers than we do."

"You mean Alex seems older than his years?"

"He's always been so independent, you know? Like he didn't even *need* me." At last, her hands settled on her stomach, at rest. She turned her head toward the window, glancing up at the clouds. "I never wanted to be a mother. Not a nice thing to say, is it? Then when Alex was born

I fell totally in love with him. I was his number one fan. He's so amazing I can hardly believe he came out of *me*."

I waited carefully as the weight of her words settled into the silence. It was beginning to rain when I spoke. "Cindy, I think you and Alex should take a little vacation when you get out of here."

She looked puzzled for a moment. "When I get out of here?"

I nodded. "It doesn't need to be anywhere expensive. But I think it would be a good idea for the two of you to have some fun together. Have you ever had a day at the beach together?"

She shook her head, then laughed. "How crazy is that? Three miles from the beach and we've never been. Then again, it's never sunny, is it . . . ?"

"Even if it's *snowing*," I replied lightly, returning her grin. "When you get out of here I think you should make spending time together a priority."

She lowered her gaze and her hands started to flutter again. "Yeah. When I get out of here."


This morning I woke, having finally fallen asleep at dawn on the floor of my bedroom, with the sound of Alex's music in my head. I had to play it. I had to hear Poppy in the notes, to feel her close again. No, not just to feel close—to find answers. The echo of her composition in Alex's piece had rung out a series of echoes that filled my small flat.

When Poppy was born, she didn't breathe for two minutes. The doctors were frantic, flapping at the bottom of my legs with a suction machine, counting—*one, two, three, come on, sweetheart*—until finally a midwife plucked her up by the ankles, held her upside down, and gave her ass a firm spank. She screamed, and I felt as if a flood of relief had poured across me.

Now the trauma of that moment had a new echo—was that what caused it? Had the lack of oxygen at her birth somehow caused something in her brain to go wrong? Did schizophrenia lurk in my gene pool, striking my mother, then skipping over me to reach Poppy? Was it something I had done?

And what else could I have done to save her?

I checked my phone. Missed calls from Fi and Michael, and a number I didn't recognize. I tried calling it back, but got a busy signal. Then, after a moment's hesitation, I called Melinda at the university School of Music.

"Hey!" she said when she heard my voice. "The maestro! How're you doing?"

I asked if it would be all right if I used one of the university's practice rooms for an hour or so.

"Yes, yes, sure," she gushed. "Absolutely. No prob. Come on over and I'll get you booked in. We've a Steinway in the main practice room, how'd that be?"

"That's perfect," I replied and I hung up. My fingers were already restless. I was aching to play that music. I was searching for an answer, a missing piece of the puzzle, and I didn't even know the question.

I arrived at Melinda's office clutching a Coke and a chocolate muffin the size of a ball of Aran wool. I had decided that my period was due, that my hormones were raging, hence the reason I was slightly off kilter. That, and another temporary fling with insomnia. Melinda made drooling motions at the sight of the muffin, then took me to the practice room.

It was empty, except for a piano stool and a shiny black Steinway grand. At the sight of the NO FOOD OR DRINK sign, I tossed my Coke and muffin into the garbage pail.

Melinda frowned. "I wouldn't have said anything," she said, but I shook my head. I had no appetite, I told her. I just wanted to play.

When she shut the door behind me I began with a few arpeggios to warm up. In the last four years I had touched the keys no more than a dozen times. What intrigued me was that despite such neglect my hands retained the ghostly fingerings of the pieces I used to play over and over again. I could no longer remember the key of Rachmaninoff's second piano concerto, nor could I see in my mind's eye the notes for Ravel's "Pavane pour une Infante Défunte," but my fingers found their way to the right chords without hesitation. I felt like a puppet in reverse, my whole body tugged and jerked by the strings of the instrument.

Finally, I unfolded Alex's piece of music from my pocket. Though the melody echoed in my brain, my fingers were unfamiliar with it. I scanned the piece again, remembering Poppy's head bent over our piano.

*I love you, Mummy.*

I creased back the page until it leaned against the music stand, then slid my fingers on top of the notes. I began to play, an emphasis on the B of the right hand, a waltz in the left. I hadn't made it past the first bar when I stopped, lifting my fingers an inch off the keys. My heart was clanging in my chest at the echo of the music in the cold empty room.

This time, the memory stirred by those opening notes filled not only my head but my veins. My skin was alive with the softness of her skin when I'd held her the first time, cheek-to-chest, her whole head fitting neatly in my palm. The sensation of it was so real that it shocked me. But it was tantalizing, too. I laid my hands back on the keys and continued to play. This time, I felt the L-shape of her shoulder blades pressed into my palms as I held her after a fall from her bike. It was as if the music was a conduit between me and that moment.

I played on.

Rising up in my fingers, through my arms, and into my whole body was the warmth of her, molded against me in my bed after a nightmare, her feet tangled with mine, her perfumed hair against my chin.

By the time I had finished the first section of the piece, my heart was running and yelling through the streets of my body.

I was a few bars from the end when there was a sharp knock on the door. I stopped. "Come in," I called.

Very slowly, the door opened.

I expected it to be Melinda, or a music student who had overlooked my name written on the booking sheet pasted on the door. Instead, it was a small and very old man, hunched, dressed in a very shabby tweed suit with a yellowing shirt and muddy brown tie. I started to explain that I had permission to use this room until the hour was up, but then I stopped, realizing that something about him was intensely familiar. I struggled to place him. A deeply creased, gray face, his mouth jutting forward slightly. Bald, except for a thick, snow-white bunch of hair. He shuffled over the threshold.

"Can I help you?" I asked politely.

He stopped, straightened up slightly, and smiled. I jerked back. Even for a man of his years, he was distinctly repugnant.

"Your right hand is a little too staccato." His accent was impossible to place. "Didn't you heed the phrase marks?"

I turned to the piece of music in front of me. "Do you mean this?" I asked.

"I am the composer of the music you are playing." He bowed deeply. "I wished to introduce myself."

Stunned, I watched him as he turned slowly and closed the door behind him.

"*You* wrote this?" I said, when I could manage to speak.

"But of course I did," he replied, stepping forward. "Do you like it?"

I pushed back the piano stool and stood, bewildered.

"Who are you?" I demanded.

He was circling the piano now, arms folded behind his back, stopping occasionally to peer inside the instrument. I bent instinctively to pick up my briefcase. When I looked up he was inches from me, suddenly tall enough to meet my eyes. Only, his eyes had no irises. They were solid, cataractous, like gray marbles. I gasped and took a step backward.

"Anya," he said, watching me inch away. *"Anya."*

I could feel my heart pounding, my hands trembling. I glanced at the door.

"Would you like this piano?" he asked, grinning at me. "Or one like it?"

He was pacing around the piano once more, tracing the black wing with his twisted fingers. I stood perfectly still, my body cold, my mind struggling to work out what was happening.

"You said you wrote this piece?" I said, curiosity rising up in me despite the feeling of threat he had brought into the room.

"Yes. Aren't you going to play some more? I'd love to hear you play it."

"Someone else I know said he wrote it," I said. The man peered at the sheet of music and grinned.

"Do you know Alex?" I asked, watching him carefully as I edged toward the door.

He glanced up at the door. I swore I heard it lock.

"Just give me a moment of your time," he said serenely, sitting down in front of the piano. "I promise you won't regret it."

I could feel sweat prickling my back and under my arms, and I was telling myself to stay calm, to stop freaking out. He was at least eighty years old and if I could not defend myself against a man his age, then twenty years of circuit training had been a waste of time. But I felt myself being stripped, seduced somehow, and the light in the square little room seemed to have dimmed. Shadows were closing in on the corners, thickening.

I remembered my mobile phone. My fingers trembling, I pulled it from my pocket and began to dial. A second later, the screen went black. The battery had died.

"Alex says you're a *demon*," I said. The words sounded ridiculous in the heavy air. "Not a nice thing to call a family friend, is it? Why would he think you're a demon?"

He smiled.

"You go to university to become a demon?" I said, inching for the door.

In a flash, he was behind me, pressing against the door, his face twisted and menacing. I let out a sob. Something was very, very wrong. For a moment I believed I was having a psychotic meltdown, my hands shaking quite violently now, the floor beneath my feet turning to water.

"Are you all right?" I heard him say.

I felt myself curl up into a ball on the floor, toppled by a pain in my heart I'd felt only once before. This is what I'd felt the moment I saw Poppy at the window, and I lunged forward, but once again I am a half second too late, my hands empty, the momentum of my reach continuing in everything I do now—her absence a space of reaching.

And then, the pain stopped.

It felt as though someone had filled my body with sunlight. My eyes were still tightly shut, but the darkness retreated. I felt myself lift as if someone or something had scooped me up, then I felt weightless.

In my mind's eye, I no longer saw Poppy at the moment of her death. I saw her anxious, beautiful face right in front of me, her hands on my shoulders, shaking me. *It's okay, Mum. I'm here. I'm right here.* I wanted to open my eyes but didn't, for fear she would fade if I did so. Instead, I saw my own arms reach, cupping her face.

She turned her head slightly to kiss my hand.

"Mum, you haven't lost me. It's all really okay, you know?"

I pulled her to my chest in a tight embrace, my chest heaving with both relief and disbelief. Eventually she leaned back and looked at me. She seemed older, a teenager, her chestnut hair so long it draped around her face in Botticelli curls, her brown eyes calm and utterly without fear. Without darkness.

*Go back, now,* she said. *I love you.*


When I opened my eyes, Melinda was standing over me, slapping my face and shouting my name. I felt myself take an enormous, greedy breath, as if I'd just surfaced from the depths of the ocean. My legs and hands were numb and my brain fizzed like a bad hangover. I caught a strong whiff of Melinda's heavy patchouli perfume and landed back on earth with a sharp thud. The look on her face melted from horror to sheer relief when I struggled upright.

"Oh man—sweetie, I thought you were dead!" she cried.

I shook my head to confirm that, despite how I may have looked, I was pretty much alive. My body was tingling now, as if I'd just emerged from a warm bath or a day in the sun. "I saw her," I told Melinda. "I saw Poppy."

She threw me an odd look. I reached a trembling hand to my mouth.

"It's *freezing* in here!" she exclaimed. "Did you open a window or something?"

I shook my head, though the concern in her voice made me smile. It reassured me that I was safe. She laughed nervously.

"You'll never guess what," she said as I rose to my feet, leaning on the edge of the piano for balance.

"What?"

She folded her arms and grinned widely. "That music you showed me. It's *one hundred percent genuine.*"

I nodded in acknowledgment, glancing distractedly around the room.

"That kid is a genius," she continued. "A total child prodigy!"

I looked at the piano, then searched under it, around the floor.

"What's wrong?" Melinda said, frowning.

"It's gone," I told her. "The music has gone."

## 23
# THE THINGS
# THAT ARE REAL

ALEX

Dear Diary,

What did Pope Julius II say to Michelangelo? "Sure, come on down, son, we'll paper it."

I woke up really early today because today was a Saturday and I was going to see Mum at ten o'clock. It felt like Christmas morning. I set my alarm for seven so that I'd have time to get a shower before the others woke up and brush my teeth and clean out my ears and cut my nails. I was also afraid in case the laundry people forgot to wash my clothes so I made sure I'd have extra time to wash and dry them myself, but it was okay because when I checked my closet my shirt and trousers and waistcoat were all there, really clean and nicely ironed.

I woke before my alarm, so took a long, long time in the shower. I spent about an hour polishing my shoes and then I sat with a black marker coloring in all the scuff marks so they'd look extra clean. By this time it was only eight o'clock. So I rearranged all the photographs and drawings of our new house that I'd stuck to walls and spent a while imagining Mum and I living there, cooking together in the kitchen, sitting in the garden when it got sunny, hanging pictures of lilies and dolphins on the walls.

Then I drew Mum a picture and wrote a nice message inside. It said, "Mum, I hope you feel better soon because I love you, and if you felt as good as much as I love you, you would feel really good."

Mum was waiting for me in the living room that she shares with the other people in her ward. She was dressed in a pair of new jeans and a blue T-shirt. She had some makeup on, too, a pale pink on her eyelids and cheeks and her eyelashes were black. I was so glad to see her that I almost cried, and I felt she could see that I was upset and she almost cried, too, and hugged me really, really hard.

When she let go of me I sat across from her and smiled.

"How do you like this new school?" she said, though she said it like she wasn't glad I was going to a new school.

"It's okay," I said. "It's only temporary, right?"

She nodded. "What's this you've brought?"

I was holding my sketch pad. "I've been doing lots of new drawings," I told her. "Anya said it's good for my recovery. Shall I show you?"

Mum gave a frozen kind of smile and nodded her head.

I'd make myself stop doing any more pictures of skeletons as they seemed to upset people, so I had drawn things like the flowers growing outside my bedroom window and a scene from my classroom and a portrait of Woof. When Mum saw the picture of Woof her smile dropped clean off her face. She touched the picture for a long time and held her hand up to her mouth.

"What's wrong?" I said, worried, because she looked like she was going to cry.

She took a deep shaky breath and then held one of my hands in both of hers so tight it hurt. "Alex," she said. "I'm really sorry, but Woof has had to be moved to a new home, too."

"What do you mean?" I said.

I didn't hear all the words she said because my heart was banging so loudly, it sounded like it was in my ears, but basically it sounded something like Woof had been put in a home for dogs when Auntie Bev had gone back to Cork for a few days because there was no one at home to feed or walk him so he could pee and Auntie Bev couldn't take him with her. When Mum said a home for dogs, I knew she meant the pound. I thought of Woof being locked up there with all the other barking, miserable dogs, doing circles in a cage the size of our toilet and wondering what he'd done wrong to end up in there.

I must have been panting because all of a sudden Mum put her arms around me and said, "Oh, Alex. I'm so sorry, this is all my fault!"

"Can't we get him back?"

Mum hugged me tight and when she looked at me again her makeup was running down her face in wet black lines. "Maybe," she said. "I won't make promises to you anymore that I can't guarantee. So it's a maybe. If he's still there."

I wanted to ask whether she thought the people at the pound might put Woof down, because last time we were there I overheard someone say that they had to do that all the time because they had too many dogs. But I was scared of upsetting Mum even more.

"This is my fault," Mum said again. "If I hadn't gotten myself in here we'd all still be at home."

At last I remembered my manners and pulled my handkerchief out of my pocket. I handed it to Mum and she smiled and dabbed her face.

"When *are* you coming home?" I asked.

Mum looked away. "I don't know."

I thought for a moment about what I could do or say to make Mum happy. Right away I thought of Ruen saving my dad, but I didn't want to tell her the part about Hell because she'd definitely, definitely think I was loony.

So I said: "I know you miss my dad, Mum, and I know you've been very sad since he died. But I think that maybe someday we'll be able to see him again. You know, in Heaven."

Mum lowered my handkerchief from her face very slowly. She looked angry. *Oh no,* I thought. *I have made everything much, much worse.*

"Alex, what do you mean, *died?*" she said. Her face was very twisted now.

"I mean, when he died that morning that I found you in bed with all the pills, and Granny phoned the ambulance and . . ."

I stopped talking 'cos she was staring at me as if I'd gone nuts. Her mouth was opening and her forehead had a line into it that started to turn into a letter V.

"Mum," I said after a few moments. "I'm sorry, I suppose I shouldn't talk about it."

Then she lowered her hands and gave a sigh that was so big her shoulders stooped.

"I'm so sorry," she said, which was her twenty-ninth apology since I arrived. "I thought you understood, Alex." She looked out the window again and the sun lit up her face and for a moment she looked young again. "Granny always said I treated you older than you were, that I expected too much of you. I suppose it was because you always *seemed* so much older. Did you know you were walking at ten months old?"

My stomach was starting to turn into a knot.

She was still talking as if someone else was in the room. ". . . the visiting nurse said it was remarkable, said she'd never heard of a nineteen-month-old talk like that. Like a three- or four-year-old, she said, especially since boys are so much behind girls, usually." Her eyes smiled. "You made me so proud, Alex. I felt so scared when you were born. Didn't know how I'd feed you, look after you. Didn't know how I'd manage. Didn't know how I'd give you what you needed. But you surprised us all."

"Do you mean Dad *isn't* dead?" I said.

"You already know this, Alex. He's at Magilligan Prison, remember? I tried to take you to visit him but you said you didn't want to . . ."

I fell back as if she had just punched me in the face.

"Alex?" she said, leaning forward with her arms held out. I felt my head turn from side to side on my shoulders, as if someone was turning it for me.

"It's okay," she was saying, but then her mouth was opening and closing and I couldn't hear anything because my heart was beating so hard and it was as if I had forgotten how to speak because I couldn't get my feelings to come out as words. "He . . . but . . ." Then: "Where's Magilligan?"

"It's about seventy miles from here. Just past the Giant's Causeway." My mouth was full of spit. Mum sighed and rubbed her head.

"I want to tell you something, Alex." I got up and sat beside her but I felt like I was floating.

"You didn't deserve any of this," she said. "For a long, long time I've thought . . . well, that you didn't deserve me. That you deserve a much better mother than me. And I thought that it was because of me that my foster parents abused me. That I deserved it all."

I nodded, even though I still wasn't really sure what she was talking about. Didn't "foster parents" mean people who weren't your parents?

"But it takes time to feel good about yourself after feeling worthless your whole life."

For some reason I started thinking of LEGO.

"What do you mean by foster parents?"

Mum frowned. "See, that's the thing, Alex. I haven't been truthful with either you or me. Granny wasn't my real mum, you see. She adopted me when I was about your age."


I'm not sure what happened after Mum told me that. It was as if a huge glass tube suddenly came down from the ceiling and trapped me inside it, the way people put upside-down jars over spiders and they can't get out, and all I could hear inside the tube was my own heart racing and my own thoughts. Which were:

*Granny wasn't my Granny?*

*Auntie Bev isn't my real Auntie?*

*Dad didn't die?*

*Then who did Ruen get out of Hell?*

But I must've been making all the right noises because Mum kept talking. I think she was discussing the new house with me and all her plans for decorating when she got out of the hospital, because she kept saying things like "red paint, or maybe Tuscan orange" and "lots of fancy lamps." And while she was saying all this, a thought clanked through my head like a midnight express train:

Ruen is lying.

*Ruen is lying.*

He didn't get my dad out of Hell.

There was no cavernous building or dragons in the sky.

And what was it he'd said? My dad wanted me to *pay the debt*?

In other words, Ruen felt he could tell me a big fat fib and get some payback while he was at it.

Mum was talking mostly to herself now, going on and on about how she always wanted carpet on the stairs. She was wiping tears from her eyes but smiling at the same time.

"Maybe we can make a fresh start," she said.

I took her hand.

"Mum, I love you," I said. "But there's something I have to do."

And I left, right when she was deciding between pink and peach tiles for the bathroom.


When I left Mum I got taken back to MacNeice House. As soon as we walked through the red front door there was a big smashing sound and a lady wearing a hair net and an apron made me walk really slowly up the corridor in case I stood on any glass. "Butterfingers today," she said, holding up her fingers like she was surprised she had them on the ends of her hands. There was about eleven broken jugs all over the place and a big puddle of water. When I looked down in one of them I saw Ruen's face smiling back, but he was nowhere to be seen. He knew I was angry with him.

Miss Falls was waiting for me outside my bedroom. I walked up to her.

"I want to go swimming," I told her.

Miss Falls looked at me very seriously and I noticed her eyes and mouth were exactly like Michael's. I started to tell her that but then I thought she would only ask who Michael was so I shut up. "Alex," she said. "I'd like to talk to you about something really important."

"Right now?"

She nodded.

"I'm sorry, I can't," I said, but I didn't say why.

I didn't say that I needed to have a chat with a nine-thousand-year-old demon who fibbed about busting his way into Hell and helping my father escape just so he could hold one over me. And that I needed somewhere quiet and private to do it, because if I started shouting in my bedroom they'd come in with restraints and more white pills.

"I need to work on my butterfly crawl," I said, and I made a big show of looking at the sign for the swimming pool behind her.

Miss Falls crouched down next to me and I thought of used books with their yellow pages.

"You know, Alex," she said. "You can tell me anything. That's the beauty about having a personal tutor. Nothing you tell me can ever get you into trouble, understand?"

I nodded. I didn't understand, but when she told me this I felt the knot in my stomach turn to butter and a feeling of warmth flooded over me.

I opened my mouth. She nodded, encouraging me to speak. I wanted to tell her about Ruen. I wanted to ask her advice. So I said:

"Miss Falls, what would you do if someone you really, really trusted told you a really horrible lie?"

She smiled, and her eyes told me she knew why I was asking what I was asking, and I wondered if someone had lied to her once, the way I'd been lied to. She bent down close to me and said: "I would tell them I never want to see them again. Even if I loved them very much, I would never ever trust them again."

I nodded and she took my hand, only her hand felt like warm air. "Do you need my help, Alex?"

"Yes," I said, but then I shook my head because I didn't know how she could possibly help me with this one.

"If you ever need my help in the future, all you have to do is ask," she said.

"Thank you," I said, and I started to ask her something else but when I looked again she was gone.

I did a lot of laps up and down the pool, thumping my body into the ripples with each stroke, imagining I was fighting with Ruen. Occasionally I'd take a rest at the end of a lap, clinging to the side of the pool and muttering under my breath for Ruen to show his horrible stony face. But he didn't show.

Finally, I dragged myself out and went into the sauna. All the other boys were off playing football and the lifeguard was at the side of the pool, so I had the whole place to myself. I went in, lay down on a bench, and imagined pure hatred oozing out of my pores.

A cough. I opened my eyes. On the other side of the room I could make out an old man through the steam. He was mean-looking and he had a piranha-fish smile and was wearing a suit that was threading at one side. And the thread snaked its way through the mist and ended at the hem of my towel.

"You called?" Ruen said.

"You're a liar," I said.

"Oh?" He didn't seem bothered by the accusation, so I said:

"You told me that you got my dad out of Hell, and you didn't."

"And how did you come to that conclusion?"

I was standing now, pointing down at him as he sat on the bench opposite. "Mum told me my dad is alive and well in Magilligan Prison. So I don't know who you dragged out of Hell, Ruen. In fact I don't think you dragged anyone out. I think you made the whole thing up. And I think I don't owe you a thing."

He stood up and looked at me very crossly. For a moment I thought he was going to change shape and become a monster just to make me feel scared. But he just glanced at a spot in the corner. When I looked, I saw another demon sitting there, unfolding behind the mist. He was dressed in a tweed suit like Ruen's but it looked new and he seemed younger and timid. He seemed to be writing stuff down in a leather notebook.

"Who's that?" I said.

The demon started to introduce himself but Ruen cut him off. "That's Braze," he said. "He's an intern. Ignore him."

I picked up my towel and turned to leave. Just as I reached the door, Ruen said:

"Your mother lied, Alex."

I clenched my fists, gritted my teeth, and turned around slowly. *"What did you say?"*

"Your mother lied," Ruen said calmly.

"Just *who* do you think you . . ."

He held up a hand. "Please," he said. I was shaking with anger and my mouth felt tight as if I was really cold. He swept his hand from me to the bench, gesturing at me to sit down.

"You've got ten seconds to explain." I didn't sit down.

Ruen sighed. "The man I saved was your *real* father. The man in Magilligan Prison is not. Nobody knows your father isn't your real father, not even your father. Not even your grandmother."

All of a sudden I remembered what Mum had said about Granny: *she's not your real Granny.* The memory and truth of it hit me so hard I had to blink back tears.

"Why would Mum lie about who my dad is, huh?" I yelled. "How *dare* you call my Mum a liar . . ."

"I didn't," Ruen said. "I said she *lied*. There's a difference, dear boy. Your mother lied to protect you. Your mother lied because she loves you, and she knows all too well how much a revelation like this would hurt you. I only tell you now because you force me to."

He glanced over at the other demon, who was still writing.

I couldn't stop the tears now, nor could I stop my heart from racing or my whole body pouring with sweat, dripping down my face and arms and fingertips. A sob wormed its way out of me, and then hot tears.

Eventually, Ruen approached me. I held my face in my hands and refused to look at him. He patted my shoulder.

"It's okay," he said. "You weren't to know." Then he turned and sniffed. "You can make it up to me."

# 24
# THE NEWSPAPERS

## ANYA

I wake with a shout. A glance at the clock beside my bed bewilders me. What day is this? A quick calculation proves that I have been asleep for fifteen hours. Impossible.

I roll upright and look out the window. Brilliant sunshine lights up the small park beneath my apartment building, cars thread along the motorway to Dublin, small and bright as candy. The River Lagan flicks to my right in the distance like a silver scarf, and the city sits in the distance, a cluster of bridges and boats, mint-green domes of old buildings and shining new skyscrapers.

On mornings like this, Belfast reminds me of an old fable I once heard of identical twin sisters, separated at birth. After many years the two women were reunited, one haggard and hunched from years of service, her face dull and drawn, her eyes empty. The other sister turned heads wherever she went, her eyes shining, smile bright, her posture straight and upright. The beautiful sister made the haggard sister realize how she, too, could look, and so she became beautiful for the first time in her life. There are many times when Belfast is that haggard, weathered sister, but there are rare and wonderful days when you can catch a glimpse of the sibling's beauty.

The events of yesterday hit me like an icy shower. The sensation of passing out, falling to the floor. Poppy. The ugly old man in the music room.

The missing piece of music.

I blitz slices of apple, kiwi, and pineapple in my new blender and drink it while checking my phone for missed calls. The same unknown caller with the unfamiliar number is there. I call it.

After five rings, someone answers.

"Anya, *hi*. It's Karen, Karen Holland."

*Karen*, I think with a groan. I had forgotten to chase up our last conversation by searching microfilms of old newspaper headlines.

"Sorry, Karen," I say, my voice still husky from too long in bed. "I haven't found anything yet. Alex is at MacNeice House—"

"*I've* found something," she interrupts. "I think it's important. Do you have time to talk?"

I glance at my watch. "I've a meeting in twenty minutes. Can I see you later this afternoon?"

"Perfect."

After I hang up, yesterday's events continue to rain down on me, stark and unnerving.

For even after a solid fifteen hours' sleep, I know I saw Poppy; I know I felt her hands on my face, I heard her voice, I smelled her hair, her breath. But I have no idea how to explain it. Nor do I understand the encounter with the old man, Ruen. His face, rock-like, ancient, and those terrible empty eyes, all still burn in my brain with a force I can't quench.

After I regained consciousness, I had told Melinda about Ruen's visit to the practice room. She checked the visitors' register at reception, then CCTV footage, even contacted campus security. When she couldn't find any trace of him, we reported him to the police.

"Ruen?" the police officer had asked as I sat in Melinda's office nursing another coffee. She was skeptical. "As in *R-U-E-N*?"

"That's the only name he gave."

"And about how old?"

"Somewhere between mid-seventies and early eighties," I said.

"Did he have a knife?"

I sighed. It sounded ridiculous. I didn't mention anything of our conversation, nor how I felt. I thought of kidnap victims who discovered they had been taken hostage not at gunpoint, but by the barrel of a Magic Marker pressed against their neck. Sometimes the imagination is the true predator.

Melinda asked to speak to me for a moment and the police officer stepped aside.

"This guy," Melinda said to me. "Did he *really* give his name?"

"Yes," I said with conviction, then doubt crept in. Perhaps he hadn't said he was Ruen. Perhaps he hadn't said his name at all.

"Are you sure?" she insisted. "It's just that, from your descriptions it sounds like he could be one of the visiting professors."

"He knew my name," I interjected. "He called me Anya."

"Your name would have been on the booking sheet on the front of the door, wouldn't it?" Melinda pointed out. "The school's VPs sometimes just turn up. Some of them are very, very old. There's this one man who sounds very similar . . ."

"Do you have a picture of him?"

She nodded at the computer on her desk and we both walked around the other side to face the screen. Melinda gave the mouse a wave to close the screensaver, then typed a name into the search bar. Seconds later, the school's banner appeared in a Web browser, followed by a list of staff. Melinda scrolled down to a section marked VISITING PROFESSORS and clicked on a small thumbnail.

"Here," she said. The page reloaded. Staring back at me from the screen was a bald man, smiling, his pale eyes shielded by thick black glasses. His mouth was tombstone-shaped, his top gum broader than his small yellow teeth. He was wearing a bow tie and a tweed jacket. I leaned forward to the screen, my heart hammering.

"This is Professor Franz Amsel," Melinda told me. "He gave a paper at the School of Music a couple of nights ago. Do you think it might have been him?"

I study the wide smile and the thick glasses. The man I had seen looked older than this, I told Melinda. She shook her head dubiously.

"Most of these guys send us photos that are older than *me*," she said ruefully. "I know Professor Amsel is in his seventies, at least. Let me contact him, find out if he was here today."

I swallowed, then nodded in agreement. The police officer tapped her foot at the other end of the room. Melinda lifted the phone and dialed a number, tucking a strand of hair behind her ear.

"Hi, Professor? This is Melinda Kyle here at the School of Music at Queen's University. Yeah, hi there. I was just wondering if you visited one of our practice rooms this morning, we're in a little pickle with security for not keeping our guest register up to date. Uh-huh." She nodded deeply. "You *were* here." I felt my heart sink. She looked deeply relieved. "Oh, thank heavens. No, nothing. That's okay, Professor, I'll tell her. Thank *you*." She set down the phone and rolled her eyes. "He extends his deepest apologies and hopes he didn't upset you."

Melinda threw me a smile, then went to the police officer, explaining in a smooth, affable voice that we'd had a little misunderstanding. I sat numbly on the chair behind her desk, looking at the image of the professor on the screen. There was no denying the similarity. I felt utterly, ridiculously *stupid*. How could I have let myself stray so far from reason? How could I have believed that the man was . . . The thought of it was crazy now, and I felt furious with myself. Deep inside, I felt harrowed with fear at the workings of my own brain. If I couldn't keep it together, what future did I have as a child psychiatrist? How could I ever hope to rebuild the lives of others by helping them piece together their sense of what's real and what is not if I didn't know the difference myself?

My phone rings as I leave Karen Holland's classroom later, having spoken with Karen for almost an hour. What she has showed me there makes me want to run back to MacNeice House and speak to Alex immediately. I have already tried contacting Cindy's therapist, Trudy Messenger, without success. So when the phone rings I assume it is her.

"Trudy, I need to tell you something about Alex's father—"

A cough on the other end of the line. "It's Ursula."

"Oh. Is something wrong?"

"I need to speak to you immediately, Anya. Are you on your way back now?"

"Can I ask what this is about?" I say. "I have some calls to make—"

"I'll speak to you when you get here," she cuts in stiffly, and hangs up.

At MacNeice House I meet Ursula in the foyer and sign into the register. "You want to talk in your office?" I say, taking off my jacket.

She smiles. "Why don't we talk in yours?"

Inside my office I move the last of the boxes of books from the coffee table and invite her to sit down. I see her glancing over my posters and the dog-eared, incomprehensible paintings given to me by some patients as thank-yous for their treatment—a gift much more meaningful than any other.

"How have you settled back into Northern Ireland?" Ursula asks, clasping her hands in her lap.

I pour us both a cup of water and sit down opposite her, catching my breath. I am still wearing my jogging shoes.

"I'm actually settling back home far easier than I would have imagined," I tell her, brightly. "You never know, I might even stay."

It is a light joke, offered to break the tension. She presses her lips together.

"I heard about what happened yesterday. At the university."

I hold her gaze, feeling my heart sink. My excitement at the progress made in Alex's assessment withers. "Yes," I respond. "I'm afraid I haven't felt myself lately."

I explain to her about my unfurnished flat, how I still hadn't properly unpacked. About my patients. About my progress with Xavier's case, the effectiveness of art therapy on our newest inpatient, Ella. About my insomnia. About Alex's situation.

"Alex," she says on a sigh, as if his name is a byword.

"Yes. In fact," I tell her, "I've just had a meeting with one of Alex's old schoolteachers. I think I've just made a huge breakthrough in his treatment."

"I'm sure you have," she says dismissively, glancing at her nails. "But I'm afraid I have severe concerns about your ability to proceed here, Anya. Let's not forget about the episode yesterday." She lifts her eyes and I see disappointment there. And also—something that startles me—worry. "I'd like you to take a small period of sick leave."

"Sick leave?"

"You must understand that your episode, or whatever it was was . . . well, it was troubling, frankly. Both in terms of the future of our practice and in terms of your own personal health. Any time the police become involved it raises the level of seriousness, and with the kinds of funding bids MacNeice House is making and with the recent interest from the health minister, we don't want it to look as if—forgive me—the lunatics are running the asylum."

I am stunned. I try to respond to her, but no words come. Instead, my mind turns to what I had seen in Karen Holland's classroom less than an hour before—a photocopy of a newspaper from December 2001, bearing the headline RUINED PEOPLE'S LIVES. Beneath it was a large photograph of a shooting in progress: a masked man pointing a gun at a policeman. "Read it," Karen had told me.

> Yesterday afternoon two policemen lost their lives in what the deputy first minister described as a "monstrous act of hate targeted at the newly formed PSNI" at a checkpoint outside Armagh. Sergeant Martin Kerr, 29, the father of a two-week-old girl, was killed by a single shot to the forehead at close range. Sergeant Eamonn Douglas, 47, died from his injuries last night at the Armagh County Hospital. Two men—Alex Murphy, 30, from north Belfast, and Michael Matthews, 69, from County Kerry—were charged this morning with first-degree murder.

I had lowered the newspaper and looked at Karen. "It's the same headline as Alex's painting," she told me.

I frowned. "This is terrible. But why would Alex be so disturbed by this particular story?"

She opened a laptop on her desk and clicked on an Internet icon. "I found this on YouTube," she said, opening a new page. I watched as the screen filled with rain-smeared footage of a calm street in Belfast. A church was visible on the right side of the road, a post office on the other. The screen blurred as several women walked past pushing prams, their chatter audible but muffled through glass. Two policemen were on the road, stopping traffic and chatting to the drivers, before letting them pass on. For a moment it seemed as if nothing was out of the ordinary—it was just another checkpoint, like so many I had witnessed in Belfast. A small figure in a red school sweater was visible behind the metal fencing of the church, and a little girl in a white dress stood in the doorway of the post office.

Then, a blue car rolled up toward the checkpoint. Only one of the policemen stepped out. The other stood at the side of the road and folded his arms. I watched, my throat growing dry, as a masked man jumped out of the passenger side of the car. He pulled out a gun, pointing it at the policeman in front of him. For a moment he seemed to hesitate. Then the screen blurred as people ran past the camera, positioned, I suspected, in the back of the police van. A gunshot resounded, cracking the windscreen of the blue car. The masked man hesitated, then lifted his gun. Seconds later, there was the sound of a second gunshot, and the first policeman on the road crumpled. Another crack. The policeman by the roadside flung his arms out and fell. The gunman paused and turned his head to the boy by the church, and I gasped, afraid that the boy would be his next victim. But the gunman lowered his weapon, taking a step backward. The driver of the car signaled him, and he got into the car, which sped off.

The footage had cut from there to a mugshot of the killer, a surly-looking man in his late twenties with startling blue eyes. His name flashed beneath the photograph in white letters: ALEX MURPHY. I leaned closer.

The footage cut again, this time to a journalist holding an umbrella with one hand and a microphone with the other. *"It seems a dissident faction of the IRA was involved in what happened in this very spot just yesterday afternoon, when a masked terrorist opened fire on two policemen, supposedly in anticipation of their finding a heavy arsenal transported illegally from the southern border . . ."*

I tapped the space bar on the keyboard, freezing the film. I needed a moment to take in what I had seen. To understand its meaning. Karen walked across the room to close a window that was beginning to let in the din of the school run. I fumbled with the YouTube controls, anxious to rewind the footage. There was something about the young boy at the doorway of the post office, something familiar.

"Can we zoom in on this?" I asked Karen. She pressed something on the screen, enlarging the image. The picture was pixelated, but I was certain I knew that young, terrified face.

"I recalled something after our last meeting," Karen said. "Alex said that his mother told him that he was similar to his father. That he had his Dad *in* him. What do you make of that?"

I hit the space bar again, starting the footage from the beginning. Alex learning of his father's crime was one thing, but witnessing it . . .

The blurred footage refused to give up the boy's face. I turned to Karen.

"I think Alex knows his father was a murderer."


". . . just a couple of months," Ursula is saying, and suddenly I am snapped back into my office at MacNeice House, listening to her make arrangements for my replacement while I "recuperate."

"Ursula," I interrupt, keeping my voice and my gaze firm. "I found out something this afternoon about Alex's childhood that affects *everything* about this case."

She narrows her eyes. "Anya, Alex is—"

I raise my voice. "I've found out something about his past that puts everything about his condition in a completely new light. I urgently need to speak to him and to his mother."

"I'm sorry, Anya. But it's important that we remain vigilant as to the health of our staff as well as our patients. I'll email you the relevant forms for occupational health." She stands. "I'll initiate your period of sick leave with immediate effect." Then, with a tilt of her head: "Much better than an enforced absence. Or being fired."

I close my mouth. She eyes me coolly. "I'm sorry that it should come to this," she says, before walking to the door and closing it behind her.

ALEX

Dear Diary,

Our new house is gone. Gone gone gone gone gone gone gone gone.

Michael just came to MacNeice House to tell me. He said he was very sorry and swore a little and said his so-called friend quit his job so the new person saw that we hadn't moved in yet and moved me and Mum down "the list," as it wasn't really fair that some people were waiting for a house while we were in the hospital. I just nodded as he walked up and down my room with his hands making fists, and then as soon as he'd finished I ran to the bathroom and threw up all my lunch.

Michael said he'd try really really hard to make sure we get a house just like it. "But I liked *that* house," I told him. He took a big breath and bent his knees so our faces were at the same level and his knees made a big crack.

"I *know* you loved that house, Alex," he said. "It's just the council decided . . ." He made a fist and pressed it into his mouth and I wondered if he was actually going to bite himself. "There are loads of new houses being built at the minute in Belfast. Lots of beautiful houses just like this one." Then he leaned forward and I could see his green eyes and I felt a bit better because they told me I could trust him. "I promise you, Alex," he said. "I will make sure you get moved to a better place."

"But Mum liked that house," I said, and I knew Michael already knew this but it was much more important than whether I liked it or not. I felt for a moment like I could hardly breathe and I was scared because I knew Mum would be upset. Michael stood up and said something else but I didn't hear because I was thinking of Mum sitting in the swing next to me at the park. It was a long time ago and both of us were swinging ourselves higher and higher. It didn't matter to me if I could swing higher, it just mattered that I could hear her laughing.

When Michael left I walked out of my room and walked along the long white corridor. The other boys and girls staying here were all out of their bedrooms as it was lunchtime so they were in the cafeteria. It was a Thursday, which meant they were having a Sunday dinner with extra onions and toast. I didn't even care. My stomach was gurgly and I puked and then I locked the toilet door and sat against it.

Before I even saw Ruen I saw the dark thread of shadow on the ground, which made me jump for a second because I thought it was a snake. I saw it slide across the white tiles of the floor and then it seemed to float up and snag on my sweater.

"Where are you?" I said, because even though I couldn't see him yet I knew he was somewhere.

Ruen appeared beside the trash can as Ghost Boy. He was looking at me funny as if he wondered how I knew he was there. He had his table-tennis paddle and white ball in his hands, but instead of bouncing them he just folded his arms and scowled at me.

"Where's Braze?" I asked, because last time I'd seen him there was this other demon there, too, the one Ruen said was an intern.

"Shut up," he said, and he lifted his leg and shoved me in the stomach with his foot and I fell back onto the ground.

"What are you doing?" I shouted, and quickly he leaned forward and pushed his face into mine and said: "if you don't sit still I'll make your heart stop beating, and you'll die."

So I stopped moving and sat still as a stone on the floor.

"Good," he said, smiling. I held my breath because I wanted to pant and my heart was pounding. I hated that Ruen looked so like me just then because he was so mean and I didn't even know why.

"I'm going to show you something," he said, looking down at me. I felt scared but not of Ruen. I felt scared because the dark shadow that connected my sweater to Ruen was thicker than normal and moving the way a snake moves.

"Okay," I said to Ruen. "Then can you go away, please."

He bent down and his face looked like he was sorry for me.

"I want you to know that what I show you now is not a projection of your mind," he said, and his voice was different, like a man's. "You are not having a psychotic episode, Alex. All of this is very real, so pay attention."

I nodded and looked away from the shadow beside me, then crossed my arms across my body and pinched the undersides of my arms so I knew that I was still there and that everything was happening, because lately I hadn't been so sure. I feel so dizzy when I take the pills, especially on an empty stomach, that sometimes it feels like I'm on a ship and then sometimes I actually convince myself that I *am* on a ship and that we're floating out to sea, that my bedroom curtains are icebergs and the fields outside are the polar icecaps and the sky is really the Arctic Ocean.

"Close your eyes, Alex," Ruen whispered.

I shook my head. I was scared of the shadow.

"Don't you trust me?" he said.

"Not anymore," I said without thinking, and our faces fell at exactly the same time because we both realized it was true. Ruen frowned at me.

"Do you want your mum to live?" he said in a cruel voice.

I gasped and squeezed my eyes tight. "Look," I heard Ruen say, and right away there was this big cinema screen in my head filled with an image of Mum. It was clearer than a Wakeful Dream or a memory. It was even clearer than a film at the cinema because it was like I was right there in front of her when I closed my eyes. I could see her sitting in the common room in a red chair at the adult unit and she was watching TV.

She was wearing a long white T-shirt and her hair was tied back and her face looked blank. She kept changing position in her chair like she couldn't get comfortable.

"Is this real?" I asked Ruen, opening my eyes.

"Of course it is," he said, and I closed my eyes again and kept watching.

Mum turned to the lady in the chair next to her and said *do you have any smokes?* The lady looked at her as if she was stupid and shook her head. Mum said *thanks* in a voice that sounded annoyed and she left the room.

Then the image changed to Mum walking into her bedroom at the hospital. She looked upset and her hands were flapping and she walked up and down, talking to herself. She was saying things like, "said I was no good, he was right" and then she lay down on the bed. At first I thought she was going to sleep, and then I noticed she was reaching under her mattress for something.

I opened my eyes. "What's she doing?" I asked Ruen.

"You'll see," he said.

Part of me wanted to run out of here all the way to Mum and the other part needed to stay and see what happened.

But I already knew what was going to happen.

Mum reached her hand underneath the mattress and slowly pulled out a fat book. When she opened it I could see she had ripped out holes in the pages and hidden round white pills inside, lots of them. She sat with the book on her lap for a moment and she looked at the door, which was open, and then back at the book, and I shouted "Mum, don't!" because I knew exactly what she was thinking. I opened my eyes but the image was gone and all I could see was the orange toilet door with black scribbles on it and a rusting handle. So I closed my eyes again and instantly I saw Mum again, but this time there were no round white pills in the book and she was drinking a glass of water and crying. She rubbed her face and gave a big sigh.

"I love you, Alex. You'll be so much happier without me."

I yelled and yelled and then I opened my eyes and scrambled to my feet and I felt my fingers fumble with the lock on the toilet door and then I raced out into the corridor, though I couldn't move fast enough.

I needed to get to her, I needed to get to her. Every time now I'd been able to stop her, but this time might be too late. I started to run but it felt like my legs wouldn't move fast enough, like they were made of LEGO bricks and I had to drag them after me.

I was outside the toilets now and in the long white corridor with the long white lights in the ceiling like lightsabers. There was nobody around, not a single person. "Help!" I shouted, but my voice sounded so small. Suddenly the lights flickered off and it became very dark. It was raining outside but the rain against the glass sounded like a hiss and I felt so, so scared. There was no one to help me. I closed my eyes and I saw Mum asleep in her red chair. I started to cry.

When I opened my eyes again I saw a dark shadow at the very end of the corridor. It started off like a big black balloon hanging in the air, and then it grew and grew until it sank and splatted like a puddle of black oil that spread across the floor. I couldn't move. I was just standing there frozen to the spot. Even if the building had exploded I probably would have just stood there. All I could think about was Mum. I watched the puddle as it spread to both sides of the wall and then it started to creep up the wall and I knew what it was.

The black liquid crept up both sides and then they both floated into midair and joined and spread down to the floor to form a person. It was Ruen as Monster. He was almost as tall as the ceiling and as wide as the corridor and his eyes were tiny and yellow, his skin was a cross between black and purple. He had no ears or nose or hair and his mouth was big and full of sharp yellow teeth.

Then I heard his voice in my head, and it was soft and kind and gentle.

"Alex," he said. "Your mother is very, very ill. What will you do to help her?"

I turned and tried to run away toward the other end of the hall, but my legs wouldn't work. I made it about four doors along, but Ruen was there again, right in front of me. This time he was the Old Man, and his arms were tucked behind his back and I could see the black thread hanging from his jacket and snaking up the floor.

"Alex," he said, "Your mother is going to die." He said it like I was making it happen, like it was my fault.

I started to cry. "Help me, someone!" I shouted.

Ruen reached out to me. "*I'm* here, *I'm* helping you," he said, but I just wanted to run. I felt trapped. I turned to run again but this time I tripped and fell down with my hands outstretched and I hit my head on the floor. I wanted to get up but I didn't have the strength. I put my cheek on the ground and it was cold and I felt numb.

Then I felt Ruen stand over me.

"There is still time, Alex, but you must act quickly. Get up, get up."

I rolled over onto my back and looked up at him. "You're a demon," I told him. "Demons really do hurt people, not help people."

Ruen grinned. "It appears I'm the only one helping you right now, isn't that so?"

I looked at the ceiling. I could see the light flickering, trying to work. I wondered if there were angels up there.

"Help me," I whispered.

"I *am* helping you," Ruen said, walking around me with his arms behind his back. "Your mother will live. You just need to do one thing, Alex. Do you think you can do just one thing?"

I felt tears sliding down the sides of my face into my ears. I pressed both hands on my chest and felt myself taking breaths, in and out, and I wished I could give these breaths to my mum. There was nothing else, nothing nothing nothing that I wanted more than to stop her from dying.

Ruen bent down right beside me, so close I could smell him. It usually made me gag but it didn't then. He pressed something cold and sharp into my hand.

"Do you remember swapping cards with the other boys in the old school, Alex?"

I heard myself say yes.

"This is just like swapping cards. For your mother to live, you need to send someone else in her place."

I closed my eyes. I knew what he wanted. It was what Ruen had always wanted and even though he hadn't said so I knew it because I knew Ruen.

"Don't you want your mother to live, Alex?"

I rolled up slowly to a sitting position and looked down at what he had put into my hand. At first it looked like a knife made out of glass. I brought it close to my face and saw that it was a broken handle of a glass water jug. The end of it was so sharp that when I tapped it lightly with my finger a small red line of blood appeared above my nail a few seconds later. Ruen looked at me as I held the weapon and gave a big smile.

"I can't do it," I whispered, but then a new image of Mum flashed in my head, even though I had my eyes open. I saw her hand on the side of the chair, and even though she was asleep I saw her hand fall and I knew she was dying.

I looked up at Ruen. My mouth and eyes were sore and I felt like I was falling. I thought of my dad, my *real* dad, and what he said to Ruen: *my son will pay my debt*. And I thought of Mum, swinging beside me, going higher and higher and higher. She was laughing. When she laughed I felt like my heart would take off. I wanted to hear her laugh again.

Eventually I sat up and whispered:

"Who do you want me to kill?"

## 26
## THE CALL

## ANYA

Trudy Messenger phones me as I am at my flat, both hands filled with clothes and books that I didn't quite know whether to put back into their boxes or into the cupboards. I hear my phone ring and expect it to be Michael. Trudy sounds both angry and relieved at the same time.

"Anya? I've been in touch with the secretaries at MacNeice House, they said you would be gone for some time . . ."

I take a breath, my heart still heavy. "What can I help you with, Trudy?"

Her voice softens. "It's Alex's mother, Cindy. She's in intensive care."

"Intensive care? What happened?" But somehow I knew.

"It's so rare when this happens, usually security is so tight . . . Somehow she got hold of barbituates and . . ."

I can hear her rattle off the words *suicide attempt* and *coma* and *brain damage,* then times and procedures in a slightly shrill voice, but all at a great distance, as if a plane is taking off close by. Eventually, there is silence on the end of the line, and a terrible image unravels in my head: Ursula knocking on Alex's bedroom door with this news held in her mouth like a concealed weapon.

"Has anyone told Alex?"

"Not yet."

I sink down on the bed, my mind racing with the necessary steps. "I'm going over to see him now. When can I bring him to see Cindy?"

"That won't be possible," Trudy says. "They're doing everything they can but I don't know . . . Cindy's sister's here. She's inconsolable. It would be really traumatic for Alex to be here right now. Let's wait until things calm down and we have a better idea of Cindy's condition."

I nod at the phone, thinking hard about how I might get to see Alex without a confrontation with Ursula. Telling her about Cindy's suicide attempt would only increase her efforts to prevent me from seeing him.

Michael's green Volvo pulls into the parking lot at MacNeice House a few seconds ahead of me. Ursula appears at the top of the steps to the entrance, her arms folded. I get out of the car and walk quickly toward the steps with Michael behind, feeling Ursula's stare.

It is Michael who speaks to her first. "I think it's in the boy's interests that he speak to Anya, don't you?"

"The boy is asking for you," she says, pursing her lips. I am at the bottom of the steps, looking up at her. "He's extremely upset about his mother."

"You *told* him?"

"Somehow he already knew. He even told us where she'd stashed the pills."

I ignore her, taking the steps to the entrance two at a time. Just as I think she is going to tell me to leave or be forced to leave, she steps aside, letting us through.

"Don't sign the register," she tells Michael and me as we push through the front door. We follow quickly behind as she heads up the corridor. Michael stops at the vending machine by the doors that lead to staff offices; he fills two plastic cups, one with water, another with espresso, and hands the espresso to me.

"This is for Alex," he says, nodding at the cup of water. "You look tired. The coffee will help."

We catch up with Ursula, pushing through the heavy double doors that lead to the therapy room.

Ursula turns. "I won't note that this interview took place," she says candidly. "Looks bad to the trust if a member of staff on sick leave appears out of the blue."

I glance past her and through the glass panels of the door see Alex. He is in the armchair facing us. He's wearing a T-shirt with an image of Bart Simpson and new denim jeans, and I notice he has had a haircut. He looks different in kids' clothes. He lowers his head into his hands, his fingers crawling through his hair as if he wants to pull his head off. He begins to rock. I nod at Ursula, waiting impatiently as she turns the key in the door and pushes it open. Michael starts to go inside first.

"No," Alex says when he looks up. "You." He points at me.

Michael and I share looks. I turn back to Alex. "You just want to speak to me, Alex?"

He nods. Michael shrugs and hands me the cup of water. "I'll wait down the hall," he tells me, lifting a hand to my shoulder, then dropping it. I wait until he is out of sight before I close the door behind me. Then I sit in the chair opposite Alex. He watches me, his face pale and flat.

"What's that you're drinking?" are his first words.

I set my cup on the floor by my chair. "Espresso." I pass him the cup of water. He takes it but he doesn't drink it, nor does he say thank you, which is unusual for Alex.

"How are you today, Alex?" I ask him gently.

"Scared," he whispers.

Despite the relative stillness of his appearance, I know that his mind will be a tempest of questions and scenarios. I want to reach out to him, to fold my arms around him.

"I don't think I want to do this," he says suddenly, standing up and starting to pace.

"You don't want to speak to me?"

"No," he says, a little frantically, shaking his head. He glances at my cup of espresso, then stops pacing. "When can I see my mum?"

"As soon as the doctors say it's okay," I answer calmly. "I promise, as soon as I hear—"

". . . but it will be too late!" he screeches.

There is a knock on the door before I can reply. I open it and find Michael there, slightly breathless. He lays a hand on my shoulder and leans close.

"Bev's on her way here now," he whispers. "She just left a voicemail on my phone."

"Any word on Cindy?" I say quietly. He shakes his head. Nonetheless, I'm glad to hear that Bev is coming. Alex needs all the support he can get right now.

When I close the door and turn, I see that Alex is back in his seat.

"Are you okay, Alex? Is there anything I can do for you?"

He flicks his eyes from the corner to me, then nods nervously.

As he drains his cup of water I notice his hand is trembling. I recognize a familiar jittery energy beneath his attempt at composure, the kind I have come to associate with Ruen's visitations. I think of my meeting with Karen Holland and the YouTube footage I'd viewed. Alex watches me intently and I am careful not to let my comforting expression slip. I want to ask him about his father and the shooting, but I have already decided that today is not the day for such a discussion. I pick up my cup and drain the espresso to show I'm at ease, relaxed. It tastes terrible. I make a mental note never to get espresso from a vending machine.

Alex sits forward in his chair, wringing his hands. "I remembered some things about my dad . . ." he says.

"You did?"

He looks uncertain now, and I notice he has yet to make full eye contact. Accordingly, I get up and sit next to him instead of directly opposite. I need to show him I'm on his side, not confronting him.

"I mean, it's nothing important."

"I think it *is* important. Can you tell me?"

His eyes drift back to the corner. I resist asking if he can see Ruen.

"It happened one Saturday morning," he says slowly, his eyes gradually rising to my face. "Maybe a Sunday morning. Dad didn't talk to any of our neighbors. He'd usually come through the back door when he visited or he'd keep his baseball cap pulled down over his eyes. I was sitting on the sofa watching something on TV and I remember Dad was looking straight out the front window and then he stood up and walked to the front door. I didn't hear anyone knock. When I went after him I saw he was talking to Mrs. Beaker from three doors up. She's like a hundred years old and when she walked she was bent so far over she was staring at her feet. It was raining really heavy outside but she couldn't hold up an umbrella. So my dad says to her, 'Where are you going?' And she said, 'To do some shopping,' and Dad shook his head and smiled and told her to give him her shopping list and *he'd* do her shopping. Mrs. Beaker went back into her house and me and Dad went and bought all her groceries. Dad wouldn't even take any money from her. She was so happy she kissed him on both cheeks."

His voice has risen several decibels and he is sitting upright. Seconds pass. Suddenly his face crumples. His smile turns into a deep scowl. I notice he is holding something in his hand, hiding it between his legs.

"It's okay, Alex," I say gently. "It's good to remember nice things about your dad. It shows you are forgiving him."

He struggles to speak, his lips trembling. "But . . . but what would she have done . . . I mean, if she'd known . . ."

He doesn't finish. I glance out the glass panels of the door, hopeful that we will see Bev soon. When I turn back to Alex I see he has covered his face with his hands and I instinctively reach out to him.

"Alex," I begin. But I stop short, overwhelmed by a wave of nausea so powerful that I cover my mouth in case I throw up.

"Are you all right?" Alex says, sniffling.

"I think so. You were saying about your dad—"

"Are you feeling sleepy?" he whispers, and I shake my head, fighting nausea.

"My dad could be really kind," he says, his teeth still chattering.

*Just like you,* I want to say, but I feel a tingling in my mouth. I reach for my talisman on instinct, then realize with a stunned sense of horror that, for the first time ever, I'm not wearing it. I've left it at home. But the queasiness has passed. It's just anxiety, I scold myself.

"But what about when someone is also a murderer?" Alex is saying. "How can they really be kind if they're evil? How can anything that they did be true? It was all a lie, wasn't it?"

As I open my mouth to respond my throat tightens, and I'm choking. I lean forward to take a ragged breath, but without warning I have fallen to my hands and knees, gasping for air.

Alex stands up, his face frozen as he watches me. I see him reach behind his back, still hiding whatever he's got in his hand. I know what is happening now, but I can't explain *why* it's happening. *Anaphylactic shock,* my mind screams, *anaphylactic shock. But how? How is this happening?* I keep my mind focused on taking short breaths, using what time I have left to think of a way to tell Alex what he needs to do.

"Are you sleepy?" I hear him say. *Why is he asking that?* Painfully I raise my head, watching him through blurring vision as he steps back, bumping into the doll's house. He is sobbing now, his eyes streaming with tears.

"It's okay," I whisper, and it feels as if someone has put an invisible hand around my throat, squeezing tightly. I gag. "Help me," I beg him. "Michael—get Michael."

But Alex turns away, facing the doll's house. There is a plastic tub on the floor, tipped on its side, the small kind you'd buy from a vending machine. A jelly bean tub, maybe. Or . . . There is a trail of dust pouring out of it, like sand. And amid the sand is a pebble. No, not a pebble.

A peanut.

Quickly I roll my eyes to my left. My coffee cup has rolled beside the table leg. I have to look twice, but it's there: on the rim of the cup is a small dusting of the same beige dust.

*Keep calm, breathe, breathe . . .*

*How did he do this? Just a minute ago, I wasn't looking . . .*

*Did he pour peanut dust in my coffee? He must have . . .*

*Why is he doing this? Does he know what he is doing?*

*Does he realize he is killing me?*

Alex is speaking fast and loud, pouring out apologies and explanations. My cheek is pressed to the floor, my arms splayed, my knees bent. It is vital to keep my breathing shallow, my heartbeat as slow as possible. I can feel saliva building up in my throat, and I start to panic. It feels like I am drowning.

Alex is standing above me. He is pacing, his face screwed up in a mixture of terror and grief. I hear him mutter "Ruen," and I understand. "Ruen" is making him do this, or rather the belief he has invested subconsciously in his self-image as the child of a killer—as an inevitable killer-in-the-making. I think back to the YouTube footage, of a five-year-old Alex in the corner of the frame, watching. He was so young—too young to process the meaning of what he had seen. The media coverage afterward—newspapers, television footage—would have stirred up negative feelings toward a man he looked up to. A man he loved. His father. How many headlines had he seen like the one on the painting he did for Karen Holland's class. RUEND PEEPELS LIVES.

My eyelids sag, plunging me back into darkness. Nothing but the sound of my small little gasps. I hear Alex's feet edge closer, his whimper of fear. A muffled scraping sound. He is pushing my chair against the door, wedging it neatly beneath the handle.

"I'm sorry, I'm sorry," I hear him say. He is pleading with someone or something. "I don't want to die. I don't want to die."

I try to think of anything but the terrible alien feeling that has overwhelmed me, the thickness of my tongue in my mouth, the seductive urge to pass out. I musn't. With my last ounce of strength, I lift my head and open my eyes a fraction. At last, I see what Alex was hiding before: a thick shard of broken glass.

"Alex," I whisper, though it's a hopeless gargle of phlegm and tears and spit. Then I say what I longed to say to Poppy, "I love you, sweetheart." He bends down slightly, sobbing.

The last thing I see is Alex raising the glass shard high above him, the light glinting on its lethal edge.

ALEX

Dear Diary,

I looked at Anya on the floor and I wanted to tell her I'm sorry. I wanted to tell her not to be afraid. I wanted to tell her more about Ruen, about what he had asked me to do and why I was doing it. In my mind I could see Mum in the hospital, her face the color of vanilla ice cream, only in my mind she looks like Anya. I didn't expect her to get so sick. My hands were shaking and I thought, *she should just be falling asleep so why does she look like she's in pain?* I was so confused.

When Anya fell on the floor I felt really scared. I looked at Ruen, and he frowned at me and said, "you know what you have to do, Alex." I nodded and I felt sick. I didn't understand. I had told him I would do it. I would kill myself. I would do it to save Mum, that's what he said. He told me I had to do it in public, so everyone could see. In front of Anya. *Why?* I'd asked, but he wouldn't say. He told me to give her the peanuts if it made me feel better, so she would fall asleep straightaway and not see me do it. I felt relieved then, but scared. I didn't want to die. I wouldn't do it. But then the black shadow trailed across the floor like a snake from Ruen and wrapped around me. He squeezed it and I knew what he was saying: if I didn't do it, he would.

Anya lay on the floor, her body shivering like she was really cold. Ruen was Horn Head again, a big red horn jutting out of his faceless forehead, his body covered in hair and barbed wire. I thought, *it would be better if I just went away,* because then Ruen would come with me and the only person he would hurt is me. Mum, Anya, Michael, even Woof—they'd all be happier if I went away.

I thought of Mum again, and the picture in my head was just like the first time when she'd taken lots of pills. It was the morning Dad left—the morning he got arrested for shooting those policemen. When I found Mum in her bed she was so limp I thought she was already dead.

*Do it,* Ruen whispered, his voice in my head. But it wasn't his normal voice. It was a soft voice, not too deep and not too old and his accent wasn't English anymore; it was Irish. When I realized whose voice it was I got shivers right up my spine. It was my Dad's voice. And when I looked at the red horn I thought of the policeman my Dad shot in the head, the blood spurting out of it, and I felt sick.

"Anya!"

I turned around to see Michael pounding on the door with his fists, his eyes all wide and scared. He slammed his hands against the glass and looked down at Anya, then up at me. He looked really angry.

"Open this door!"

I could see the chair that I had pressed against the door handle move each time Michael banged against it and I knew he'd kill me when he got in.

And maybe that would be okay.

My Dad's voice whispered in my head again. *She's dying, Alex. Your mother is dying.*

"Please let my Mum be okay," I whispered to Ruen, because I knew he was angry that Michael was getting through the door and I was doing nothing to stop him. He had changed his appearance and was Ghost Boy now, his hands by his sides and his eyes all black and angry, and his clothes were exactly like mine, as if I was looking into a mirror.

Michael was still banging on the glass, shouting, and there were lots of people behind him now. Then someone hit the glass with a hammer and started trying to break it. A big crack formed across the glass in the shape of a W.

I looked down, and for a moment it wasn't Anya lying there—it was her little girl, Poppy, just the way Ruen had described her. She had dark hair like Anya's and had fallen from a terrible height and she wasn't moving. I blinked again and saw it was Anya. I wanted to reach down and fix her arm to make sure she was comfortable. But before I could do anything there was a gigantic crash and I screamed. The glass in the door smashed and scattered to the floor.

"Anya!"

Michael reached through the broken glass and swept away all the shards with his hand before pushing the chair away from the door handle. I saw there was blood on his hand but he didn't notice. Then Ruen tightened his grip around me and I started to yell because it hurt a lot.

*The only way to save her is to kill yourself,* he said. *You're nothing. You don't deserve this life. You should have saved her.*

I lifted the glass handle from the floor. My mind was playing the image of Mum over and over, her hand on the bed opening loosely like a petal.

I knew what Ruen was telling me.

I was going to grow up to be just like my Dad. And that was a bad thing, because my Dad was a murderer. I didn't want to hurt anybody. But I was already doing it. I was hurting me. I was hurting Anya. And I was never going to be free of him.

But he had lied. He said I was unlovable. But Anya said she loved me, didn't she?

"I'm not nothing," I told Ruen. "I'm Alex. I can be anything I want to be."

I lifted the glass higher. Then I slashed it down over the thick black link between me and Ruen, and Ruen roared as the shadow shattered and every vein in my body felt like it was going to explode.

Someone grabbed my arms and yelled "She's going!" and Michael shouted, "What have you done?" and then there was nothing but blackness.

# 28
# THE ANSWERS

## ANYA

I woke up in Belfast city hospital, a venue in which I had never spent any time during the thirty years I lived here but which was now startlingly familiar. I was in a ward with two other women, a heart monitor bleeping close by, but oddly, no wires were attached like last time. No drip, no signs of medical intervention. Just my alarmingly thin legs poking out from beneath a white hospital gown, a sour smell of body odor that suggested it had been days since I'd arrived. A bunch of red roses sat in a vase close to the bed. I lay in a blank daze as the wheels of thought warmed up again, wondering how long I'd been out for and—deep in the roots of my suspicions—if I really was alive. Gradually a series of aches and throbs announced themselves all over my body—my throat, my neck and shoulders, my stomach—and I realized with relief that I *was* alive.

A young black-haired nurse walked past and threw me a smile, then doubled back as it occurred to her that I had surfaced. She checked my vitals, read my chart.

"Well, well," she said brightly. "Back in the land of the living. How are you feeling?"

"Where's Alex?" I asked.

"Who?"

"Michael," I corrected myself. She would probably be a stranger to the situation; Michael would know about Alex. "Michael Jones, he must have brought me in. Is he around?"

She considered while strapping a blood pressure gauge around my right bicep. "Don't know a Michael Jones," she said cheerfully.

She flipped open my chart and scribbled a figure in a column. "I'll arrange for you to get some soup. You must be starving."

Just then, footsteps made their way toward my bed. I looked up and saw Michael standing there. The nurse glanced at me.

"This is who you meant?" She smiled, then left the room.

Michael pulled a chair close to the bed and sat down. He had fresh silver stubble on his jaw; his eyes were puffy with lack of sleep.

"You look great," he said, smiling.

"Where's Alex?" I whispered. The memory of what had happened was creeping back like a slow tide.

Michael's smile crumpled. He ran his fingers through his hair, visibly reluctant to tell me. I felt my heart sink.

"He's dead, isn't he?"

He took my hand. "You don't mind, do you?" he asked. I shook my head. I was remembering it all now: Alex's face, raw with tears and grief. The trickle of dust on my espresso cup. The sensation of drowning.

He swallowed, then looked away. "He's not dead."

I felt a surge of relief, so great that I felt my eyes sting with tears. An enormous weight left my heart. The feeling was familiar. It was exactly how I felt on those nights when I dreamed Poppy had not jumped. That, instead, she had closed the window and stepped back inside. That she had lived.

But then Michael looked back at me, his gaze intense and searching.

"What's wrong?" I asked, frightened.

He shifted in his seat, pressing his palms together and adopting a poise that seemed familiar—it was one I often assumed when attempting to put patients at ease. "Anya, I have to tell you something, and I need you to listen and try to understand. Okay?"

I nodded, my heart pounding.

His voice was soft, his gaze unyielding. "Alex doesn't exist."

I blinked at him, certain that I'd heard him wrong and waiting for him to repeat the sentence in a different form. A long time passed before he spoke again.

"He's not real."

"What do you mean, *not real*?" I said, exasperated.

He was so close that I could make out the whiskered lines at the sides of his eyes—deeper when he hadn't had enough sleep—and the look there that said he wasn't kidding. "Listen carefully . . ."

"I *am* listening carefully," I snapped. "Michael, what are you saying? No, *why* are you saying this? This is ridiculous. And it's not helpful . . ."

His fingers tightened on my hand. "Anya, I have been treating you for several months now."

"*Treating* me? What are you talking about? Treating me? For what?"

He cleared his throat, opening and closing his mouth as if testing the words before he spoke them. "You had a breakdown back in May, on the anniversary of Poppy's death. I should have seen it coming. You had become more and more withdrawn, even from me. You began to tell me your mother had had schizophrenia."

"My mother *did* have schizophrenia," I snapped. My mind was reeling. Breakdown? What was he saying? Was I still unconscious, dreaming this?

He was shaking his head. "No, she didn't. Your mother died from cancer, ten years ago. It was you . . ." He trailed off, reluctant to say any more. I stared at him, waiting for an explanation, but instead he stood and nodded to someone. I leaned forward as he pulled the curtain around the bed, and as he swished the faded yellow fabric past my face I caught a glimpse of who he was addressing: Ursula, but not as I knew her. She seemed to have gained a considerable amount of weight in the last day or so, and her hair glinted with additional streaks of silver.

Something was very, very wrong, I decided. I watched numbly as Michael carefully tugged the curtain across the last inch of light so that we were completely alone. I jumped when he sat back down, and he saw.

"Anya," he said, reaching for my hand again. I pulled away from him. He looked wounded. "I'm not going to hurt you," he said gently, holding up his hands. "Quite the opposite. I'm here to help you."

"Help me?" I looked around me, noticing again the lack of wires. My body would need serious intervention to help it recover from anaphylactic shock, and yet there was nothing. I told Michael this, and he seemed mildly bemused.

"Blackouts," he said, his face serious. "They became more and more regular once you began to make progress."

"Progress?"

"You can't . . . you can't see any of them now?"

I glanced around the cubicle. "See who?"

"Alex. Ruen. Cindy. Any of them?"

"Michael, don't be absurd! You're scaring me—"

He nodded. "This is good. Ironically, you've been gaining clarity after each blackout. The last one was so serious I thought I'd lost you entirely."

A new possibility struck me. "Am I dead?" I said then, very serious.

"No. But it was mentioned once or twice."

"Mentioned?"

"You wanted to die, Anya. When you told me Ruen wanted Alex to kill himself, I knew what it meant."

"Michael, please." I wanted him to stop. "We've been working together on Alex's treatment since early May. Why are you saying this?"

Several moments passed before he answered. "When I met you at the conference all those years ago . . . well, I was intimidated. You were this rising star, everyone was talking about how good you were. When you came to MacNeice House last year it took me ages before I could summon up the courage to ask you on a date." He shook his head in disbelief. "Luckily, we never became lovers. Otherwise they'd never have let me treat you."

"Last year? I only started working at MacNeice House a couple of months ago . . . Where's Alex? What has happened to him? Tell me!" I suddenly needed proof, hard evidence, anything to shoot down these ridiculous claims he was making.

"No, Anya. Look, I'm sorry to have to lay all this on you so soon. I thought I'd guide you out of your psychosis gently, give you time."

"Time for what?" I thought of Alex: I didn't want him to face the consequences of what he had done, and yet I needed to find out why he had done it. Why he had tried to kill me.

Michael's face flushed. "I thought you were coming closer to seeing the truth, especially when you said you saw Poppy."

"What *truth*, Michael?"

He held my gaze. "You really want me to spell it all out?"

"Damn it, yes!"

He took a deep breath, pressing his palms together—the way he always did when presenting a patient's symptoms. "I only found out about your history when we became close. Your medical history. You had suffered delusions as a child, freaked out your parents when you claimed to be playing with a twin sister . . ."

"That was *you*, Michael!" I protested.

He shook his head. "You had a twin, Anya. She died when you were born. The delusions grew stronger. But you overcame them. With treatment and your own study of the illness, you overcame it all, Anya. Quite unheard of for a psychiatrist with a history of psychosis to rise to your heights."

I stared at him. Surely he was talking about someone else.

"When your daughter displayed similar symptoms, you were convinced you could treat her. Her psychiatrist suggested that she be institutionalized, and you agreed. But then Poppy attacked you. You knew how badly she didn't want to be separated from you, and so you decided to treat her at home. And later, when she jumped, you blamed yourself."

It was suddenly all too much. There was a roar in my head that threatened to burst my eardrums if I didn't press my hands against my ears and hold them there. When I opened my eyes again I was back on the bed, the curtain pulled back and the light from the windows pouring through, so that the nurse standing above me appeared haloed by sun. She inspected the monitor by my bed before producing several pills and a cup of water. Michael stood at her elbow, watching.

"I want my voice recorder."

"What voice recorder?"

"The recorder I used for all my interviews with Alex." I slid from the

bed carefully and shuffled toward the small cupboard, certain that my
handbag and briefcase would be stored there. I found only a small
white plastic bag containing a copy of *Hamlet*, a framed photograph of
Poppy, a set of keys, a makeup bag full of elastic bands, and a leather
journal that I deduced was a notebook I'd forgotten about. At the bottom of the bag I found my tape recorder. I pulled it out, triumphant.
"Look," I told Michael, as if the thing itself was evidence. "Better yet,
*listen*." And I pressed PLAY.

Michael sat down and leaned back into his seat with a sigh. I glared
at him, waiting for my or Alex's recorded voice to break the silence. To
prove to him that he was wrong. When nothing came, I glanced at the
volume dial, flicking it with my thumb. The sound of static merely in-
creased to hiss. "You erased the tapes."

"Anya . . ."

With trembling hands I plucked the cassette tape out of the recorder, flipping it over to the other side. Still nothing but static when
I pressed PLAY. "Why would you do that? Why would you go to such
lengths?"

"Believe me when I say that I wish I could have taken a little more
time to guide you back to reality, but the events over the last few weeks
have proven that too much is at stake. So what I need you to do right
now is step back inside your role as a psychiatrist, Dr. Molokova, and
help me solve the riddle posed by my most challenging patient."

I searched his face for a few seconds, reluctant to play along. "Go
on."

He seemed visibly pleased by my response. "For the sake of argument we'll refer to the patient as Patient A."

"History?"

"Parental bereavement. Witnessed an only child plunging to her
death. Patient A was medically trained to deal with the condition the
child was afflicted with, but ultimately could not prevent this terrible
tragedy. Possible psychological impact?"

I drew a breath, certain he was talking about me, but he immediately held up a chiding finger. "Please retain your professional focus,
Dr. Molokova."

I nodded, feeling a spike of fury at the game he was insisting on playing. "Okay. Possible psychological trauma, ranging from guilt to severe depression and reenactment."

"Psychosis?"

I blinked. "Potentially. Of course, that depends on other factors."

He continued in a perplexingly hypothetical tone. "Patient A experiences psychotic episodes of an escalating intensity. Is delusional, and given medication for delusions."

"Risperidone?"

He nodded. "These delusions have strong ties to the deceased child."

"Such as?"

"Patient A reports a primary delusion in the form of a child with a similar condition as the deceased, a condition Patient A works tirelessly to treat."

"Go on," I said carefully.

"Many other delusions seem to be founded on memories."

"Gives the delusions strength," I reminded him. "It's essentially building fiction on the foundations of undeniable fact. What are the delusions?"

"The home of the child that Patient A believes they are treating. The child's mother. The child's social worker . . ."

"You're a social worker."

He shook his head, sadly. "I *was* a social worker when we met six years ago. You believe I'm Alex's social worker, when in fact I'm a psychiatrist working at MacNeice House, just like you." He leaned forward. "You once said you came back to Northern Ireland to rebuild lives. Now help me rebuild your own."

Panicked, I thought quickly to what I remembered about the moment before I lost consciousness. Alex, his face wet with tears. But somewhere in the background I could hear echoes of another voice: "What have you done? Anya, what have you done?"

"You said I came to MacNeice House a year ago," I said, recalling the day I met him—handsome and serious in his navy suit, how I had had to flex my hand after our handshake. That was only months ago, wasn't it?

"Yes." He nodded. "And you were fine. More than fine, actually. You were changing things, exactly as you said. You rented an apartment. You were treating patients. I took you to see *Hamlet* at the Grand Opera House. And then you changed. You didn't want to see me anymore. You started working at home. Only 'home' wasn't your apartment. You moved so I wouldn't know where you lived. And when I tracked you down, I was certain something was wrong."

I nodded, thinking frantically. Proof. It would be easy to erase cassette tapes, but my notes on Alex would be at my office. I could contact Karen Holland, Jojo. I could show Michael the YouTube footage. We were so close to bringing Alex to realizing what he feared all along: that he was going to turn out to be a murderer, just like his father.

The roar in my head was getting louder and louder. I closed my eyes against it. "You said Patient A's delusions were grounded in memories," I said.

"Yes," he said, so tenderly that I opened my eyes. "Memories of meetings with colleagues, interviews with previous patients, each of them compounded to inform the primary delusion. The problem is, Patient A is not conscious of these memories. Reality and irreality have become so confused that they've switched in Patient A's mind, meaning that memories are now perceived as elements of subconscious fantasy. Or in other words . . ."

"Dreams," I said. He nodded.

"What do you remember?" he said gently.

I opened my mouth to speak but found I could barely articulate what I wanted to say. Instead, more and more images seemed to flood into my mind: a memory of me cooking up onions in Alex's house, the feel of the metallic handle cold in my hand, the view from the kitchen window overlooking the weed-spotted patch of concrete the council called a garden. The blue armchair positioned in front of the television. Try as I might, I could not summon Bev's face, or Alex's. I could make out the nicotine-stained lace curtains hanging on the bay windows, the tuneless piano in the hall, the damp-ridden walls of Alex's bedroom . . .

But a psychiatrist would never enter a child's bedroom. Not without reason or a parent's consent. I knew I had never been inside his room. And yet, I could remember it. How could I? Which of my memories were real?

"Please," I said, steadying my voice. "Take me to Alex's house. I need to go there, Michael. Please."

I watched the faces of Belfast unfold before me as Michael drove his ailing Volvo through its streets, my spirits lifted by the sight of the murals we had visited together, by a gleam of sunshine falling on the River Lagan, turning it for a moment into a gold ribbon. We slipped up an alley close to the Opera House and continued on the narrowing streets toward Alex's neighborhood, and it was then that Michael broke his silence.

"After your breakdown you came back to work, remember? Ursula said it was fine, but I was uneasy. I tried to get you to confide in me, but I should have known better. Anytime I tried to get close, you backed away, until one day I showed up at your apartment with a bouquet and a bottle of wine and found a sixty-year-old barrister living there. You'd moved out some time ago. And so I followed you home." He glanced at me. "I hope you don't mind."

I felt the car start to slow down, creeping along the pavement of a street I recognized instantly. Alex's house was visible through the windscreen. The broken windowpane causing the familiar lace curtains to billow out into the front garden. I breathed a sigh of relief. I hadn't imagined this.

"We've no way of getting inside," I told him. "Unless *lock picker* is on your list of former occupations."

He reached down and grabbed the plastic bag from the backseat, giving it a shake. "The key's in here, isn't it?"

He smiled and held out his arm for me to take. I walked with him toward the house, noticing the decrepit blue car parked outside the house, both wheels flat, its windscreen shattered. Teenage boys heckled us from the house opposite, but Michael ignored them.

"It did strike me as odd that you would choose such a neighborhood to reside in," he said, taking the keys from the bag. "And as you would never admit to it, I had to work it out all by myself. But I think I cracked it."

"You do?"

"You're anonymous here. No one to disturb your work."

"My work?"

He slipped the key into the lock. "The creation of Alex Connolly."

I stepped inside, shivering.

Everything was exactly as I remembered it, with one small omission: the piano that Cindy had kept in the hallway. It was missing, but at the spot where it once sat were four distinct grooves from its brass wheels.

In the living room I spotted the blue armchair in front of the ancient television, the round table where I had sat with Alex, the electrical socket hanging off the wall.

"And now that I'm finally inside, it all makes sense," Michael continued, glancing around the room. On the mantelpiece, the school photographs of Alex that had once rested there in cardboard frames were gone, as was the framed portrait of him and Cindy. There was nothing there, now. Not even holes in the peeling wallpaper from the nail upon which the portrait had hung.

"What makes sense?" I said distracted.

"When you first mentioned Alex I believed he was as real as you did. You complained about the state of the house he lived in, the bad neighborhood. It was soon after that that you moved out of your flat. It makes sense. You went looking for Alex. And you came across this place. You started off carrying out your 'interviews' here. And then, when Alex took hold, you moved in."

I nodded, less agreeing with him than processing the information he was giving me, piece by piece. So far, the pieces fit. I had to think of the person he was describing exactly as he had offered—as Patient A. Only by remaining objective could I begin to understand how or why the things he was saying might be true—whatever that truth might be.

"I want to go upstairs," I said.

I looked into each of the bedrooms, noticing my own suitcase on the floor of the room with a double bed. "What about Cindy?" I said levelly. "You say Alex was a delusion. What about Cindy? Did I make her up, too?"

"Poppy's death was your breaking point, Anya. Your fears were so deep inside you that only Cindy could give voice to them. Cindy. A woman full of sin. You believed you were a bad mother, Anya."

I contemplated this. Much of it rang true, but I said nothing, glancing at the second stairwell and indicating that I wanted to continue upward. And so we continued on, mounting the creaking, carpetless staircase that led to the top floor and Alex's bedroom.

The door to the room was closed. Michael stepped forward and leaned against it, pushing it open.

Inside, the room was freezing. The large dormer window was completely gone except for a single jagged shard hanging down like a fang. There was no bed, no posters, and no wardrobe. But there *were* two items in the room. A small stool, and before it a piano.

"Anya, careful," Michael warned as I took a nervous step toward it. "It's not safe up here. Whoever moved a piano here needs their head examined. That floor is unsafe."

"I moved it here." I sat down at the piano, suddenly recalling the two men I'd hired to shift the thing up three rickety flights of stairs. I'd paid them generously; they'd taken one look at the wad of cash and another at the scar on my face, then set to work without asking questions.

"You say that Alex doesn't exist," I said to Michael. "Yet I remember you and me—we interviewed him together in the therapy room."

He shook his head and rubbed his hands to keep warm. "I interviewed *you* in the therapy room, Anya, when you claimed you had a patient in there and I found nothing but thin air."

"What about the hospital visits? Our meetings with Harold and Ursula?"

"We had many hospital visits and meetings, but always about other patients." He hesitated. "Patient A's primary delusion was a small boy who believed he could release his own father from Hell, the father he loved but whom he feared he was becoming. Hypothesis: Patient A was attempting to release herself from her own hell. She was struggling with the two sides of her character: the side she saw as virtuous, loving, and the side she perceived as demonic, unloving."

My fingers slid up the yellowed ivory of the keys, the notes of Ruen's music blooming vibrantly in my mind. I played the first bar, then, wincing at the tuneless chime of the piano, turned back to Michael. "You want to know why Patient A suffered from those particular delusions?"

He cocked his head to one side, his expression changing. I played the second bar of the music slowly, the music rising sourly into the icy air.

"Patient A believed that she was a murderer for not preventing the loss of her child. Patient A's psyche could not tolerate the fact that she possessed the tools to heal her child and did not use those tools effectively, and so a gaping hole was torn in the fabric of Patient A's life." I closed my eyes, Poppy's face rising up in my mind. Her voice. *It feels like a hole, Mum*. I felt my breaths shorten, the wind beginning to howl its way through the broken window and the cracks in the walls.

"Go on," Michael said softly.

"A common response to such grief would be manic depression or suicide. But there was an additional element to Patient A's situation."

"What was that?"

"Love," I answered. "Patient A believed that her lack of love caused the child to die. Patient A was convinced that, even if the child had lived, she had been doomed from the outset by the fact that her mother knew too little of love to save her completely. That's where you're wrong, Michael."

"Oh?"

"How else would any patient deal with such crippling emotions, and with the knowledge that there was something she could have done to save her daughter, but didn't?"

He nodded, but his expression was one of fear. "Come back from the window."

I realized I was no longer sitting at the piano but standing by the window, looking down over Belfast. For a moment I saw Poppy's face as she sat by the window of our apartment in Edinburgh, her smile as she turned to me. *I love you, Mummy.* What had it felt like, I wondered, when she fell? Was it relief? Was it so much better than living with me?

"Don't," Michael said tersely, glancing at the window. His face was white with terror. "Poppy died, Anya. She was off medication. That wasn't your fault. You can't let this destroy you, too."

I considered that as I looked out to the street below. It would be so easy to let go, to slip out of reality entirely, to step out of life. Is that how Poppy had felt?

And right then, as if he had read my thoughts, Michael said: "You know, it took me a while to figure out why you kept that diary. Why you wrote entry after entry in Alex's voice. And now I think I know why."

I stretched a hand out to lean against the window frame, dizzy with confusion. "You do?"

"Anya."

From the corner of my eye I saw him holding up the leather journal that I'd found inside the bag. "You will never know how Poppy felt. Couching her inside Alex didn't help you work out what was going on inside her head. Her death was an accident, Anya. A terrible accident. You were not responsible for it."

I was close enough now to step forward without him being able to reach me; the distance between us was so great that I'd be out the window before he could react in time. He raised his voice.

"You told me once that you believe everything can be overcome. But can you stare at yourself in the mirror and see a demon looking back and still overcome that aspect of yourself enough to become human again?" He paused. "That is the question."

I flicked my eyes at the shard of glass hanging loosely down from the frame, the insistent wind tugging at it like a child's tooth. A second ago I had glimpsed my own face reflected there, the scar on my face like an asterisk. Now another face had appeared, and I was frightened to look at it. But I knew who it was. Ruen. When I summoned up the courage to look, he smiled, his green eyes malevolent, willing me to jump. I looked down, focusing on the cracks in the floorboards, taking my last step forward, into the open air.

But Michael lunged, fast enough to grab the back of my shirt and, holding on to the shard of glass hanging from the frame, yanked me backward. We both fell to the floor, the wind howling after me.

"Are you okay?" I whispered weakly.

Michael looked at his palm, streaked with blood. Quickly he wrapped the sleeve of his jacket around the gash. Then: "You know I was wrong before. He's alive, Anya."

"Who is?"

"Alex."

I searched his face, wondering for a moment if had lost his mind. "What?"

"In your psyche. Alex never died. And he survived precisely because you saved him. You told me that you had managed to convince him that he wasn't a murderer, but Ruen wouldn't let up. It's this that you have to work through now. You have to know that you loved her, how much you loved her. Play the song."

"The song?"

He nodded. "You know which one."

I glanced at the piano. "The music's gone, Michael. I don't have it . . ."

He struggled to his feet, holding out his good hand to help me up. "You wrote that music. And I believe the reason you wrote it was so that there could be some completion to the bond between you and Poppy. You finished what she had started. It's not a 'love song for Anya' at all. It's a love song for Poppy, a reminder that she loved you. You once said, 'Hell is when no treatment is given.' I am offering you that treatment, Anya, but I need your help. I need your willingness to step away from the abyss. If you believe you can, if you can only take my hand and begin the climb, I need you to play. *Play.*"

Reluctantly I inched around the piano toward the seat, flinching at the reflection of Ruen, changing through all four of his guises in the sheen of the wood. Could I ever be free of him? Could I ever accept that the demonic and angelic lurked in my own nature, and that I had a choice between which to act upon?

I thought of Alex, surviving somewhere in the corners of my mind. He had overcome all his obstacles. He was free of his fear of becoming like his father. He was free of Ruen. Could I do the same?

I sat down and slid my fingers up the keys, finding a high B with the third finger of my right hand. *Poppy,* I thought, her face bright in my head.

And I began to play.

DEMONS DO NOT EXIST ANY MORE THAN
GODS DO, BEING ONLY THE PRODUCTS
OF THE PSYCHIC ACTIVITY OF MAN.

—SIGMUND FREUD

# ACKNOWLEDGMENTS

First and foremost, I wish to thank my husband, Jared Jess-Cooke. Thank you, my love, for your patience, for Alex's jokes, for generally putting up with me while I wrote this, and for your endless encouragement.

To my agent, Madeleine Milburn, a kung-fu bow of respect, love, and a debt of appreciation for reminding me to follow my instinct. To my U.S. editor, Kate Miciak, thank you so much for your marvelous creativity and passion for this book. To my U.K. editor, Emma Beswetherick, Lucy Icke, and the rest of the team at Piatkus, I thank you all warmly for your help and for cheering me on.

The research I carried out for this book gave me a lot of respect for the people involved in children's mental health in the U.K., particularly in Northern Ireland. In this regard, I am indebted to Dr. Marinos Kyriakopoulos, who helped enormously with my inquiries into early-onset schizophrenia, and who was generous enough to do not one but two very thorough fact-checking reads of drafts of this book. Thanks also to Dr. Stephen Westgarth for his help and advice on childhood psychotic disorders, to Dr. Aditya Sharma for his generosity and insights, and to Helen Stew for information on social services. All errors—including my deliberate sidesteps from fact during the pursuit of good fiction—are mine.

Love and thanks to my friends and family who championed me throughout, especially my mother-in-law, Evita Cooke, who was there to help out with child care at a moment's notice. Having someone who was willing to feed, bathe, and put the children to bed while I was nine months pregnant and struggling to finish the first draft of this book was a true (and characteristic) act of generosity and kindness.

A warm thank-you to those readers whose kind e-mails—often including the line "don't stop writing!"—serendipitously reached my in-box on those days when I most needed encouragement.

Finally, I want to thank my little ones—Melody, Phoenix, Summer, and Willow. There is no greater inspiration in my life than the four of you.

## ABOUT THE AUTHOR

CAROLYN JESS-COOKE was born to a musical family in Belfast, Northern Ireland. She is an award-winning author of poems and novels, as well as four nonfiction books. Her first poetry collection, *Inroads,* won the Tyrone Guthrie Award, an Eric Gregory Award from the Society of Authors, a Northern Promise Award, and was shortlisted for the London New Poetry Award. Her bestselling novel *The Guardian Angel's Journal* has been translated into twenty-one languages.

www.carolynjesscooke.com